ALEX SHEARER

I WAS A SCHOOLBOY BRIDEGROOM

Also by Alex Shearer

The Fugitives
The Great Switcheroonie
The Greatest Store in the World
Sea Legs

ALEX SHEARER

I WAS A SCHOOLBOY BRIDE GROOM

*Hodder
Children's
Books*

a division of Hodder Headline Limited

First published in Great Britain in 2006
by Hodder Children's Books

1

A Catalogue record for this book is available from the British Library

ISBN-10: 0 340 93028 4
ISBN-13: 978034093028 4

Typeset in NewBaskerville by Avon DataSet Ltd,
Bidford-on-Avon, Warwickshire

Printed and bound in Great Britain by
Bookmarque Ltd, Croydon, Surrey

The paper and board used in this paperback are natural
recyclable products made from wood grown in sustainable
forests. The manufacturing processes conform to the
environmental regulations of the country of origin.

Hodder Children's Books
a division of Hachette Children's Books
338 Euston Road
London NW1 3BH

I WAS A SCHOOLBOY BRIDEGROOM
(*a true life story*)

Your father and I are of the opinion, Bosworth, that it might help no end with your school work for you to have some stability in your life and a plan ahead of you. In fact, we think it might be a very good idea for you to get engaged.

'Engaged?' I said, puzzled. 'But engaged to do what, Mum?'

'Engaged, Bosworth . . .' she explained, '. . . to be married.'

1

Bosworth in the Middle

To be perfectly honest, I wasn't even thinking of getting married, as I had quite enough on my plate as it was with my rabbits. (Not that the rabbits were actually on a plate. I don't mean I was eating them.)

It's a bit of a full-time job looking after rabbits, what with cleaning them out and chopping up carrots for them and chasing them round the garden, trying to get them back into the hutch. They take up a lot of your free time, energy and Elastoplast, do rabbits, and in some ways you're better off with a pet stick.

Then, on top of all that, there was also all my homework to do, plus my internet surfing to get on with, my on-line games to play, my books to read, my music to listen to and my DVDs to watch, so as you can imagine, the last thing on my mind right then was getting married to anyone. Let alone

Veronica Angelica Belinda Melling. In fact I had not even heard of Veronica Angelica Belinda Melling back then, and had no reason to believe that she existed.

I was going along quite happily, as a matter of fact, back in the old days, before she came along. I won't say that I didn't have a care in the world, as everybody has *some* cares, but I didn't have many, and the ones I did have weren't that big, not as cares go.

No, I had quite a nice little life going. There was school, which wasn't too bad. I handed my homework in and kept my head down, and if I never got many distinctions, well, I never got many detentions either, which was fine by me. There weren't many A stars, but nor were there many D minuses. And while I wouldn't have said that I was Mr Popularity, I wasn't Mr Unpopularity either. I was always Mr Average, somehow. Yes, that was me – Bosworth in the middle.

So there I was with my nice little life, with my various amusements and the odd friend or two. I lived in quite a nice house, with quite nice parents (I thought), having quite nice holidays in the summer and with two quite nice rabbits. It was quite nice really.

And then the trouble started.

Up until that time, trouble was something I had mostly stayed out of. Some people are like that

2

with swimming pools. 'Don't like them and never go in them,' they say. 'The water's too cold, the pool's too crowded, I hate being splashed and I don't like the chlorine.'

I was like that with trouble. Some people thrive on it, I know. See a drop of trouble and they're straight in doing lengths. They've got on the old trouble costume and the trouble goggles and they're off. But me, I'd go out of my way to avoid it. I'd take a two-mile detour to avoid trouble. I always liked the quiet life.

Looking back now, I can see whose fault it was. It was all the fault of the Old Bombay Indian Restaurant, where Dad used to get his takeaway curries. He came back one evening with his usual Friday night bag of six foil trays, plus nan breads, chapatis and popadoms (sometimes he got some food for us as well) and he sat down at the kitchen table and announced in his usual I've-got-a-great-plan-my-lightbulb's-just-gone-on way he has that, 'Those people from India have got the right idea.'

Mum looked at him from across the table, where she was toying with a raw potato, wondering what this new bee in his bonnet was. Mum does not eat curries as they are fattening. Dad does eat curries, but funnily enough, he doesn't get fat. It is Mum, who never eats curries, who is always on a diet.

That time, she was on the potato diet. She had been on it all day and had already weighed herself several times to see how much weight she had lost. (None, so far, but it was early days yet.) Her latest diet – the raw potato diet – involved eating nothing but uncooked potatoes for a month. If, by the end of that time, you had not lost at least ten pounds, you could return the *Raw Potato Diet Book* to the shop you had bought it from and get a complete refund.

Dad gave me half a nan bread and some curried lentils to play with. Mum looked on enviously, turning her potato around and inspecting it from all angles, probably wondering where to bite into it first.

'What do you mean?' she asked Dad. 'About Indian people having the right idea? The right idea about what?'

'Food, for a start,' Dad said, scooping up a big dab of vindaloo with his chapati. 'Delicious, it is.'

'Fattening, though,' Mum said wistfully, as if remembering long ago and far away, when she had been one of those girls you see at bus stops who are so skinny they could be the bus stop, if they were only a bit taller.

'But it's not just food,' Dad said. 'It's the culture.'

Mum went to the drawer for a sharp knife to cut her potato with. It was too large to swallow whole and too tough to bite into.

'It's a whole way of life,' Dad said. 'A different approach to things. I was chatting to Ravi behind the counter and he was telling me that when it comes to life and family, that back home in India, they leave nothing to chance.'

'Oh?' Mum said. 'Is that a fact?'

To put you in the picture, Mum was a little bit suspicious of things Indian and had been so ever since her unfortunate experience with the red-hot Indian chilli diet. It was true that she had lost over seven pounds on it, but as she had also lost some of her hair, her eyebrows, the contents of her stomach and several days off work, she did not regard it as a success. On top of that, she soon put the seven pounds back on again, thanks to the cake, ice cream and chocolate diet, which she falls back on in times of stress.

Dad was tucking into his curry big time now. We never bothered with a tablecloth when Dad was having curry. Mum just put a bit of newspaper down and hid the breakable ornaments.

'So in what way are things in India better?' Mum asked, biting into a slice of raw potato with no evidence of enjoyment. Dad gave me half a popadom and a dunk of mango chutney.

'All sorts of ways,' Dad expounded, suddenly becoming aware of the cat by his feet, looking up at him, kind of willing him to drop some food on the floor.

It is not all cats who like curry, but ours does. Our cat will eat anything, including rabbits, which is why we have to keep him locked in the house when they are out in the garden.

'For instance?' Mum said. I don't think she was really all that interested in what Dad had to say. She just needed something to take her mind off food.

'Well, take getting married, for example,' Dad said, waving his chapati around. A bit of chicken wing went flying across the kitchen; the cat had it before it hit the floor. 'They don't leave important things like that to chance in India. They have it all sorted out years in advance.'

I looked at him blankly. I was starting to think that maybe there were drugs in the curry and I shouldn't have any more in case I started hallucinating. But then I thought that I might quite like to try hallucinating, so I pushed my plate over for a dollop more.

'What, Donald,' Mum said, 'are you on about? I presume you mean the dowry system, do you?' And she had a long suck of her spud.

'Yes, exactly – the dowry system,' Dad said. 'And apparently it works very well. The way Ravi explained it, it kicks off when your children are still quite young. You search around, find another family you like the look of, and then . . . well, now, say you've got a boy, like we have, like young Bosworth here . . .' (I'll explain about the name Bosworth later) '. . . well, if you've got a spare boy, you go looking for a family with a spare girl. And if you've got a spare girl, you go looking for a nice respectable family with a spare boy.'

Mum chewed on her potato – which I noticed was starting to go brown.

'What do you mean "spare", Dad?' I said.

'You know, unattached,' he said. 'Not committed. Nothing on the calendar, nothing in the diary, so to speak. Not engaged. Not spoken for. Not married yet.'

Still the warning bells didn't ring. They should have rung by then, but they didn't. They probably hadn't been oiled in a long time, or maybe the batteries were flat.

'So?' Mum said, rather snappily too, I thought. 'We know what the dowry system is. So what about it?' Mum always got snappy when she was on diets. I don't think the poster she had stuck on the fridge door saying 'Food Is The Enemy, Eat It And Die' helped with her moods all that much either. 'Are you saying you think it's a good idea?'

'Well, it does save a lot of messing around,' Dad said. 'All that dating business, and hanging round in discos. Your kids don't have to bother with any of that because you've already got them somebody lined up.'

Mum looked at Dad with a strange expression on her face, as if he had turned into a large, raw potato himself, and her diet book said she was going to have to eat him.

'But what about the rest of it?' she said.

It was Dad's turn to look blank.

'What rest of it?' he said.

'*Love*,' Mum said. 'Falling in love! Romance! Deciding for yourself who you want to be with. And not having somebody foisted on you by your parents. I dare say the arranged marriage system's got its merits, but I'd rather make my own mistakes, thanks very much.'

Dad went a bit quiet, as he mopped up some korma sauce with a chapati.

'What do you mean . . . mistake?' he said.

Mum did her best to laugh it off.

'I'm just saying that surely love should come first and marriage after, that's all. Not the other way round.'

But Dad wasn't deterred in the least.

'But that's what's so clever about it,' he said. 'By all accounts, in most of these arranged marriages, the two people *do* come to love each other in the end. I'm not saying it's a perfect system. Of course it doesn't always work out. But the other thing to remember is there's money in it.'

My ears went up. (It was a trick I'd learned from my rabbits.) Dad had my full attention now.

'Money in it, Dad?' I said. 'How do you mean? How can there be money in getting engaged to be married at a young and tender age? Tell me more, do.'

'Ah, well,' Dad said, sounding like he was already backtracking, 'when I say money in it, Bos . . .'

(That was me. Bos is short for Bosworth. This is typical of parents, to my mind. They give you some crummy name which they think is a great idea, and then later on, they have second thoughts, especially when everyone starts saying, 'Bosworth? What kind of name is that? It sounds like a rare breed of pig or a big chicken.' So they try to disguise your real name by shortening it, or simply call you something else.)

'When I say money in it, Bos,' Dad said, 'what I mean is there's only money in it if you're a boy.'

'I'm a boy, Dad,' I reminded him, in case he had forgotten.

'But there's no money in it if you're a girl. Which I admit some people might see as sexist and unfair,' Dad added, with a glance at Mum.

'Not me, Dad,' I told him. 'I don't see it that way. People paying boys to go and marry girls sounds absolutely fine in my opinion. I mean, you wouldn't go and marry one for any other reason, would you, Dad?'

'Well . . .'

He was looking at Mum again and she was looking at him, as if she wanted a little private word about the nature of my upbringing.

Before she could ask for a brief adjournment, however, and a confidential adult word, I just needed to get the facts straight, to make sure I hadn't misheard or failed to understand things.

'So just to get this right, Dad,' I said. 'What you're saying is that boys like me can make money out of getting engaged to girls? People will pay them to do that? And when they get their hands on the dosh, they can go and spend it all? On themselves?'

'Well, sort of,' Dad said. 'Something like that.'

He looked rather uncomfortable as he spoke. I thought maybe his curry was too spicy. But when I followed his gaze and saw that he was looking at the expression on Mum's face, I realized the cause of his discomfort.

There was something Mum did not approve of. Something she didn't like at all. I thought it was maybe the raw potato that was doing it, or perhaps that was only part of the reason.

'Hmm,' I said, going into thoughtful mode. 'Money . . . for getting married? Hmm. I might be interested in that.'

Then I heard a kind of licking noise, and realized that the cat was up on the table, with his head in a foil tray.

Mum saw him a second after I did.

He didn't stay there long.

2

Show Me the Money

'Tell me more about the money, Dad,' I said as we moved seamlessly on to the puddings. 'Describe it to me in fine detail. Is it big money we're talking about here, Dad, as that's the kind I like the most. Though even little money's better than none.'

There was a pause as he set the puddings out – a selection of Indian sweets and tasty fudge-type things.

'Pudding, Mum?' I said, proffering the plate, in an effort to be polite.

'It's all right thank you, Bosworth,' she said. 'I've not finished my raw potato yet. In fact I don't know if I ever will.'

So Dad and I had to eat them on our own. He selected a gulab jam. I decided to do the same.

'So then, Dad,' I prompted again. 'Tell me more about this dowry business, eh?'

'Well,' he said, reaching for a piece of the fudgy

stuff to wash the gulab jam down with. 'To be honest with you, Bosworth, the reason why a dowry has to be paid to a boy's family is because in some parts of the world women aren't thought to be worth as much as men.'

'Not here though,' Mum reminded him. 'I think you'll find in this house, they're worth a great deal more.'

'Yes, dear,' Dad agreed. (For although there was only one of Mum and two of me and Dad, it was understood by all of us that she was still worth far more on her own than Dad and me put together.) 'I'm only reporting what some people believe. Not saying I agree with them.'

'But, Dad,' I said, anxious to hear more about this money-making opportunity, yet still a little bewildered by it. 'How come boys can get paid to marry girls, when according to all the pop songs you hear, you're lucky to get a girl to even look at you? In most songs there's usually some bloke going on about how his heart is broken because some girl won't go out with him, as she thinks he's a smelly loser with spots. You get the impression that he'd have to pay *her* just to say hello.'

'Well,' Dad nodded, taking another sweet from the selection, 'that's as maybe, son. I agree it seems that way in the pop charts. But it's not like that in other places. It's what is known as cultural differences.'

'Ah, right, Dad,' I said. 'I've heard of those. We're always doing them at school, cultural differences, and learning why one man's turban is another man's skullcap, and why some people can't eat cheese on Sundays unless there's a Z in the month.'

'Quite,' Dad said, and Mum gave me one of her funny looks as if she thought I hadn't been paying attention at school again. 'Anyway, under the dowry system, a girl's parents give money and presents to the boy and his family to encourage him to marry their daughter. You see?'

I chewed this information over along with some almond-flavoured fudge.

'You mean otherwise, if they didn't do that, she'd be cluttering the house up for the rest of her life? And they'd never get rid of her? Is that what you're saying, Dad? That the girl's parents basically pay you to come and take her away? Same as the rubbish truck comes round on Fridays to shift the bin bags?'

Dad glanced at Mum, who was looking a bit tight-lipped. He was looking increasingly nervous.

'Perhaps your mother would like to answer that one,' he said.

'It's nothing of the sort, Bosworth,' she said. 'What you have to remember is that families often have both girls and boys in them. For every dowry you'd receive for marrying off a son, you'd also have to pay one for marrying off a daughter. So it's swings and roundabouts.'

The gulab jams and fudgy things were sadly nearing an end. I licked the end of my finger and used it to dab up the crumbs.

'Manners, Bosworth,' Mum said.

'Sorry, Mum,' I said, and went on doing it anyway. I often find that an apology is all you need to excuse your poor manners and bad behaviour. You don't actually have to stop anything. You just say you're sorry for being who you are and then carry on as normal. I don't think people really expect you to change but they appreciate it if you're a bit humble.

'Anyway,' Mum said, 'it can't always be so wonderful for the children involved in these dowry arrangements. Finding yourself engaged to a complete stranger. I don't know if that's a recipe for a good marriage or a formula for disaster.'

I thought it was interesting to hear that there were recipes for getting married. If I ever got married when I grew up and things went sour with the wife, maybe I could stick her in the oven on a low heat with a couple of baked potatoes.

'Why, under the dowry system, a boy and girl might get engaged, and then not see each other again for seven years or more – not until the day of their wedding,' Mum said.

My ears lit up on hearing this. (I know that strictly speaking it is eyes that light up and not ears, but those of you with a poetical nature will know what I am getting at.)

'Not see her, Mum?' I said. 'For seven or eight years?'

'That's right,' she said. 'A boy might get engaged to a girl from another village or town, hundreds of miles away. They meet as children, a portion of the dowry is handed over, then the girl's parents take her back home. Next time they meet, they're two grown-up people, dressed in their wedding clothes.'

But I'd more or less switched off by then. My mind was away in other places. My brain was boldly going where brains had never gone before. All I could think of was dosh.

I mean, when you're still a kid, what are years? Years are great big meaningless things. A year is like a mist on a far horizon. A year is massive, a year is immense, a year goes on forever.

And as for seven years, well, that's as good as a lifetime. In fact for some animals, it is a lifetime – several lifetimes. And if somebody says to you that in seven years' time you have to get married, to you that's virtually the same as never having to get married at all.

It's so far into the future as to be unimaginable. You can't see the day ever coming. It's like contemplating the ice caps melting or the sun going out or the end of the world. You know it'll happen, but you'll never be there to see it. A debt to be repaid in seven years' time is a debt you never have to pay at all.

You think.

Though of course, that isn't true. It's like in those stories about people who sell their souls to the devil for forty years of riches and fame, thinking the forty years will never pass, or that the devil will forget all about them and never come back to claim his side of the bargain.

But they do. And he does. He always does. Devils and elephants never forget. Time catches up with everyone in the end, and debts and dowries have to be settled.

Not that all this meant anything to me. Seven or eight years was an eternity away. All I could think of was wodges of dosh and being paid to get married to someone.

I even started thinking that if I could find enough girls wanting to get married, and if I was sneaky about it, I could get engaged to several at once, and have so much dowry coming in that I could set up my own business on eBay, buying and selling events tickets.

It looked like a big money-spinner, as far as I could tell, with absolutely no down side at all. Except the big reckoning, maybe, waiting at the end of the seven-year tunnel. But as I say, that was so far in the future, it was as good as not there.

I picked the last of the crumbs from the plate, and licked them from my finger. The cat gave me a funny look, as if licking crumbs was his job.

'You know, Dad,' I said, 'this dowry lark sounds like not a bad idea to me. I can see that it's a bit of a foreign notion, but none the worse for that. For after all, as Miss Wedgely our teacher tells us, the world's a great melting pot of race and culture these days. So if you've got anybody lined up, who you think might like to marry me, and whose parents are big in the old dosh department, well, I might be prepared to give her the once-over and the benefit of my experience.'

What experience that was, I didn't know, but I thought it sounded good, so I said it.

I realized Mum was staring at me, her mostly uneaten raw potato still on her plate.

'Mum,' I said. 'Your mouth's open.' (She was always telling me when mine was, so I thought I ought to return the favour.)

She waggled a finger in her ear. Then she turned to Dad.

'Did I just hear right?' she said. 'Did I really hear what I just heard? Or am I imagining it due to low blood sugar and lack of proper nourishment?'

Dad looked slightly smug and kind of pleased with himself.

'You see, Muriel,' he said. 'I told you it was a good idea. It might be just the thing for Bosworth.' Then he turned to me. 'So would you like me to look into it then, son?' he said.

'What, Dad?' I said – more shocked than slow

on the uptake. I hadn't expected anyone to take me seriously.

'Look into finding someone,' he said.

'S-someone for what, Dad,' I stuttered.

'Someone for you to get married to, of course, Bosworth,' Dad said. 'Would you like us to take some soundings? See if there's a good family with a nice girl, who are looking to marry her off at some time in the future, and who'd want her to get engaged for now. A fairly well-off sort of family, who could afford a decent dowry.'

'A d-dowry, Dad?' I said, still stuttering, a bit shellshocked from the swift and rapidly accelerating pace of events.

'Yes, son,' Dad said. 'What do you think of that? How do you feel on that score? What would you say? Would you like us to find you a wife?'

'Ehhhhh . . .' I said. And then I said it again. 'Ehhhhh . . .' And again. And again after that.

And then I remembered, with a sudden jolt, that I hadn't fed my rabbits.

3

A Cause for Concern

The matter of getting married one day, and of finding nice girls to get engaged to (and getting paid for it into the bargain), sort of fell by the wayside after that. Not only did I forget about it, Mum and Dad seemed to have forgotten about it too. It had just been one of those things that you talk about over dinner and immediately put out of your mind as soon as you've done the washing-up. (Not that there had been a lot of washing-up, it had mostly been foil trays.)

So I just got on with looking after my rabbits (Arbuthnot and Grizelda) and with the occasionally complicated business of being Bosworth Hartie.

Being a Hartie was bad enough sometimes with people saying things like, 'Are you hearty then? Are you a hearty chap?' like they didn't know the two words were spelled differently – I don't think.

That my parents had saddled me with 'Bosworth' to go with 'Hartie' was a little on the unforgivable side. Apparently it had been Mum's idea. She had seen the name in a newspaper and had thought it sounded distinguished. Dad hadn't been so impressed, so I later found out.

'You can't call him Bosworth,' he said. 'It's the name of a battle, isn't it? The Battle of Bosworth. You may as well call him Waterloo, or Trafalgar, or Second World War Hartie or Spanish Armada Hartie, or Charge of the Light Brigade Hartie, or Bunch of Fives Hartie, or Smack in the Gob Hartie or . . .'

But Mum was not to be dissuaded, and so Bosworth it was. The only concession she made was to agree to the name Dad had wanted being put down as my middle name. So my full title was Bosworth David Hartie. Little by little, in a sort of stealthy way, I was edging out the Bosworth and more concentrating on the David. It was my intention to dump the Bosworth altogether at some point, and start a fresh life with a new identity, first as plain Dave Hartie and then as Dave Smith. It might even mean a whole change of personality and a new social circle. But as I didn't really have much of a social circle, that wasn't too great a problem.

Sometimes I used to wonder why I never had any brothers or sisters, but I think the main reason was that Mum and Dad could not agree on what the next one ought to be called.

I'd never had that trouble with my rabbits. I'd said to the man in the shop, the moment I saw them, 'That one's an Arbuthnot,' I said, 'and that one there is a sure-fire Grizelda, or my name's not Dave.'

The pet shop man gave me a look then.

'You do know that your Grizelda is a bloke rabbit,' he said. 'And your Arbuthnot is a girl.'

'Makes no odds to me,' I told him, because I'm a boy who sticks with his decisions, once he's made his mind up – even if his information is completely wrong. It is best to do this, in my opinion, for to do otherwise is a sign of weakness which can cause people to take advantage, once they know that you're prepared to back down.

Anyway, names aside, the conversation about dowries, weddings, long engagements and all the rest just seemed to fall by the wayside. And by that same wayside it might have stayed forever, had it not been for The Disastrous Exam Results.

You may well be wondering why The Disastrous Exam Results are in capital letters. The reason is because from the moment they arrived in the house, that was how they were referred to – In Big Capital Letters. All The Time.

Now I'd be the first to admit that maybe my concentration and my devotion to homework had slackened off a little during that term, but as my grandad was always saying, 'There's more to life than school, sure as one and one make three.'

Which is true. There were my rabbits, my DVDs, my stunning collection of computer games. I won't list all the distractions there were, as I've mentioned them already, but I admit that I had let them distract me, and I hadn't done much work.

So OK, I deserved a bit of a telling-off and a bit of a talking-to. I'd have knuckled down again come the start of the following term, and got back up to my usual high standard of being just about average. So yes, I admit that I deserved the bad report and the poor results and the red underlinings.

But I didn't deserve the Capital Letters – All The Time.

It was Capital Letters at home for weeks, after the exam results arrived. Not only did we have The Disastrous Exam Results, we also had the Where Did We Go Wrongs along with the It's All Your Fault The Way You Give In To That Boy And Always Let Him Have His Own Ways, usually accompanied by the My Fault? What Do You Mean? It's You And Your Nagging That Have Turned Him Off School Work.

And on it went.

It was a bad time for all of us round at my house.

Even my rabbits weren't happy bunnies.

I had become a Cause For Concern.

Mum, initially, was of the opinion that He Should Go And See A Good Psychiatrist. Dad, however, was worried about the cost. Grandma's view was that A Good Kick Up The Backside Would Soon Sort Him Out, but as Dad pointed out to her, you were no longer allowed to give children of tender years good kicks up the backside, as if you did they would sue you and you would end up in prison sharing a cell with murderers and a bucket for a toilet.

There were a lot of whispered conversations behind closed doors after that, conversations I wasn't privy to. And even though I put a glass tumbler to the wall and my ear to the base of the tumbler (which acts as a sort of amplifier) I was still unable to make out much more than odd phrases, things like: . . . *thinking about what we said before . . . the love of a good woman . . . girls mature so much earlier . . . set an example . . . provide stability and encouragement . . . the chance to grow . . . development of the inner self . . . something to aim for . . .* and other grown-up catch-phrases and buzz-words which adults like to use when they are endeavouring to confuse you and impress themselves by sounding knowledgeable.

But if I ever walked into the room where these whispered conversations were going on, the whispering would immediately stop, and the capital letters would resume, or Mum and Dad would look all innocent and say things like . . . *Yes, I must make an appointment to get my hair done as I mentioned,* and, *Yes, it does seem like rain.*

One Saturday morning, while I was on the computer doing some homework (and I really was doing it, I wasn't just pretending and actually playing on-line *Killers of the Subway*), there was a bit of bustling and rustling and coughing out in the corridor, and then Mum and Dad came in mob-handed, all two of them together, and they said the terrible words that all children dread to hear from their parents.

'Son,' they said. 'We'd like to have a word with you.'

In my opinion, if you ever hear those words addressed to you by your mum and/or dad, your best plan is to run screaming from the house, right out of the front door, and not to stop running until you get to Australia. (Unless you are in Australia to start with, in which case don't stop running until you've got to Moscow. (Unless you're starting off in Moscow, of course, in which case, go somewhere else.))

Yes, 'We'd like to have a word with you' – I think it has to be one of the most frightening sentences ever constructed. It is up there along with other such horrifying expressions as, 'We've found a magazine under your bed,' and, 'Where did you get all that money from?' and, 'There's a girl at the door with a baby,' and, 'Why is there a horse in the wardrobe?'

You can imagine my state of mind, therefore,

when Mum and Dad came into the room and made their simple – but strangely frightening – request.

My mind went on a quick search and spooled rapidly through all the events of the past weeks. But I couldn't think of a single thing I had done wrong – apart from not very well in the exams. Other than that, my life was an open book, with not a smudge on its pages. I was, as far as I knew, an innocent man. But I was still worried, for being innocent is no guarantee of not being found guilty. Or, as my grandad likes to put it, 'When there's been a robbery in the toffee factory, don't walk past the gates chewing.'

Dad closed the door behind him.

'Yes,' he said. 'We'd like to have a little word with you, Bos, if we may.'

'That's right,' Mum said, giving me what I think was supposed to be a reassuring smile – though it could have been the start of toothache. 'We would.'

'Sit down, Bosworth,' Dad invited.

'I am sitting down, Dad,' I pointed out.

'Then sit down again,' he said.

'But I haven't stood up, Dad,' I said. 'So how can—'

'Look, why don't *we* sit down?' Mum said. 'And then we'll all be sitting down and it'll be nice and cosy.'

Nice and cosy is a worrying expression too, in my experience. In films, whenever people want to get nice and cosy with anyone, it is usually to pull their toenails out. (At least it is in the films I watch, though other people might have different experiences.)

There was only one chair in the room where we had the computer, so Mum and Dad did a very strange thing, they sat on the floor.

'There,' Mum said, looking up at me. 'So we're all nice and cosy now.'

(Which sounded like the toenails again to me.)

'OK,' Dad said. 'So who's to start?'

They looked at each other.

'How about you . . . I . . . either of us . . . how about I . . .'

'OK, I will. The thing is, Bos—' Dad began. But Mum interrupted him and immediately took over.

'The thing is, Bosworth,' she said, 'is that we have been very worried and concerned about you recently, especially ever since your Disastrous Exam Results.'

'Oh, you needn't worry about them, Mum,' I said. 'I'll be cracking the books big time, soon as I'm back at school and—'

But she wasn't listening.

'Your father and I are of the opinion,' she said, 'that you have come to that stage in life where you ought to be given more responsibilities, and that they will help you to settle down and to mature.'

'But I've got responsibilities,' I pointed out. 'I've got my rabbits.'

'We mean bigger responsibilities, Bosworth.'

'What – bigger rabbits? Or were you thinking more of some badgers?'

'No, not bigger rabbits,' Mum said. 'Or badgers. We are thinking more of a guiding hand, a steadying influence, a light touch upon the tiller for those who are having difficulties navigating a steady course.'

'Oh,' I said, a touch flummoxed and not quite catching her drift. 'So what did you have in mind exactly?'

'I think . . .' Mum began. Then she changed it to, 'We think . . .' Then to, 'Your father and I think . . .' and she nudged Dad in the ribs with her elbow a few times until he started nodding his head (and then she nudged him again to get him to stop). 'That is to say, we are of the opinion, Bosworth, that it might do you a lot of good to start thinking about settling down.'

'But, Mum,' I said, 'why do I need to settle down when I haven't even got unsettled or settled up yet?'

'Nevertheless,' Mum went on, 'your father and I feel that it would help no end with your school work for you to have a plan ahead of you, Bosworth, something to aim for, something for your studies to lead to – a goal, as it were. We feel that would be very beneficial for you.'

'Oh,' I said. 'So what do you think I should do then, Mum?' I asked. 'Do you think I ought to go to Disneyland?'

'No, Bosworth,' Mum said. 'Not Disneyland. No, we feel that what you need is a good woman to set you straight. We are of the opinion, Bosworth, that it might be a very good idea for you to get . . . well . . .'

'What, Mum?' I demanded impatiently. 'Get what?'

'Well,' she said, with a look at Dad, '. . . a good idea for you to get . . . engaged.'

'Engaged?' I said, puzzled.

'Yes,' she said. 'Engaged.'

'But engaged to do what?'

'Engaged, Bosworth . . .' she explained, '. . . to be married.'

4

The Cupid's Bow Introductions Bureau

It has always seemed to me that there are only two things in life that are ever engaged. The first one is courting couples and the second one is public toilets. Plainly, as I was not a public toilet (despite rumours to the contrary), Mum had to mean 'engaged' as in 'courting couples'.

At first I was surprised – even stunned – to hear Mum come out with this idea, especially when she had been so lukewarm about the dowry and the arranged marriage business when Dad had first broached the matter over his vindaloo and gulab jam.

'Engaged, Mum?' I said. 'How do you mean, engaged?'

'Engaged,' she explained, 'to a girl.'

'But to what girl, Mum?' I said. 'I don't know any girls. Well, no, I do. I know the girls in my class at school. But nobody would ever want to get engaged to any of them as they are rough and unruly types, who probably couldn't even fry a tea bag, never mind bring up babies and make sardine sandwiches. Half of them wouldn't even know how to put oven chips in the toaster.'

'No, Bosworth,' Mum said, 'a girl from your class might be a little close to home. Your father and I were thinking of a nice girl with prospects for you, from a good, clean, orderly and respectable family, but not someone right on the doorstep.'

'Oh,' I said. 'I see. And would there be any dowry involved?'

Mum and Dad shared a look.

'Well, we might, I think, ask for a small dowry as a sign of good faith,' Mum said. 'Not from greed or to line our pockets, more as evidence of proper commitment.'

'Oh,' I said again. 'And so who would be getting this dowry then, Mum?' I asked. 'Who exactly would it belong to?'

'Well, strictly speaking,' she said, 'as you would be the one getting engaged, Bosworth, ultimately the dowry, I suppose, should go to you.'

'Oh,' I said. And then I said it again, because once didn't seem like enough. 'Oh.'

'So what do you think then, son?' Dad asked. 'We don't want to force you into anything, but your mother has a point. A little commitment in your life and some serious future plans might be just what you need to get you back on the straight and narrow path for examination success.'

'Oh,' I said, 'I don't know, really...' (And I didn't either. But had I known then what I know now, if I had had even the faintest idea of what getting engaged would involve, I would have run screaming from the room, yelling, 'No, no, no. Anything but that,' and legged it down the road.)

'Well, think it over, son,' Dad said. 'We'll give you some time to mull it over in your mind.'

'You've got till lunchtime,' Mum said. 'And I'll expect the answer to be the one I want.'

She seemed to be a bit irritable to me that morning. But I didn't think it was anything personal. I put it down to the new celery and parsnips diet. Not that I have anything against celery and parsnips, but I wouldn't fancy them for breakfast.

They left me alone with the computer then, to think about their proposition. As far as I could tell, I had everything to gain and nothing to lose from getting engaged. For starters, I would get a big load of dowry out of it, and then I wouldn't have to see the girl again for another seven years, by which time I would have spent all the money and – with a bit of luck – she might have forgotten all about the arrangement or have met somebody else.

So as there was no way I could lose, I went along to the kitchen, where Mum was steaming a parsnip for lunch, to tell her and Dad that I was agreeable to getting engaged as long as the terms were acceptable and as long as it didn't interfere with my homework.

They agreed that being engaged ought not to interfere with my homework, as the intention was quite the opposite.

'OK,' I said. 'So where are these girls who want to get married to me then, Mum? The ones with all the dosh, ready to pay for the privilege? Bring on the totty,' I said. 'Show me these groovy chicks. Just call me Bosworth the love machine. I hope you've got a few good-looking ones lined up, as although beauty is only skin deep, it's the skin you see first. I'd also prefer one who wasn't too much on the big side, as I might feel intimidated. My preferred choice would be a girl with regular white teeth and no moustache, as they're the ones who seem the nicest. I don't mind if she has braces – but not if she's wearing them to keep her knickers up.'

'Well, to be honest, Bosworth,' Dad said, 'we don't actually have any one girl in particular lined up at the moment, as it is early days yet and we are but putting a toe in the water, so to speak. But if you've got a spare moment later on in the day, I see in the paper that there is a highly recommended introductions bureau in town, and we could all maybe take a stroll down there and see if they have anything half-decent on the books.'

'I'm afraid you two will have to go on your own,' Mum said, 'as I'm busy later, having my nails done at Beautiful Fingers.'

'What happened to the place you usually go to?' Dad asked. 'Rub 'Em and Scrub 'Em?'

'I've stopped going there,' Mum said. 'They were too rough.'

'OK, Bosworth,' Dad said. 'Looks like it's you and me then, son. It's the men.'

(I may have imagined it, but I thought Mum made a derogatory sort of snorting noise at that point. But she could have just been sneezing as a result of the steamed parsnip vapour.)

So Dad got on the phone straightaway and he rang up the introductions bureau he had seen advertised in the newspaper and made an appointment for half past two. The bureau was in the High Street, in a small office suite on the first floor of a building which also housed Webster's Wet Fish and Cockle Shop at the ground level. The business was called the Cupid's Bow Introduction Bureau (Prop: Mrs Maria Knuckell) and so we rang a bell and went up the stairs, leaving the sound of the Wet Fish and Cockle Shop behind us (if not the smell).

Mrs Knuckell's secretary was sitting in a small office typing on her computer; she invited us to take a seat, saying that Mrs Knuckell was busy with a client but that she wouldn't be long. She also gave me a searching, lingering look, as if she was not used to seeing boys of my age round at introductions bureaux.

After five minutes, the door to Mrs Knuckell's room opened and she emerged, ushering out a middle-aged lady who I presumed was looking for love and who was seeking Mrs Knuckell's assistance in tracking it down as she had so far been unable to locate it on her own.

'So don't you worry, Miss Spood,' Mrs Knuckell said as she showed her out. 'I'm sure we will have a gentleman for you very soon, to match your high requirements. Tall, dark, young and handsome millionaires looking for ladies twice their age with warts on the ends of their noses are not easy to find, but rest assured that we will find one for you – or the nearest thing to it – nevertheless.'

Miss Spood thanked her and left, whereupon Mrs Knuckell turned to her secretary and said, 'Send her the details of Mr Honker, Laurel, if you would. I feel they might be compatible.'

'But he's not tall, dark, rich and handsome,' Laurel objected. 'He's short, fat, out of breath and living on a pension.'

'Close enough,' Mrs Knuckell said. Then, dismissing the matter from her mind, she turned around, her smile like the revolving light on a lighthouse, and she gave Dad and me the full 200 watts' worth of teeth.

'Ah – you must be Mr Hartie,' she said to Dad, extending her hand in greeting. And then she saw me sitting next to him. 'Oh,' she said. 'I didn't realize that you were a single parent. Men with boys can be hard to shift. Especially boys with learning difficulties, if appearances are anything to go by. But don't despair, I'm sure we'll have someone on the books who isn't too fussy. Come into my office and I'll take some details. This way.'

Before Dad could clarify the situation or raise any objections, Mrs Knuckell had disappeared into her office, so we had no choice than to follow.

'Please, sit down,' she invited. 'Now,' she said, 'if I can take a few particulars, Mr Hartie. First of all, what kind of relationship are you searching for? Serious? Deep? Meaningful? What? Or are you basically just looking for an unpaid cleaner?'

'Eh, no,' Dad said. 'The thing is, I'm not actually looking for a relationship at all.'

'You aren't?'

'No.'

'And why is that?'

'I've already got one.'

'Have you indeed?' Mrs Knuckell said, starting to sound a bit haughty.

'Yes. I have. I'm married.' He indicated me. 'To his mother.'

'I see. So why are you here then, Mr Hartie? Is one relationship not enough for you? I hope that you are not here looking for bits on the side, as it isn't that kind of bureau.'

'What's a bit on the side, Dad?' I asked hopefully, as the expression sounded a bit grown up, like something you'd want to find out about but your parents wouldn't want you to know.

'It's like salad,' Dad said. 'That you have on the side of your plate.'

It seemed odd to me that Mrs Knuckell would be doing salads as well as introductions, but I didn't pursue the point.

'I'm afraid your secretary must have got the wrong impression when I rang up and arranged the appointment,' Dad said. 'I'm not here because I'm looking for an introduction for myself . . .'

'Then why are you here?' Mrs Knuckell asked, assuming a no-nonsense, I'm a busy woman, please don't waste my time, tone.

'We're here for him,' Dad said.

'Him?' Mrs Knuckell said, searching around the room. 'And who exactly is him?'

Dad pointed at me with the sharp part of his elbow.

'Him,' he said. 'Bosworth.'

Mrs Knuckell stared at me.

'Him?' she said. 'Him! You're looking for somebody to marry . . . him?'

'Well, no, not straightaway,' Dad said. 'It's more a long engagement we're looking for.'

'With a big dowry,' I chipped in.

'Leave the dowry for now, son,' Dad whispered. 'We'll sort that out later.'

Mrs Knuckell was looking at me with some intensity by now, her eyes like little laser beams.

'Him?' she repeated. 'Him? But he's just a boy.'

'Big for my age, though,' I said, taking a couple of deep breaths so as to expand my chest.

'Yes, I know he's too young to be getting married right now,' Dad said. 'But he's been a bit wayward recently and his mother and I think that he needs a shape to his life.'

'Shape? Really?'

'And commitment. And responsibility. And getting engaged to the right girl would give him that, we feel . . .'

'Along with a big dowry,' I chirped up again, feeling that to some extent the essence of the matter was being overlooked.

Mrs Knuckell peered at us through her spectacles.

'Well,' she said. 'In all my years of match-making . . .' (which surprised me somewhat, to hear that she had worked in a match factory) '. . . I have never been asked to do anything like this. I'm afraid that I don't have any dealings with, or any experience of, arrangements of this nature. And I have no one on my books under the age of twenty-two. I do have an eighty-year-old lady who might be prepared to wait a few years, if I explain the situation to her. But you must appreciate that by the time he's old enough to marry her, she may no longer be with us.'

'How is she in the dowry department?' I asked, feeling that someone who was going to kick the bucket soon might be the perfect candidate.

'Let's leave the dowry for now, son,' Dad said. 'We're not in this for the money, you know.'

But I felt, on that account, he should only speak for himself.

'No, it's someone of his own age we're looking for,' Dad said. 'A sensible sort of girl with good exam results who'll lead by example and show him the way ahead.'

'Ask about the dowry, Dad,' I whispered. But he didn't seem to be listening to me any more.

'Well, I'm sorry,' Mrs Knuckell said, 'but I'm afraid I can't help you. I'm not in the long-term arranged marriage business. If that's what you're looking for, I suggest that you try Patel's Partners (Arranged Marriages a Speciality). Mr Patel has far more experience in that line than I do, and he may be able to fix your son up with a suitable girl – though I have to warn you that his standards are very high and before he takes your son on, he may wish to see his examination results.'

Dad looked dismayed. But possibly no more than I did, now suddenly seeing all hopes of dowry slip away.

'Examination results?' Dad said. 'Why would he want to see those?'

'Well, plainly,' Mrs Knuckell said, 'because any girl who is prepared to enter a long-term marriage arrangement will be looking for the best possible candidate. Her parents will want the best for her, and they will be seeking a boy with good prospects ahead and a history of solid achievement behind him.'

'Oh,' Dad said. 'Yes, I see. Maybe I should have thought of that.'

'Indeed,' Mrs Knuckell said. 'It is a competitive world out there, Mr Hartie. There are millions of boys in the big city and your son is but one of them. What does he have to offer a girl that other boys don't – this is what you must ask yourself. What makes him stand out from the crowd?'

'I do have a very interesting collection of unused airline sick bags from around the world,' I said.

'Maybe so,' Mrs Knuckell said, 'but could you support a wife and family on them?'

'Well, I don't know about that,' I said, 'but we'd be all right on long car journeys.'

'Maybe,' she said, 'but I cannot say, young man, that I am overly impressed. As a mother of daughters myself, I would hope that when it comes to matrimony they could do a little better for themselves than unused sick bags.'

'Hmm,' I said. I could see what she was getting at, but was reluctant to concede that there was any serious truth in it. I looked over at Dad, who seemed a little depressed and downcast, as if things were not going as he had expected.

'So you think this Patel bloke would want to see our Bosworth's examination results before he takes him on?'

'Quite possibly,' Mrs Knuckell confirmed. 'More than probably, in fact. Of course, exam results are not the be-all and end-all. Many a child has not been good academically but has still gone on to great success. Academic success is but one manifestation of intelligence and ability. There are many other outlets for natural talent. Are there any other fields in which young Bosworth here has proved precocious?'

There was a slightly embarrassing pause then, while Dad mulled things over. In the end I had to give him a nudge.

'There is my collection, Dad,' I reminded him, 'of unused airline . . .'

'Yes, we know about that, son.'

'. . . from around the world.'

'So are there any other qualities,' Mrs Knuckell said, 'which would commend your son to a girl's parents?'

'Well, he's good with rabbits,' Dad said.

'I am,' I agreed. 'Very good.'

'And he's kind,' Dad said.

'That's right,' I said.

'And considerate – when he remembers.'

'When I remember, yeah.'

'And he's got a good memory.'

'Have I? Oh yes, of course I have. I'd forgotten about that.'

'And he's pretty clean. On the whole.'

'Baths every Wednesday,' I said. 'Armpits twice a week.'

'And he's affectionate.'

'I love my food,' I said. 'Ask anyone.'

'And he's got many interests.'

'Sit me down in front of that telly,' I said. 'I can watch it for hours. Wonderful concentration.'

'And he's keen on sports.'

'Loved seeing the Olympics,' I said. 'Sitting there watching people running, it doesn't half keep you fit.'

'And so maybe he might not exactly *excel* in a lot of areas,' Dad said, 'but if he studies and applies himself and does his homework, there's no reason why one day, he couldn't aspire to be just about average. In fact I think that Bosworth here could easily end up as outstandingly mediocre.'

'So there you are,' I said. 'What more could a girl ask for? All this and good looks too.'

But Mrs Knuckell's years in the lonely hearts trade had plainly jaundiced her view of human nature.

'Hmm,' she murmured. 'Well, I've had some tough cases on my books in the past, Mr Hartie,' she said. 'Some of which I thought I'd never get rid of.

There was the one-legged tightrope hopper – he was on my books for years. There was the bearded lady – I never thought I'd get rid of her until one day the bearded man turned up. But I'm afraid that this is one I couldn't even contemplate taking on. No, I'm sorry, but this isn't my field of work. I suggest you either try Patel's Partners (Arranged Marriages a Speciality) or go it alone and try a small ad in the personal columns of the local newspaper. Other than that advice, I cannot help you. Now, as I am a busy woman, with many of the lonely and the lovelorn to pair up, you'll excuse me if I press on with my matchmaking. I shall bid you good luck and good day.'

And with that, she stood up and opened the door for us, and out of it we had to go.

'Don't worry, son,' Dad said, as we walked back to the car in the multistorey car park. 'Don't you be discouraged by what she said. There are plenty of pebbles on the beach and plenty of fish in the sea.'

'There were quite a lot of them in Webster's Wet Fish and Cockle Shop too,' I said. 'If the pong was anything to go by.'

'There's a girl for you out there somewhere, son,' he said. 'It's just a question of us finding her. I'm sure that even as we speak, there's a family somewhere, and they've got a daughter of your age, and they're looking at her and they're thinking to themselves, "How are we ever going to get rid of this one?" And that'll be the girl for you.'

'What, the one they can't get rid off?'

'That's the one,' Dad said cheerfully.

'The one nobody else wants?'

'That's her,' he said. 'So don't you get despondent, Bos. We'll find her for you. It's just a matter of making a few enquiries and of tracking her down. There must be a family somewhere that's so desperate they'll be only too happy to have you as a son-in-law. Come on, let's go home and talk to your mother and plan what our next move should be.'

I followed him up the concrete stairs to level 3, feeling somehow depressed and out of sorts. I was sure he meant well, but I didn't know if I wanted to get engaged to the girl that nobody else wanted. Because if nobody else wanted her, why would I? But then, on the other hand, if nobody else wanted her, there might be a bigger load of dowry coming my way, by way of sugaring the medicine.

I moved on with a lighter step then, feeling optimistic for the future. I decided to go on the internet when I got home, and check out the price of new digital cameras, and also have a look on eBay to see if any unused airline sick bags had come on that I didn't have in my collection.

You never knew – I might get lucky.

5

Arranged Marriages a Speciality

Despite Mrs Knuckell's discouraging words in regard to Patel's Partners (Arranged Marriages a Speciality) and the chances of a boy with undistinguished exam results making any headway round there, we called upon him just the same. After all, nothing ventured, nothing gained, and if you don't go gambling, then you can't lose all your money.

Mum took me this time, and if Mr Patel looked surprised to see us, he didn't say so, or indicate as much, not even by a twitch of a facial muscle. He sat impassively, reading my school report and slowly shaking his head.

Finally, he looked up.

'This boy,' he said, 'is going to be difficult. You're not going to find any brain surgeons' daughters in a hurry to get engaged to this one.'

'She needn't be a brain surgeon's daughter,'

Mum said. 'We weren't expecting that.'

'Just having a brain would do,' I chipped in, so as to let Mr Patel know that I wasn't one of those fussy types, who are never satisfied with anything, no matter what people do. 'It needn't be a big one.'

'Let me look on my computer,' Mr Patel said, 'and see who I have. There might be someone from overseas for instance . . . hmm . . .' He spent a while looking at details on the screen. Then, 'I do have a gentleman in Delhi in India,' he said, 'who is looking to marry off his daughter in six or seven years' time and is willing to consider an immediate engagement. He's prepared to put down a dowry of five hundred rupees.'

'What's that in pounds?' I asked.

'About a fiver,' Mr Patel said. Which was rather less than I had been expecting.

'What does this gentleman in Delhi do?' Mum asked.

'He pulls a rickshaw,' Mr Patel said.

'You're pulling my leg,' Mum said.

'No, a rickshaw,' Mr Patel insisted. 'And very successful at it he is too.'

'Delhi does seem rather far away though,' Mum said. 'Do you have anyone nearer home?'

'I do,' Mr Patel said. 'But all these parents seem to be looking for at least A grades in all subjects. Some are even wanting nothing but A stars. It's an all-round, A-star boy for their daughters, or nothing.' Mr Patel turned and fixed me with his eye. 'Tell me, boy,' he said. 'Have you ever got any stars?'

'Not stars exactly,' I said. 'But me and the rest of the second eleven football team did all moon out of the school bus window once as we were driving past the convent and—'

'Bosworth!' Mum said. 'That'll do.'

'So – no stars?' Mr Patel said. 'Just moons?'

'No stars as yet,' Mum qualified. 'But one day – right, Bosworth?'

'Right,' I said, trying to sound positive and confident.

'I see. Yes.' And Mr Patel went back to his computer screen. He clicked with his mouse and he turned the little wheel in it, but the further through his records he went, the more downcast he became. 'Another trouble,' he said, 'is that you don't have any Indian heritage. Most of my customers here are looking for a nice boy with some Indian ancestry and possibly some rich relatives and a penthouse in Calcutta, or someone related to Bollywood film stars. No offence, but that's just how it is.'

'I'm afraid that isn't Bosworth, really,' Mum said. 'Most of our ancestors came from Crouch End.'

'But I'm very adaptable,' I said. 'I mean, I don't mind putting on a sari if it helps.'

Mum gave me one of her don't-be-stupid looks.

'Saris are what ladies wear,' she said.

'All right,' I said. 'I'll wear a charpoy then.'

It was Mr Patel's turn to sigh.

'A charpoy is a rope bed,' he said.

'Oh,' I said. 'So what about a charlady? What's that in India?'

'It's a woman who does the cleaning,' he said.

'What a coincidence,' I said. 'It's exactly the same here. Small world or what?'

Mr Patel appeared to be coming to both the end of his list and the end of his tether at, conveniently, the same time.

'To be perfectly honest, Mrs Hartie,' he said, 'I don't know if I can help you today. It might be better if you left it a year or two. I don't really feel that your son Nosworth—'

'Bosworth,' I corrected.

'That your son Dogsworth here is ready for any kind of a long-term commitment. He doesn't give me the impression that he is ready for marriage yet. Maybe in twenty or thirty years' time he might have matured a little. If I were you, Mrs Hartie, I would leave things a while, or try a small advertisement of my own in the newspaper – the small ads, you know, the personal columns.'

'The under-a-tenner sort of thing?' I said.

'Sort of,' Mr Patel agreed.

'Or maybe I could auction myself on eBay?'

'Yes, yes,' Mr Patel nodded, 'it's a possibility. They do say that you can get rid of anything on eBay, so I hear, and there's a mug born every minute.'

'What's that got to do with anything?' Mum demanded.

'Nothing, nothing, Mrs Hartie,' Mr Patel said hastily. 'But what you have to remember is that arranged marriages and long engagements are not as great a part of your tradition as they are of those who came here from other places. And even back in India, things have moved on. So even if you do put an advertisement in the personals, you may not, I fear, get any great response.'

(Though he proved to be wrong about that.)

Mum started to get up from her chair.

'All right. Thank you anyway, Mr Patel,' she said. 'And thank you for your time.'

'Not at all, Mrs Hartie,' he said, showing us out. 'Sorry I couldn't be more positive.'

'That's all right. Thanks for trying.'

We were at the door.

'If you ever get divorced, dear lady,' Mr Patel called after us, 'do come back and see me. I've plenty of elderly gentlemen on the books, looking for well-built ladies with a bit of meat on their bones. I'm sure we could do good business.'

Mum grunted something in reply and we walked on down the road. We happened to pass a bookshop on our way back to the car, and Mum announced that we were going in for five minutes.

'I'll see if they've got any new diet books in,' she said.

So that was what we did. It was quite a good bookshop too, with a little coffee shop in it. I got a book as well. Then Mum sat and pored over her new diet manual while we had hot chocolate and cakes.

'Why leave happiness to chance? It is said that marriage is a lottery. Increase your daughter's chances of picking a winning ticket by arranging everything well in advance. Young lad from good home seeks similar . . .'

'No, hang on, Dad,' I said. 'That doesn't sound right.'

'What do you mean?'

'Young lad from good home seeks similar – well, that sounds like I'm looking for another young lad to get engaged to.'

'Ah.'

'Wouldn't it be better to specify a girl first, and we could see how we got on from there, and then if that didn't work out, we could always think again afterwards.'

'Oh, yes. See what you mean. I'll rephrase that.'

Dad deleted what he had just written and started the sentence again.

Young lad from good home seeks young lady of similar background . . . appeared on the computer screen.

'How's that?'

'Better.'

. . . *young lady of similar background to provide mutual*

*support and stability with view to eventual marriage.
Long-term engagement envisaged. Dowry negotiable.*

'What else should I put?' Dad asked.

'Write, *No Two Baggers*,' I said.

He gave me a blank look.

'What's a two bagger?'

'It's a girl who's so horrible that one bag over the head isn't enough,' I explained.

'Let's not have any pots and kettles, please, Bosworth,' Dad said.

'Eh?' I said. 'What do you mean, Dad? Do you mean I'm a two bagger? Because if you do, I feel I ought to mention that people often say to me: "Bosworth, you're the spitting image of your dad, you know. In fact, if you were just a few stone heavier, with a bald head and wrinkles, the two of you could easily be taken for twins." '

'Is that a fact?' Dad said, sounding a bit niggled for some reason. 'Well, all the same, we'll drop the *No Two Baggers* bit, if you don't mind. So, where were we . . . oh yes . . .'

He again read out what he had just written.

'. . . *young lady of similar background to provide mutual support and stability with view to eventual marriage. Long-term engagement envisaged. Dowry negotiable.*'

'How about *No Three Baggers* then?' I said. 'If we can't say *Two*?'

'I don't really think that we want to mention any kinds of baggers at all, to be honest, son,' Dad said.

'OK. Leave the baggers bit out then,' I said. 'And if anyone answers the advertisement who is a three bagger, we can just make some excuse.'

'That's it, son,' Dad said. 'We can do it tactfully.'

'Like by running away screaming, eh, Dad?' I said. 'Subtle stuff like that.'

Dad worked on in silence for a while until he had composed the advertisement for the personal column to his satisfaction.

Young lad from good home seeks young lady of similar background to provide mutual support and stability with view to eventual marriage. Long-term engagement envisaged. Dowry negotiable. Girl with good exam grades and strong future earning potential will stand best chance.

'Could you add, *No Elephants*? Dad,' I asked.

'No,' he said. 'I couldn't. I'm not adding *No Elephants*, I'm not adding *No Two Baggers*, I'm not adding *No Three Baggers*, and I'm not adding *No Elephant Three Baggers* either before you suggest it. You'll just have to take what you can get, Bosworth, and be grateful for it. It's the support and guidance of a good woman that you need. They say girls mature earlier than boys, and that's what you need, a bit of maturity. Looks are secondary to character. You take my word for it, Bosworth, you don't want one of these flighty bits of things who swank about like models in their skimpy outfits, showing off their belly-buttons and embarrassing their parents.'

'Don't I, Dad?'

'No, son. It's a down-to-earth, sensible kind of girl you need, with proper shoes. One who's got her feet planted on the ground and who isn't afraid to get her hands dirty and who won't get blown over by a gust of wind – no matter where it comes from.'

'If you say so, Dad,' I said, as I was a bit tired of it all by then and didn't think it was going to lead to anything anyway. I thought if I just went along with it for a while to keep everyone happy, then sooner or later Mum or Dad – or both – would get bored with it, and they'd forget about the whole thing, and we could all go back to normal apathy.

'OK. That's it, then,' Dad said, hitting the print button. 'I'll print that out and show it to your mother.'

The sheet of paper rolled off the printer.

The final version read:

Young lad from good home seeks young lady of similar background to provide mutual support and stability with view to eventual marriage. Long-term engagement envisaged. Dowry negotiable. Girl with good exam grades and strong future earning potential will stand best chance. Apply in writing (enclosing passport-sized photo) in first instance to . . .

'To where?' I said, as the writing stopped there.

'The newspaper will give us a box number,' Dad said. 'That way we can stay anonymous initially.'

'And get rid of all the two baggers.'

'You seem a bit overly concerned with two baggers, if you ask me, Bosworth.'

'Stitch in time, Dad,' I said. 'Baggers can't be choosers.'

'Anyway, do you think that'll do?'

'I suppose so,' I shrugged, anxious to get on to the computer myself and to start surfing my favourite websites. 'Why not go and show Mum?'

He did, and I got the computer to myself for a while. He was back later on though with some suggested amendments, which were in due course made. The ad then appeared the following Friday in the Personal Column under the Ideal Partners heading. I read it and then forgot all about it for the rest of the weekend and most of the week.

But on the following Friday, the mail started to arrive.

Dear Sir,

Further to your advertisement in Ideal Partners, we are looking for a future husband for our daughter Gladioli (photo enclosed) who is aged 12 and a half. Gladioli is interested in getting married when she is old enough to leave school and is looking for someone who will do as he is told and who will take the dustbins out on Friday. She would expect her future husband to be good at bicycle maintenance, able to fix punctures, change tyres, and pump inner tubes up. In return for this we can offer a room at the back and use of a shed for the young couple until such time as they are able to afford a house of their own.

Regarding dowry, we will be willing to accept whatever you can afford. Looking forward to hearing from you.

Yours sincerely

Mr and Mrs B. N. Pendleton

That wasn't the only one to have got hold of the wrong end of the dowry stick. Several more arrived, in similar vein, some polite, some not so polite, some direct and blunt to the point of rudeness.

Dear Sir,

We can only assume that your son is an out-and-out two bagger (possibly even a five bagger) if he is so ugly-looking that you have to pay someone to take him away.

Fortunately for you, however, I am in the scrap business, and therefore used to getting rid of unwanted items. My daughter, Petunia-Jane, who you might have seen recently on the television, featured in the Cause for Concern documentary series (it was the episode titled 'Child Pizza Addicts') is – luckily for you – not all that fussy, and therefore willing to consider getting engaged to your son if the money is right. She is not able to get out of the house at present, not until we get the door frame widened or the window taken out, but will be happy for your son to visit at a convenient time.

She does have an aversion, however, to boys called

Rupert, so if that is your son's name, I would advise him to change it before he comes round here, at least if he wants to go home with as many teeth as he arrived with. (Assuming he has some.)

Looking forward to hearing from you at your earliest convenience,

Big Kenny (of Big Kenny's Car Scrappers).

PS – When you call, don't worry about the dogs. They are only trying to be friendly and though they seem to want to jump up and bite you in the throat, they are only playing. They are quite harmless and have never killed anyone yet.

PPS – We weren't able to fit all of Petunia-Jane on to one photo, but if you set the three enclosed ones together, you will get a good idea of what most of her looks like.

There were several other letters of that kind, and most of them went in the bin.

'Pay!' my mum said indignantly. 'Pay some girl to marry my Bosworth! My boy Bosworth! What a cheek.'

(I was plainly in temporary good standing. I am not often 'my boy Bosworth'. I am usually 'your son Bosworth' or 'my husband's son, Bosworth' or 'my mother's grandson, Bosworth' or 'that boy, Bosworth' or 'him' or 'you' or 'the bad smell in the corner'.)

'These people,' Mum continued, 'have plainly no idea of how the dowry system works. Us pay them indeed. The very idea. What a nerve. If we don't get any proper replies, we shall have to give the whole idea up.'

And then she opened the cream envelope. It was the last one too. It had to be the last one. Just when you think you're safe, just when you think the coast is clear and the trials are over, there it is, the envelope marked 'Fate' with the letter marked 'Doom' inside it.

This is what it said.

Dear Advertisers,

We were very interested to see your advertisement in the columns of the personal ads this weekend in which you expressed a wish to find a future marriage partner for your son.

We are great admirers of this traditional way of doing things and feel that the arranged marriage system has much to commend it. Why leave such things to chance and to the impetuous desires of wayward youth? Far better to follow heads rather than hearts. Parental guidance in these matters can be invaluable and can avoid many mistakes and much heartache for one's children.

We have a daughter, Veronica Angelica Belinda (photograph enclosed, though it doesn't do her full justice), for whom we are anxious to find a suitable partner as a future spouse.

Obviously, such a thing as an actual wedding would be a long way in the future, but we feel – as

we presume you do – that now is the time to forge
links and build alliances for the future.

We are not rich people, but reasonably well
off, and would be willing to pay a token sum in
dowry as a gesture of serious commitment and
good faith.

Perhaps you would like to get in touch with us
over the telephone for an initial chat, and then we
can take things from there and – if all goes well –
meet up in person, and then arrange for our
daughter and your son to get together and to see how
they hit it off.

Looking forward to hearing from you.

Yours sincerely,

Mr and Mrs L. Melling.

'Well,' Mum said, passing the letter over for Dad
and me to see. 'That one sounds promising. Don't
you think?'

I didn't think so at all. It smelled like a rat to me.
I didn't care for the sound of it one bit. The name
alone was enough to make me nervous – Veronica
Angelica Belinda. How could anybody with a name
like that be fully functioning and in possession and
control of all her faculties?

'Hmm, it sounds all right, doesn't it?' Dad said.
'And she looks like quite a nice girl too, Bosworth,
don't you think?'

He handed me a photograph. It had obviously

been taken with a digital camera and printed out on a home computer.

It was a picture of a girl. A harmless-looking girl, many would have thought, or so it might have seemed to the untrained adult eye. But one look at it and I got a bad feeling in my bones. Call it superstition, call it gut reaction, call it panic; but behind those butter-wouldn't-melt expressions and those nice-as-pie looks lay hidden and treacherous depths – I was sure of it.

'She looks like a nice girl, doesn't she, Bosworth?' Mum persisted. 'Don't you agree?'

Of course I had to agree. There was no denying it. Yes, she did look like a nice girl, very much so indeed. She *looked* like a nice girl. She was probably very good at *looking* like a nice girl. In fact, looking like a nice girl was doubtlessly a technique which she had honed to perfection over the years, as a front for her criminal activities.

So, 'Yes, Dad,' I had to admit. 'She does look like a nice girl, yes.'

But that didn't mean she was. Not one bit. It probably meant just the opposite.

6

Sign Here

I seemed to become a bit irrelevant for a few weeks after that letter from Mr and Mrs Melling (whom I had already begun to think of as the Smelly Mellings) arrived. In fact I spent a lot of time with my rabbits.

Rabbits can be very restful animals in times of stress, and there is nothing like chasing your rabbits round the garden with a big net for an hour or so to get the juices flowing and to keep you fit.

My two rabbits, Grizelda and Arbuthnot, each had their own separate hutch. To start with, I'd tried to put them in one big hutch together for company's sake, thinking that as one was a man rabbit and one was a lady rabbit, they ought to get on. But all they did was fight, and when I came out to see what the noise was, I found Grizelda with half his fur missing and his legs trembling and Arbuthnot with a bleeding paw and her whiskers standing on end.

This did not bode well in my mind for myself and Veronica Angelica Belinda Melling (whom – even though we hadn't met yet – I had already mentally nicknamed The Virus). If two small creatures like a couple of rabbits couldn't get on and live in peace and harmony together without tearing each other's hair out, what hope for the larger mammals, I thought?

And then I looked again at the photograph of Veronica (The Virus) Melling with her butter-wouldn't-melt looks and her what-*me*-cause-trouble? demeanour and I got those feelings in my stomach that you get when peering down into great depths from the roofs of high buildings with no railings around the sides.

I dreaded the thought of being stuck in a hutch with the girl in that photograph. Not only would my legs be trembling, my knees would be knocking together like coconuts in a hurricane.

Mum and Dad seemed oblivious to it though. They were having a great time, corresponding with the Smelly Mellings and ringing them up on the phone and negotiating what the dowry ought to be and how much of it should be paid in hard cash and how much of it should arrive in the form of bedding plants for Mum's garden and tins of lager for the fridge.

I appeared to have been forgotten about completely. Which is typical to my mind. This is adults all over, as far as I can see, and whenever you hear a grown-up say, 'We're doing it all for you, you know. We've made years of sacrifices, and it was all for you,' well, nine times out of ten, it wasn't. It was for them and for the fun they got out of it – even if the only fun they got was being able to moan and complain.

Take playing the violin. How come parents want their children to learn it, but they never go and learn it themselves? Or studying for exams. If exams are so great, why don't parents go and sit a few? Or cross-country runs. Why don't they go on those? And why don't a few parents go to fat camp? I'm sure there must be some vacancies.

But I suppose that these things are what are known as life's mysteries, the answers to which will one day be revealed – like when you're grown up yourself and when you've sat all your exams and you can just lounge about now and not have to do any more. You can spend your days telling other people that studying and homework are good for them, but not having to do any yourself.

Mum and Dad arranged to meet the Smelly Mellings in a pub somewhere in order to 'hammer out the details' and 'iron out the small print'. One meeting wasn't enough so they went and had a few more. They all seemed to be having a great old time, but all the while I was out in the garden with my rabbits, growing more worried and concerned at the prospect of getting engaged soon to The Virus – whom I still hadn't met.

But that day was soon to come.

After the fourth round of dowry negotiations, Mum and Dad came home with a bulky-looking contract full of expressions such as 'party of the first part' and 'party of the second part'. I couldn't make out any parties of any third parts, but had I been a lawyer, I dare say I might have found some.

'Here you are, son,' Dad said. 'We've hammered out a deal for you, and we think we've done all right. We'll just go through it with you, then you can sign it at the bottom, and then we'll exchange contracts with the Mellings, and the thing will be done.'

'Yes, but, Dad—' I protested. But I got no further.

'OK. Now, first of all, Mr and Mrs Melling have agreed to buy £200 worth of premium bonds in your name – we know it's not a huge sum, but it's a sign of good faith, and you could get lucky and win a lot more.'

'But—'

'And that, along with any winnings, will be held in trust for you until you're eighteen.'

'Eighteen! But I'll be dead by then. I'll be an old man by the time I'm eighteen.'

'But there's more, son. That's not just all.'

'Oh. Do I get some cash as well, then?'

'No, not exactly . . .'

'Don't be so materialistic, Bosworth,' Mum said.

'This isn't about money. This is about securing your future and setting you on the straight and narrow path. This is about finding a sensible girl who will be as a guiding star to your storm-tossed ship as it sails through the blustery oceans of life . . .'

'Oh. Yeah,' I said. 'Right. I forgot.'

'Indeed,' Mum said. 'As your father will tell you, the love and support of a good woman is a priceless thing beyond rubies and pearls. Isn't that so, Donald?'

'Yes, dear. Whatever you say,' Dad agreed – a little too quickly, I thought.

'Why,' Mum went on, 'if your father hadn't met me when he did, just think where he would be today.'

'Yes, just think,' Dad sighed. 'I'd be on a beach in the Bahamas . . .'

'He would be lying in a gutter somewhere,' Mum said, 'with a six-pack of strong lager, heading for an early grave. Isn't that right, Donald?'

'I suppose so, dear,' Dad said. 'If you say so.'

'No suppose about it,' Mum said. 'And what I have done for your father, Bosworth, this delightful young girl, Veronica Angelica Belinda Melling – a jewel amongst jewels and a gem amongst gems, by all accounts – will one day do for you.'

'Oh.'

'Oh yes. She will take you by the scruff of the neck, Bosworth, and propel you out into the world.

She will see to it that you will succeed, for she will not let you fail. She will be as a life-jacket to you, Bosworth.'

'You mean I'll have to blow her up?'

'I mean she will be as the Coastguard for you. As the Mountain Rescue Service.'

'You mean she's got a helicopter?'

'No, Bosworth, I mean that she will be there to save you.'

'From what, Mum?' I said, a little perplexed as to what I needed to be saved from.

Her eyes narrowed into slits, as small as little letterboxes. She looked like a photo I'd seen of Ned Kelly the outlaw in his suit of home-made armour.

'From yourself, Bosworth,' Mum said. 'From yourself.' Then she sighed again and she looked at me with a motherly expression and put a hand on my shoulder. 'Oh, Bozzie, Bozzboo, Bozzikins,' she said. 'My dear little Bozzie-wozzie-woo! What's to become of you if we let you go on drifting like this – with your slap-happy approach to lessons and homework, with your "that'll do" attitudes and your "don't worry about it, dude" outlook on life. You do see that all this is for your own good, don't you?'

'Yes, Mum,' I said. 'I suppose so.'

'You appreciate, don't you, Bosworth, that there is more to success in life than thuggish rabbits with psychopathic tendencies and a somewhat unhealthy and obsessive interest in unused airline sick bags from around the world . . .'

'It's only a hobby,' I protested. 'At least I don't collect the used ones any more.'

'Even so. As long as we understand each other. We do understand each other, don't we, Bosworth?'

'Yes, Mum.'

'Good. Now then – the rest of the engagement contract if you would, Donald, please.'

'OK,' Dad said, turning a few more pages. 'Now where was I? What had we got up to?'

'We'd just done the dowry.'

'Ah yes. We've agreed that you and whatshername . . .'

'Veronica Angelica Belinda, Donald,' Mum said. 'Really. The least you can do is to remember the name of your future daughter-in-law.'

'Right, yes, this Veronica Angelica . . . Belinda . . . whatever . . . we've agreed, son, that you and she are to meet each other and see how you get on, and then after that we can all keep in touch with regular – if occasional – visits and bulletins. You're both to sit all your exams, hopefully go on to A-levels after GCSEs, and maybe to college after, though that remains to be seen. And then we'll have the wedding. We're paying for that fifty-fifty, though the Mellings have promised to pay for the honeymoon.'

'Maybe we can come with you on that, Bosworth,' Mum interrupted.

'That'll be nice,' I said.

'Then after that, Mr and Mrs Melling have promised the two of you their spare bedroom to start married life in. Any questions?'

'Yes. What about my rabbits?' I said.

'What about them, Bosworth?'

'Who's going to look after my rabbits while I'm on honeymoon? Or can I take them with me?'

'Take your rabbits? On your honeymoon? I never heard of such a thing,' Mum said.

'No worse than taking your mother,' Dad pointed out. But Mum just gave him a cold look, and didn't respond to that.

'Frankly, Bosworth,' Mum said, 'I hate to say this, but there is a very good chance that by the time you get married, your rabbits . . . your rabbits . . .'

'Yes?' I said, feeling my lower lip start to tremble. 'What? What about my rabbits?'

'Well . . . your rabbits . . . I'm afraid to say . . . will probably . . . be . . . dead.'

'My rabbits!' I wailed. 'My rabbits! I want my rabbits! I don't want my rabbits to die. I don't want to live without my rabbits. If I have to live without my rabbits I don't want to live at all. I love my rabbits. I want to marry my rabbits. My rabbits love me and I love them and I want to marry them now! Dowry or not!'

'Now see what you've done,' Dad said. But Mum was in no mood for reproaches.

'Don't be ridiculous, Bosworth,' she said. 'You can't possibly marry your rabbits. Certainly not two of them, for that would be bigamy, and anyway, one of them's a boy. And what would the neighbours say, if they found out that you had married a rabbit. The shame of it. I would never be able to hold my head up at Weight Watchers again. Imagine it, people stopping me in the street and asking how the daughter-in-law is, and my having to admit that she was a rabbit. How can you, Bosworth? How can you even suggest it? You're a wicked boy sometimes. I know you don't mean to be, oh but you certainly know how to turn the knife in a mother's heart, Bosworth. For here I am, with nothing but your best interests in mind, arranging the best possible marriage I can for you, and you spurn my efforts and tell me that instead of this lovely girl, you would rather marry a rabbit. It's cruel, Bosworth. Cruel is what it is. There are times when you are a hard and a heartless boy. And this would appear to be one of them. A rabbit. Just imagine it. Hopping up the aisle. The discrepancy in sizes for one thing. And the dinner afterwards. Sitting there at the top table with a carrot and a plate of lettuce. It would completely spoil the day.'

'Muriel, love,' Dad said. 'I don't think Bosworth was altogether serious about marrying his rabbits. It was more a manner of speaking, you know.'

'Oh. Yes. Well, be that as it may . . . however . . .

continue reading out the contract if you would, Donald, so that Bosworth knows what he's agreeing to.'

'Right, well, where was I now? Oh yes. So, yes, now see here, Bosworth, there are various exclusion clauses here, to cater for contingencies.'

'What contingencies, Dad? What do you mean?'

'I mean the contract ceases to be binding if certain things happen.'

'Like for instance?'

'Like if you go mad, say, son. She's not obliged to marry you if you go mad.'

'What about if she goes mad?'

'Let me just check the contract about that . . . ah . . . here it is . . . no, right enough. You don't have to marry her either.'

'What about if I have a bad accident or contract a nasty illness and lose my looks, what's the situation then?'

Dad seemed momentarily perplexed. 'Looks, Bosworth?' he said. 'What looks are these, son?'

'You know,' I said. 'Me. My looks. My good looks. That I inherited from you. Those looks.'

'Oh, those. No, well, I don't know about that. No. I think she has to take you as you are. After all, this is what marriage is all about, son. It's for better, for worse. For richer, for poorer. If you marry someone and they lose their looks or put on five stone in weight you're still lumbered with them, like it or lump it.'

'Or if you find out that they snore like a train coming through a tunnel with all hooters blaring, there's not much you can do about that either,' Mum chipped in.

'Go on,' I said. 'Anything else I need to know?'

'No, I think we've covered everything. Haven't we, dear?'

'Yes,' Mum agreed. 'You'll find we've been very thorough, Bosworth, and nothing has been overlooked.'

'Em, there is one thing, Mum . . .'

'What?'

'Well, didn't you put a certain clause in, a certain crucial sort of clause, I would have thought.'

'Which is what, Bosworth?'

'Well, the thing is, Mum, this Veronica Angelica or whoever, we haven't actually met up yet, have we?'

'No.'

'So what if . . .'

'Yes?'

'I mean, what if . . .'

'Yes?'

'I'm not saying this would happen . . .'

'No . . .'

'But what if . . .'

'What if, yes?'

'What if . . .'

'What if what, Bosworth?'

'Will you come to the point, lad?'

'Either tell us what you're going on about, Bosworth, or drop the subject.'

'Well, I only wondered if you'd made provision in the contract for the remote possibility – not that I'm saying this would ever happen, of course – but the tiniest, remotest possibility that . . . well . . .'

'That what?'

'That this Veronica Angelica whoever . . . what if . . . we don't . . .'

'What?'

'. . . like each other?'

It was as if I had dropped a bomb. A bomb with a bad smell in it. Yes, it was as if I had dropped a very large stink bomb in a very small room. One with no air-conditioning, and no windows.

There was a long and terrible silence. The kind of silence which you must get on an aeroplane when the pilot looks out of the window to see that both the engines have dropped off.

'Not like each other, Bosworth? Why on earth would you not like each other? A lovely girl like Veronica Angelica Belinda here, who, going by her photo, is the sweetest thing since iced lollipops. Why would you not like Veronica Angelica Belinda?'

'I don't know, Mum. And I'm not saying I won't like her. But what if I don't? We don't still have to get engaged if we don't like each other, do we?'

'Donald,' Mum said. 'Did we make provision for that?'

'Eh, I don't know . . .' Dad said, scanning the contract, 'I don't think . . . that any of us ever considered it as a possibility.'

'Well, I'm sure that's not going to happen,' Mum said with blithe and carefree confidence. 'And even if there is the odd difference of opinion, it's unlikely to be anything serious. All couples have the odd little tiff and the occasional disagreement. Why, even your father and I don't always see eye to eye on everything, do we, Donald?'

'Whatever you say, dear,' Dad said.

'But those things teach us tolerance and how to make allowances and serve only to forge and to strengthen the bonds of a relationship. Don't they, Donald?'

'If you say so, dear.'

'Well, you don't have to agree with me if you think I'm wrong, Donald.'

'Of course not, dear,' Dad said. 'Wrong?' he said. 'You?'

'So don't worry, Bosworth,' Mum said. 'We have selected this girl very carefully for you, and we are quite convinced that you are completely compatible. You're bound to like each other. We can as good as guarantee that. Can't we?'

'Yes,' Dad nodded. 'I'm sure we can.'

'So in that case, when,' I said, 'do I get to meet her?'

'Well . . .' Dad looked at Mum quizzically. 'This weekend?' he suggested.

'I don't see why not,' she said. 'Just as soon as the ink is dry on the contract and everyone has signed it.'

'This weekend?' I said.

'Yes. I'll ring the Mellings and arrange it.'

'Us go there or them come here?'

'Whichever is the most convenient.'

I suddenly realized that somebody had put a pen into my hand.

'If you just sign there, then, Bosworth. Put your name above that dotted line.'

I hesitated. Some unseen, powerful force held me back.

I think it's that thing which is commonly known as fear.

'But, Mum,' I said, 'Dad . . . don't you think . . . before I sign the contract . . . it might be better if I met her first. Meet her first and then get engaged, rather than the other way round?'

'Well, I do think you're splitting hairs a little now, Bosworth, and being a tiny bit picky here. After all the trouble we've gone to. And I don't think the Mellings are going to be very happy if we start raising petty objections at this advanced stage.'

'But . . .'

'It's only a formality, Bosworth. It's not as if you won't like the girl. Look at her photo. What's not to like?'

So I did it. I did the deed. Everything in me said

not to sign – my fingers, my thumbs, my fibres, my nerves, my rabbits, my collection of unused airline sick bags. I could see them in my mind's eye and hear them in my mind's ear.

'Don't sign, Bosworth,' they chorused. 'Don't sign till you've seen the goods. It's a pig in a poke. It's a cat in a sack. Don't commit yourself to something you might regret for the rest of your days. You've got your whole life ahead of you, Bosworth, so whatever you do, don't sign anything.'

And I knew, I knew, even as I applied pen to paper, that I was doing the wrong thing. Even as I signed my signature – that distinctive and stylish signature which I had been practising and developing for years, in case I got famous one day and people asked for my autograph – even as I signed it, I knew it was wrong. I knew I'd regret it. I knew it was all a big mistake.

But I went and did it anyway.

I always go and do it anyway, even when I know that I shouldn't. In fact I do it *especially* when I know that I shouldn't. In some ways, I do it *because* I know I shouldn't.

It's been the story of my life.

7

Not Love at First Sight

The weekend approached and Veronica Angelica Belinda Melling (The Virus) approached with it.

'Where shall I suggest that we meet up?' I overheard my mother ask, as she wandered into the living room for the cordless phone handset. 'Our house, or theirs?'

'Maybe neutral territory might be best,' Dad said. 'For a first encounter. There might not be so much stress that way.'

'How about we meet up at the zoo then?' Mum said. 'Shall I suggest that?'

'Yes,' Dad said. 'Good idea. That should take the pressure off. We can all wander round and have a little chat and look at the animals while Bosworth and Veronica get to know each other. Then we can go to the tea-rooms for a drink and some cake. Yes. That sounds like a good way to break the ice. If the Mellings are agreeable to it, then the zoo it is.'

So the zoo it was. I said the skating rink might be a better place, if we wanted to break any ice, but as usual nobody listened to my suggestions.

We got there at about two on the Saturday afternoon, bought our tickets, and went inside.

'Where did you say we'd meet them?' Dad asked.

'We arranged to meet up by the monkey house,' Mum said.

This did nothing for my confidence. I'd been getting increasingly nervous as the week had gone by, and while I wouldn't have said I was actually dreading this first encounter with Veronica Melling (Mrs Bosworth Hartie to be) I was full of trepidation and felt a strange and heavy sense of foreboding and doom. Sometimes the foreboding was so heavy, it seemed like five-boding to me.

The fact that we were meeting up outside the monkey house only undermined my confidence further. I thought, why the monkey house? Did Veronica Melling and monkeys have some kind of attraction for each other, some close bond? Did she – despite the evidence of her photograph – look like a monkey, or, worse, smell like one, or even worse, did she stand there scratching herself and eating bananas and not care who was watching when she went to the toilet?

'Come along, Bosworth, don't dawdle.'

We passed by the penguins. I wished I was a penguin. If I'd been a penguin, I thought, I wouldn't be on my way now to get acquainted with a fiancée I'd never met. It was better to be a penguin. It was easier for them. Things were simpler and more black and white for penguins, whereas for people, they were complicated and all shades of grey.

'Ah, I think I see them. There they are.'

'There?' I said, stopping abruptly and staring ahead. 'There? There? Is that them? Is that the Mellings? There?'

I was determined not to go a step further.

'No, Bosworth,' Mum said. 'Those aren't the Mellings that you're looking at. Those are the African wart hogs. The Mellings are over there to the left, standing on the path there by the monkey enclosure.'

There they were. And there was Veronica Angelica Belinda Melling, her photo come to life. She was about my height and of medium build and looks. There was nothing actually wrong with her, not that you could have specified, yet as she turned and looked away from the monkeys to see the three of us advancing along the path, and as she nudged her parents to let them know that we were there, I knew we were doomed.

I couldn't put my finger on why, I could find no rational explanation. It was an emotional response, I suppose, on both sides. Because I looked at her, and she looked at me, and it was mutual loathing at first sight. One-sided loathing would have been bad enough, but I could tell she didn't like me every bit as much as I didn't like her. We were like north and north, or south and south, like the same poles of a magnet – we repelled each other.

I could tell she was trouble. In fact I wouldn't have been surprised to hear that she was known to the police (in several countries) and had even been in and out of prison. She just had this look about her of criminal intent. I knew why her mum and dad had got involved in this whole engagement. It was in the hope of a steadying hand and a mature influence; it was to get *her* on to the straight and narrow.

'Mum,' I said. 'D-dad,' I stuttered. 'Let's go home.'

'Nonsense, Bosworth, we've only just got here. Let's all go and introduce you.'

'No, let's go and look at the penguins, Mum.'

'Bosworth, we've seen the penguins.'

'Let's go and see them again. They might be missing us already.'

'Later, Bosworth.'

'Let's go see the crocodiles, Mum. Let's go feed ourselves to them.'

'Bosworth, whatever has got into you?'

'Nothing's got into me, I just want to go and get into a crocodile.'

'Bosworth, that's enough.'

'Let's go and look at the lions then, Mum. Perhaps the big lion will open his mouth and let me put my head into his gob to have a look at his teeth.'

'Bosworth, you can't do a thing like that. It would be positively suicidal.'

'Let's go see the piranha fish, Mum. Let's go and have a little swim with them.'

'No, Bosworth. Oh look, Mrs Melling is waving. Hello, Josephine. How are you, dear? Smile, Bosworth, wave.'

'Can I throw up?'

'Certainly not.'

'Let's go see the electric eels, Mum, and jump in the tank. It might be painful, but at least it'll be quick.'

'Bosworth, do stop dragging your feet and please let go of my coat.'

'I don't want to go, Mum, let's go home.'

'Bosworth, really. Don't do that. Do get up off the ground and kindly release my ankles. People are starting to stare.'

'I don't want to get engaged any more, Mum. I think it might be a bad idea. I've decided I've got a religious vocation and I'm going to become a monk.'

'Bosworth, don't be silly. You know nothing about monks. Monking wouldn't suit you at all. You'd have to get up very early in the mornings and wear itchy underpants. And who would do your washing? And there's no honey nut crunch for breakfast either.'

'Come on, son,' Dad said encouragingly. 'It's only nerves. I felt the same the day I married your mother. I got to the church and my first instinct was to make a run for it and not stop running until I got to South America.'

'Oh, was it, indeed?' Mum said. 'Is that so?'

But before we could debate the issue any further, the Mellings were upon us.

'Donald, Muriel!' Mr Melling said.

'Frank, Josephine,' Dad responded.

'Muriel, Donald,' Mrs Melling said.

'Josephine, Frank,' Mum replied.

'Lord,' I thought, 'help me.' (But I don't think he heard.)

'So this must be Bosworth,' Mrs Melling said, eyeing me up like a potential dinner. 'Isn't he a fine-looking boy, Veronica?' But Veronica neither agreed nor disagreed. She just stood there looking surly, seeming to size me up, as if wondering which two ribs to stick the knife between.

'And this must be Veronica that we've heard so much about too,' Mum said. 'My, isn't she pretty, Bosworth?'

('No prettier than the monkeys,' I thought to say, but I kept my views to myself for the time being. I just grunted and sort of shrugged, as if I couldn't really say, one way or the other.)

'She's even prettier than her photograph,' Mum said.

('What photograph is that, Mum?' I thought. 'The mugshot round at the police station with "Public Enemy Number One" written underneath it, "Wanted For Crime On Seven Continents. Do Not Tackle Alone." Is that the photo you mean?')

'Well, Veronica, say hello to Bosworth,' Mrs Melling told her daughter.

'Bosworth, say hello to Veronica,' Mum said.

'Your fiancé and husband-to-be one day, Veronica,' Mrs Melling went on. (Followed by titter-titter-titter.)

'Your fiancée and lovely bride-to-be one day, Bosworth,' Mum said. (Followed by more titter-titter-titter. When people's mothers start titter-titter-tittering, it always bodes trouble, as far as I can see, and usually for their offspring.)

'Say hello to Veronica, Bosworth.'

'Hi.'

'That wasn't very friendly.'

'Hello.'

'Hello who?'

'V'rnica.'

'That's better.'

'Your turn now, Veronica. Say hello to Bosworth.'

'What for?'

'That's not very nice. Because he's said hello to you, of course.'

'Hi.'

'A little bit more effusive, Veronica?'

'Lo.'

'Hello who, Veronica?'

'Hello, Fat Face.'

'No, Veronica, your father and I did explain to you before we left the house, his name is Bosworth, not Fat Face.'

'Hello, Bumsworth.'

'Bumsworth yourself, Verruca,' I muttered under my breath.

'Don't you call me Verruca, Bumsworth,' she muttered back, loudly enough for me to hear, but not the adults. 'Or I'll knock your teeth into the middle of next week and then I'll knock the rest of you after them.'

Her mother went on talking, quite oblivious to these threats. 'No, Veronica. It's not Bumsworth, it's Bosworth. Say it properly now,' Mrs Melling insisted, and then she kind of giggled a bit, as if to laugh it all off, and said, 'You'll have to excuse Veronica, she's a little bit shy.'

Shy, I thought? She wouldn't know the meaning of the word. She looked about as shy as a bulldozer to me. She probably had a thicker skin than the rhino.

'Well, Veronica, we're all waiting.'

Finally she said it.

'Hello, Bosworth, how very nice to meet you,' and she gave a big smile and a small curtsey.

'There, that's better.'

'Oh, lovely,' my mum said. 'What a charming girl.'

And then, as she straightened up from her curtsey, she gave me a dead leg with her knee. But it was all so swiftly and subtly done that nobody noticed.

'Bosworth, what are you doing, what are you staggering around like that for?'

'Don't play the fool please, son,'

'But, Dad, she—'

'No telling tales now, son.'

'Kneed me in the—'

'That'll do, Bosworth.'

'But—'

I never got any further. Mum chimed in with a suggestion as to how we should now all proceed.

'What say we all have a walk around the zoo together now? I'll walk with you, Josephine, while Donald and Frank can have a chat together about the football and angle-grinders or whatever it is men talk about, and Veronica and Bosworth can follow along and try to get to know each other.'

'Splendid!'

'Wonderful!'

'Good idea!'

'Excellent!'

But it wasn't me who said any of those words, and it wasn't Veronica Angelica Belinda Melling either. Yet, without bothering to consult us on our opinions, the adults took our agreement for granted, and walked off, expecting us to follow. Which we didn't. At least not straightaway.

We just stood there looking at each other. It was a kind of staring match, a trial of strength, if you like, one of those who'll-blink-first contests.

'You give me another dead leg like that,' I warned her, 'and I won't care if you're a girl or not, I'll give you double dead legs back for it, plus a dead brain as well. Though if appearances are anything to go by, you might have one of those already.'

'Listen, Bumsworth,' she said. 'I don't know who you are or why my mum and dad got me into this, but I tell you here and now that I'd rather drink a pint of toilet cleaner than marry you. And if you ever call me Verruca again I'll shove your head so far up that hippo over there's rear end that you'll be looking at the back of its teeth.'

'Oh, will you now?' I said. 'Well, if you call me Bumsworth again, I'll throw you into the snake pit, and the next time you open your eyes, you'll be wearing a python.'

'Veronica!'

'Bosworth!'

'Don't dawdle!'

Reluctantly, we shuffled on our way, following our parents. Some start to married life this is, I thought, getting threatened with being inserted into the wrong end of a hippo. I was better off in my single days, when it was just me and the rabbits. I told her as much.

'I was better off in my single days,' I said. 'Before I got engaged to you. Back when it was just me and my rabbits.'

'Go and marry your stupid rabbits then,' she said.

'I will,' I said. But I wasn't all that confident about it. I just said it out of defiance.

We walked on into the insect house then, following our parents. There were some giant land slugs in a glass case. It didn't seem like a bad life being a giant land slug. Not to me. I stopped by the glass case to have a better look at them.

'Saying hello to your relatives?' Veronica Melling sneered.

I turned and looked at her.

'Wait till we get to the hairy three-toed sloths,' I said, 'and you'll be able to say hello to yours.'

We walked on in silence, vaguely together, yet totally ignoring each other. I realized that a lot of people were doing that.

Finally, I couldn't stand the silence any more and tried to make an effort at conversation.

'Got any hobbies?' I asked.

'Only one,' she said.

'What's that?'

'Sticking people called Bosworth into buckets of horse dung.'

'Keep you busy?' I said.

84

'It will do one day,' she said.

Then there was another lengthy silence while we inspected a large termite mound.

'I've got a hobby,' I said.

'What – being an idiot?' she asked.

'No, besides that,' I said.

'I'm supposed to ask what it is, am I?' she sighed.

'Could do.'

'All right then. So what is it?'

'I collect,' I said, 'airline sick bags from around the world.'

She looked at me sideways.

'You're a nutter,' she said.

'I mean the unused ones,' I said.

'Used or unused, it makes no difference. It's the stupidest hobby I've ever heard of.'

'They'll be worth a lot of money one day.'

'I doubt it.'

'Could be worth millions.'

'How many have you got?'

'Seventy-two.'

'You need therapy.'

'No, I don't,' I said. 'I just need the love of a good woman. That's what my mum says.'

'Well, you won't find it here, Fartsworth,' she said.

'What did you call me?'

'Never mind what I called you. Come here!'

Before I knew what was happening, she had me by the arm and was pulling me through a door and into the nocturnal animal house. It was dark and clammy in there, humid and smelling of ripe fruit. Some bats were behind a wire mesh, hanging by their feet from a branch. She got me into a dark corner.

'Now look,' Veronica Melling said, 'let's get something straight. I'm not engaged to you because I want to be. I'm only engaged to you because of my parents. I've been wandering off the rails a bit, I have, see, and not doing my homework and stuff.'

'What a coincidence,' I said, 'because I—'

But I never got to finish the sentence.

'Be quiet,' she said. 'Veronica's talking. Now my mum and dad got me into this, because they think that my getting engaged to you is going to turn things around and set me on the straight and narrow way and stop me being a spoilt, selfish, self-interested only child who's used to getting her own way all the time.'

'But—'

'I warned you about interrupting me, didn't I? That's your second warning now. Next time, it'll be another dead leg. Now you listen to me and listen good. My parents may have got me into this, but I'm not going along with it. I'm never going to marry you. I would rather set up home in that bat colony.'

'I'd like to see you do it,' I said. 'I'd like to see you hang upside down by your feet for hours on end.'

'Well it happens to be my sporting activity for

my Duke of Edinburgh's Award as a matter of fact – hanging upside down from trees, gold medal standard.'

'You're lying.'

'You just stay out of my way, Bosworth, and stay out of my face. I may have to go along with this so far, but only so far and no further. I'm warning you now that I'm dangerous material and you don't want to tangle with me. And if you think you're going to be a good influence, well, you aren't. We don't want any goody-two-shoes mummy's boys round here.'

'Wait a minute,' I said. 'Hold on. It's you who's supposed to be the good influence, not me. You're supposed to be helping me, not the other way round.'

She looked a bit shocked. Even in the darkness. She had a shocked sort of outline.

'Who said that?' she said.

'My mum and dad.'

'Did they?'

'Yes.'

'But my mum and dad told me that you were a mature and sensible boy and a general all-round good influence.'

'No, that's you,' I said. 'Apart from the being a boy bit.'

'Then . . . do you mean to say . . . that means . . .'

'What?'

'It means I've got engaged to you under false pretences! You tricked me!'

'I did no such thing. You tricked me!'

'You lied to me from the start.'

'I did not. If anyone's doing any lying round here, it's not me.'

'Well, I'm telling you, Snotsworth, that I'm never ever going to marry you, no matter what. I don't like the look of you or the sound of you. So you stay out of my face and stay out of my hair.'

'Why?' I said. 'Are there nits in it?'

'I'm warning you, Spoonsworth . . .'

Even in the darkness of the nocturnal house I could sense her raising her knee for another dead leg. I was just getting ready to slip out of the way when a far door opened, admitting some light, along with two faces, one of which belonged to my mother, the other of which was Mrs Melling's.

'Oh, there you two are!'

'Oh, how romantic!'

'They want to be alone in the dark together already!'

'We thought we'd lost you.'

'But we've found you now.'

'Come along then, Veronica,' Mrs Melling said.

'Yes, come along, you lovebirds,' Mum cooed, and then there was a bit more generalized titter-tittering.

'We're all going to have some tea now.'

'And cakes.'

'In the zoo cafeteria.'

'So, if you two can tear yourselves away from each other . . .'

(If I could just get my hands clamped round Veronica Melling's neck, I thought, nothing would tear me away from her.)

'Are you coming, Veronica . . . ?'

'Bosworth?'

We left the nocturnal house and staggered, blinking, into the light. We walked past the primates, held in a big cage. A huge gorilla sat inside an old tractor tyre, picking what might have been fleas off his chest and eating them. He looked sad and depressed, and who could have blamed him. He should have been out in the wild, roaming free.

I feel like that, I thought, caged in and trapped.

The feeling of claustrophobia got worse when we arrived at the cafeteria and sat down at a table.

'You'll be pleased to hear, Bosworth,' Mum said, 'that while you and Veronica were getting to know each other, Mrs Melling and I had a little talk. And guess who it was about?'

'Who, Mum?' I said. (As if I didn't know.)

'Why, you and Veronica, of course. And guess what we decided we would do?'

'What, Mum?'

'We decided, Bosworth, that we would have a party. An engagement party for you and Veronica. A little public celebration.'

'Yes, we can hire the church hall,' Mrs Melling said.

'And invite everyone,' Mum said. 'Our friends, Josephine and Frank's friends, your friends at school too, Bosworth, and Veronica's friends. In fact, we can invite everyone in your class. How would you like that? That would be wonderful, wouldn't it? They can all come to meet your bride-to-be.'

'We could even have a little ceremony,' Mrs Melling said. 'Nothing official, of course. Just symbolic. And Veronica and Bosworth can both get up in front of all their friends and classmates and exchange their promises that one day, when they are grown up, they will love and cherish each other all their days, and settle down to happily married life. You know, sort of plight your troth, as it were.'

(I didn't really know what a troth was. The only troths I'd heard of were the ones horses drank out of. But I certainly wasn't going to plight one.)

'So what do you say, Bosworth?'

'What do you think, Veronica?'

'What do you say, Bosworth, dear? What do you say to that?'

I didn't say anything. I just sat there, staring at all the expectant, grown-up faces. My slice of coffee and walnut cake had turned to sawdust and ashes in my mouth.

And that was the moment – I know now, as I look back – yes, that was definitely the precise time and the very moment when I realized what I would have to do.

Yes, it was there at the table in the cafe at the zoo that I saw I had no alternative, and that there was only one course open to me.

I would have to run away from home and start a new life elsewhere. Somehow, some way, I had to escape from Veronica Angelica Belinda Melling.

8

Goodbye Cruel Parents

There is no one more stubborn and unreasonable than a person who is doing things 'for your own good'.

I must have tried to broach the subject a dozen times.

'Dad,' I'd start to say. 'About this Veronica, I've got a very bad feeling about all this . . .'

'That's quite enough, Bosworth. I don't want to hear another word on the subject. Do you think we've gone to all this trouble for our own pleasure? Do you think we've spent days tracking down a suitable bride-to-be for you for our own amusement? We've done it for your sake, Bosworth. We've done it . . .'

That's right. They'd done it for my own good.

'Mum, could I have a word with you? You see, the thing is, I've been having second thoughts about this engagement business and—'

'Stop right there, Bosworth. Not another syllable. You're only going to make me angry if you go on like this. When we've gone to all this expense and inconvenience, and all . . .'.

Yes, you guessed it, *all for my own good*.

I sometimes feel the world would be a better place if people didn't go round doing unwanted favours. I mean, doing someone a good turn when they've asked you to, that's one thing. But when they never even asked, when they don't even want . . . well, it turns a good turn into a bad one, as far as I can see. It isn't a favour any more, it's interference.

'Just you be grateful, Bosworth, that we didn't find some rough girl for you from a family where they spend all their time watching telly and getting pizza cheese off the carpets.'

'Yes but—'

'No buts, Bosworth. We have found a fine girl of good stock for you.'

'I thought stock was what you made soup out of. Does that mean I can make soup out of Veronica Melling?'

'No, Bosworth, it does not.'

'No, I didn't think so really.'

'Bosworth, son, one day you'll thank us for this.'

But that, I could never imagine.

I suppose, if they hadn't planned the engagement party and had just kept things quiet, I might have been able to put up with it. But not if they were going to ask everybody in my class and all the neighbours as well. The shame alone would have killed me. I'd never have heard the end of it at school. It would have been stuff like, 'Oh look, it's Bosworth. Are we off courting after school today? Are we meeting our own true love at the school gates this afternoon then, Bosworth? Will we be carving our initials on any tree trunks today? Or will we just be holding hands and sitting on the park bench watching the sun go down?'

No, my life wouldn't have been worth living when they all found out that I was engaged to be married to Veronica Angelica Belinda Melling.

'Playing football at four o'clock then, Bos? Or do you have to get home to the wife?'

They'd make my life a misery forever. And that was just my friends. I couldn't imagine what my enemies would do. They'd probably get a lawn mower and mow a message into the cricket pitch: *Bosworth loves Veronica.* Or spray-paint it on the back of the changing block: *Bos 4 Veronica 4 Ever.* They'd send me text messages. They'd send me honeymoon brochures from the speciality travel firms, and details of starter homes from the estate agents. They'd send me books such as *Making Your Marriage Work* and *Women Are from Germany, Men Are from Wales* and *How to Have a Baby for Beginners.*

I knew they'd do all that, because if it had been

someone else who'd got engaged, and not me, it's what I would have done.

I sat up in my bedroom and contemplated my options. Running away from home was my only answer. It was just a matter of how and a question of when.

To be honest (again), it would not be the first time that I had run away from home, though on previous occasions I had never got any further than the garden shed. I had just gone there to put the wind up people and so that they would realize how badly they had treated me, when they discovered I had gone, and how they ought to have appreciated me while I was still there, but they hadn't, and now I wasn't any more.

Half an hour usually seemed to do the trick, and then either Mum would turn up, tapping on the shed door and saying, 'Bosworth, do come back inside. It's damp out here in the shed and you might catch some kind of fungus,' or Dad would hammer at the window and say, 'Get out of that shed, Bosworth, before I lose my rag. And don't touch my jug of home-made potato cider. If you upset that, your days will be numbered.'

But real, serious, proper, never-coming-back running away, I had never done before. So I started to make plans.

First I had to decide what to take. I compiled a list. At the top of the page I wrote 'Running Away

Stuff', and I underlined it. Then, underneath that, I wrote the number '1', and next to that I wrote 'Biscuits'.

I ran out of steam and ideas a bit after that, but at least I had the basics for survival. Over the ensuing days I added some other things such as money, sleeping bag, toothbrush, small TV, small TV table, shelf, gloves and thick socks. On reflection I decided to leave the shelf, and by a process of revision and addition, I had soon complied a decent list of essentials to help me to survive in the wild.

I also decided to pack my *Real Commando Handbook*, which I had got for Christmas. It not only told you how to build a bivouac, but also described how to strangle people with a coat hanger and told you which wild plants you could eat without poisoning yourself. Once you had strangled somebody with your coat hanger, the book said that you could then straighten it out and use it either as a fishing rod or for hanging your trousers up (not that I was thinking of taking them off as it would have been cold).

My plans, once I had run away, were a little on the vague side. But I was sure that once I had been away for a time everyone would soon be very sorry that they had treated me badly and got me engaged to a girl like Veronica Melling and had tried to ruin my life with terminal embarrassment by having a party about it, even though I had tried to plead with them not to, but they simply wouldn't listen.

Yes, sometimes the only way you can get people to pay any attention to you is not to be there, to simply disappear.

I decided to write a note to leave on the kitchen table, explaining why I had run away and why I would not ever be coming back unless there were big changes.

I didn't want to jump the gun, however, and to run away unnecessarily, so I decided that I would leave running away until the very last moment, hoping that in the meantime something would intervene to stop the engagement party ever taking place.

Plans for the party were well underway though. Mum had decided that she would rent me a morning suit so that I could look like 'a regular little bridegroom' (her words) and Mrs Melling was getting Veronica measured up for 'something a bit wedding-dressy' so that she could look as big an idiot as I did when the day finally came.

The event was not being billed as an engagement party, as that would have given too much away. Cards were sent out inviting people to a 'big surprise'. Well, it was definitely going to be that all right, because I wasn't going to be there.

Mum and Mrs Melling had got quite pally in the meantime, and Mrs Melling spent a lot of time round at our house, sitting in the kitchen drinking cups of tea while she and Mum decided who to invite to the party and who to leave out. The way they carried on, you would have thought that a real wedding was on the books, and not just some party down at the church hall to let people know that a marriage had been arranged for some years ahead.

'And we'll have to order a cake,' I heard Mrs Melling say, 'with a little icing-sugar bride and groom on the top, and with their names iced on as well. Along with a few words like, "We can hardly wait!" '

'Yes,' Mum said, 'or "Looking forward to marrying you one day".'

'Or "I yearn to be yours",' Mrs Melling said.

'Or how about "Be my sweety-pie"?'

'Or "All my love forever".'

'Or how about "I might go and kill myself after all",' I thought, and I went up to my room and closed the door.

I could think of nothing more embarrassing than a cake with a little icing-sugar bride and groom on top, and a message iced into the surface saying 'Be My Tweety Pie' or whatever it was. Things like that can cause untold psychological damage to children of a sensitive disposition, such as myself. They can find themselves in court in later life for shop-lifting or for stealing millions of pounds in internet fraud, and it is all due to mental trauma and childhood scars caused by things like imitation wedding cakes with 'I Love Tweety Pie' written on them.

As the day of the engagement party approached,

I made one last-ditch attempt to stop it happening. I found Dad in the shed one evening, checking on his cider, and I tried to talk to him, man to man.

'Hi, Dad,' I said, wandering in and pretending to seem casual and unconcerned.

'Hi, Bos,' he said. 'So how are you? Looking forward to the big day?'

'Now, I'm glad you brought that up, Dad,' I said. 'Because, to be honest, I'm not really looking forward to it at all.'

'Quite understandable,' Dad said. 'You're bound to get nerves with a thing like that looming up.'

'No, it's not nerves exactly, Dad, it's more along the lines of desperation.'

'Ah, good old Bosworth,' he said, pouring himself a glass of cider. 'That's my boy. You haven't lost your sense of humour, I'm glad to see. Always there with the little jokes.'

'No, Dad, I—'

'You'll be all right, son,' Dad said. 'As long as you keep a sense of humour, you won't have too many problems with married life.'

'No, Dad—'

'As long as you can still have a laugh, you'll be fine. That's the way to do it, son. As long as you can face the firing squad with a smile playing about your lips and a twinkle in your eye, you'll die a happy man.'

'Dad, what's getting engaged got to do with facing firing squads?'

'Nothing, nothing, absolutely nothing. Forget I ever said that. Nothing at all.'

'Dad, I've got to be honest here, I'm thinking of running away from home. I'll run away from home, Dad, rather than get engaged to The Virus.'

'Who?'

'Smelly Melling. Her – Veronica.'

Dad slapped his knee and took another swig of his home-made potato cider.

'There you go again,' he said. 'Cracking me up with your jokes and your little quips. Run away from home, eh? "The Virus", eh? You've got an affectionate little pet name for her already. You're a case, you are, Bosworth. You keep us all smiling, you do. Run away from home! That's a good one. Very good indeed.'

Then he slapped his other knee so it wouldn't feel left out or jealous of the first one and would see that he was slapping both knees equally, and he lifted his glass of cider again.

I was plainly going to get nowhere. I was a misunderstood child who could not communicate with his parents. Far from being a dream and a fantasy, running away from home was now my only option and my sole means of self-preservation.

So I went up to my room to make a start on my running away note, the one which I was to leave behind on the kitchen table, for them to find when I had gone, and which would explain why I had vanished.

I went through several drafts, trying to hit the correct tone, but I finally realized that it was never going to be perfect or contain all the things that I wanted to say, so I just wrote it from the heart and then left it like that, unrevised and uncorrected.

Dear Mum and Dad, I wrote. *Or, if you would prefer, Dear Dad and Mum. I wouldn't want you to think that I was having favourites by putting either of you before the other as I love you both equally and am fed up with you both equally too.*

By the time you read this note, I will have run away from home. It is no use coming looking for me, as I do not know where I'm going, so it is most unlikely that you will ever find me, as I shall probably not be there.

As you know, I am not one to bear a grudge particularly, nor one to sacrifice his creature comforts unnecessarily or unless severely provoked — which I am and have been by this getting married business which, to my mind, has got completely out of hand.

I don't doubt that in the beginning you both meant well and only wanted to find a nice girl for me so as to help me settle down to doing well at school and being a credit to you and a useful member of society and to avoid embarking on a life of crime and drug dealing — which I know is your greatest fear – and that I will end up in prison one day with people who've got Love and Hate tattooed on their knuckles and with half their teeth missing. But I have to say, to my mind, there are far worse things than tattoos on your knuckles and missing teeth. There is Veronica Melling for one, and there is getting engaged to her for another.

It seems to me that all this getting engaged stuff has taken on a life of its own and everyone has forgotten about me and that it is just a big excuse for people to feel good about themselves and have a party.

Now I'm not saying that arranged marriages are necessarily a bad thing for everyone, but they don't suit me. I can think of nothing more horrible than having to spend the rest of my life with Veronica Melling. I would rather stick a garden spade in my head – or, to be more truthful, I would rather stick a garden spade in her head. But I would never actually do a thing like that, as it would be wrong, and not much good for the spade either. So, dear Mum and Dad, much as I love you both, you give me no choice than to go.

I think you started all this for my sake and with good intentions, but you have lost sight of the purpose of it all somewhere along the way and now this arranged marriage thing is like a runaway train. If someone doesn't put the brakes on soon, there is going to be a terrible accident and a big crash.

As you can imagine, the hardest thing for me about running away from home is to leave Grizelda and Arbuthnot, my rabbits, behind. I did consider taking them with me but felt that it would be cruel to stuff two rabbits into my rucksack as they would not be able to see where they were going and might also get squashed if I forgot that they were in there and sat on the rucksack by mistake.

I hope that you won't mind looking after them for me and feeding them occasionally. You will find some carrots for them up in my room underneath my pillow and half a cabbage in my clean underpants drawer.

So goodbye then, Mum and Dad (or Dad and Mum if you would rather have it that way round). I'm sorry to have to leave you as we had some good times together, especially at Christmas when you bought me all the presents. I suppose that I would probably leave home one day anyway, and am just doing it a bit earlier than expected, so there is no real need to be upset.

I hope to be in touch again in a few years' time, probably when the threat of Veronica Melling has evaporated, and when she is safely married to somebody else.

Don't worry about me. I will be all right. You always brought me up to be able to look after myself and I am sure that is what I will do.

If you get hard up for money while I am away,

please feel free to sell off my collection of unused airline sick bags – but only as a last resort. Or if you get really ill, you can use one of them.

Please look after yourselves and don't forget to wash, especially behind the ears. I am sure I shall miss you both very much, but I dare say I'll get over it.

I'm sorry I have to run away, but it seems to me that I have no alternative.

Don't forget to let the cat out at night.

With much sorrow and lots of love,

Your son,

Bosworth

I folded the note in two and hid it in one of my homework books. It was Thursday night and the engagement party was scheduled for Sunday.

'We'll have the reception in the afternoon, shall we?' Mrs Melling had said. 'Just like a real wedding.'

That left two clear days for some horrible disaster to take place – for Veronica Melling to fall down a mine shaft or be abducted by aliens – which would render my running away from home unnecessary.

But the horrible disaster did not come and the aliens did not want her. Instead the preparations went ahead. The clock hands went round and the time drew nearer, until finally it was Saturday night, and it was no longer a question of *if*, it was a matter of *when*, then a matter of *soon*, then a matter of *now* – or never.

It was after midnight. My rucksack was packed, all was ready. I had some money, some clothes, a carton of milk and a few biscuits.

The house was quiet. Mum and Dad were both asleep. I tiptoed down the stairs and went into the kitchen. I left the note on the table and put the salt cellar on top of it so it wouldn't blow away. Then I silently opened the back door and went out into the garden, where I said goodbye to my rabbits.

Then, with a heavy heart, and with no real sense of where I was going, just the certainty that I had to get away, I crept along the path to the back gate and slipped out into the lane. The gate rattled shut behind me. I froze a moment, waiting for the light to go on in the bedroom window. But it didn't. Mum and Dad slept on.

I walked on down the lane and came to the street.

Where to go now? Where to head for? Where to spend the night?

I decided to make for the railway station. It seemed like a good place to go. They were always busy, were railway stations, and I wouldn't stand out or be especially conspicuous there, I would be just another traveller. And besides, there were always warm waiting rooms at railway stations, with benches that you could curl up on and go to sleep.

Of course there were officials too, and railway

policemen, and guards, and platform attendants, and other travellers, who might get a bit nosy about what a boy of my age was doing out on his own at that time of night.

But even if I got discovered and got dragged back home, it would at least have taught them all a lesson. They'd have seen sense then and called the engagement off, when they realized how desperate I was – to the extent that I'd flee from home to get away from it.

So on I walked, feeling a bit small and alone in the night. I tried to keep to the back streets as much as possible and away from the crowds of pub and club goers and revellers who I could hear in the distance. They were probably all queueing for taxis and waiting at kebab stalls or heading for yet another disco.

At length I got near to the station. I could see the glow of its lights and hear the sound of the trains as they rumbled in to the platforms.

But then I saw something else too – a figure approaching the railway station entrance, just the same as I was, but coming from the opposite direction.

It wasn't a grown-up figure. It was more a child-sized one. It was somebody of about my own age, as far as I could make out. It was carrying a backpack, just like I was, and it had its jacket hood pulled down low, over its forehead.

From a distance it was hard to tell if it was a boy or a girl. But as we got closer, I could see that it was definitely a girl. In fact I had a weird feeling that it was somebody I knew.

Then, as we got closer still, I saw that it most definitely was somebody I knew. And not only was it the last person on earth that I had expected to see, it was also the last person on earth that I wanted to see.

We came within two metres of each other and then stopped dead.

'You!' I heard a voice say.

'You!' I said in turn.

There was no doubt at all then, there was absolutely no mistake.

The person who was standing in front of me was Veronica Angelica Belinda Melling.

It was her.

It was The Virus in person.

9

The Waiting Room

Veronica Melling stood and gawped at me, and not wishing to be rude I returned the compliment and gawped back.

'What are you doing out?' I demanded. 'It's half past midnight. Do the police know you're on the loose?'

'Never mind what I'm doing out,' she said. 'What are you doing here?'

'I'm getting a train,' I said.

'Train to where?' she wanted to know.

'Haven't decided yet,' I said. 'Not that it's really any of your business. But if you want to know the truth of it, I've run away from home. So there.'

She seemed to get a bit angry then. With her coat hood pulled down low over her eyes, she looked like a large, demented peanut. But I didn't tell her this as I felt it would not be tactful.

'What do you mean you've run away from home?' she said. 'And what exactly have you run away from home for?'

'I've run away from home,' I said, 'to get away from you.'

'Oh, and have you now?' she said. 'Well, it may interest you to know that I've beaten you to it. Because I've already run away from home first to get away from you.'

I gave her a hard stare.

'How do you know that you ran away from home before me?'

'Because I live further away from the station and if we've arrived here at the same time it stands to reason that I must have left home earlier.'

'Ah, but I took the long way round,' I said.

'So did I,' she said.

I could see this argument was leading nowhere.

'Well, you can go back now,' I told her. 'Because as I am running away, there's no need for you to. You can buzz off home and go back to bed, or to your basket, or your nest in the loft, or whatever it is you sleep in.'

'Certainly not!' she said. 'And have everyone think that you stood me up at this engagement party, when the truth is that I ran away to avoid you, and it was me who stood you up? No thank you. So you go home, and I'll stay here.'

'Not likely,' I said. 'I'd never be able to hold my

head up again. I can't have people thinking that I was left at the altar, so to speak, when it's quite the opposite. Or them thinking that the party's off because you've done a runner, and there I am, broken-hearted. No way. I want the world to know the facts – and the facts are that I'd rather marry a donkey than marry you.'

'No,' she said. 'The facts are that not even a donkey would marry you. Not even a stupid one. And I would rather marry a clam than marry you, as not only would it be better-looking, it would also have a bigger brain and better personal hygiene.'

'Well, I'm not going home,' I said.

'Well, neither am I!'

'You better had,' I told her. 'Or you'll get into trouble.'

'Doesn't bother me. I'm used to it.'

'And besides, it's dangerous for girls to be out on their own at nights.'

'Not as dangerous as it is for bird-brained halfwits to be out on their own at any time of day.'

'Well, you said it,' I said.

'Yes, I did, didn't I?' she said.

So at least we agreed on something . . . though I wasn't sure exactly what.

'Well, excuse me then,' I said, in a somewhat cold and unfriendly tone. 'But I cannot waste any more time chitchatting with the likes of you. I've got important running away business on and you're interfering with my timetable. So, if you don't mind, I'll say cheerio, and I'll be off.'

'Me? Mind you saying cheerio?' she said. 'You must be joking. I hoped you'd say cheerio the first time I saw you.'

'And I hoped you'd get lost the first time I saw you.'

'And I hoped . . .'

And so it went on for a while, until I could see that it was getting neither of us anywhere, so I didn't bother replying to her last remark and instead went on into the station, still uncertain as to where I was going to go, but not wanting to seem as if I lacked a plan or confidence.

I went to look at the train times and destinations, up on a board. As I stood, gazing upwards, I detected movement out of the corner of my eye.

The Virus was standing right beside me.

'Are you following me?' I said.

'Don't be ridiculous,' she said. 'Who in their right mind would ever want to follow a bad smell like you?'

'You're in your right mind then, are you?' I said. 'Or is there some doubt about it?'

'Any dog getting a whiff of you would plead for someone to stick a cork up its nose,' she said.

'Any dog getting a whiff of you would plead for someone to stick a cork up your bu—'

'Do you mind? I'm trying to read the timetable,'

she said. 'Kindly don't pester me, or I shall call a porter over and have you arrested.'

'And if you go on talking to me,' I said, 'I shall ring up the loony bin and have you committed.'

'How childish,' she said. 'Now go away.'

She then made a big display of getting out a pen and a small notebook and she made a lot of I'm-studying-the-timetable-don't-bother-me faces and she sucked the end of her pen and made hmm-that's-very-interesting noises and then she jotted down train times in her notebook in a sort of yes-I-think-I'll-probably-go-there manner.

I tried to take a peek over her shoulder just to see where she was thinking of going so that I could avoid the place. But when she saw me looking, she twisted away so that I couldn't see what she had written, but it didn't really bother me as I wasn't that interested anyway.

She closed her notebook with a decisive snap and put the pen back into her pocket.

'That's me then!' she said. 'See you around, Bozo.'

'Bosworth,' I corrected her. 'Not Bozo.'

'All sounds the same to me,' she said. 'So good riddance to bad rubbish. Nothing personal, but meeting you was worse than measles. Enjoy the rest of your life, because I'm going to enjoy the rest of mine – the main reason being that I'm not getting married to you. And whatever happens after a narrow escape like that has got to be great by comparison. So see you.'

'Not if I see you first,' I said. And then she made a rude sort of gesture, and she stomped off towards the platforms and disappeared from sight.

I was left on my own – which suited me fine. The station was still busy with people catching the last trains, but once they had gone, it would be a long wait until morning and the first trains of the daytime.

I wondered what to do. A cold wind blew along the concourse. I shivered a bit and wished I had taken my warmer coat. Still, too late to do anything about that now.

Unless I went home, of course. I could simply have gone back, sneaked in, ripped up my note before anyone read it, and have gone back to bed. And then in the morning I could have looked all surprised when they woke me up with the glad tidings – sorry, bad news, I meant to say – that Veronica Melling had legged it.

Only if I did that, everyone would think I had been stood up, and I wasn't having that. I wasn't going to be stood up by Veronica Melling, I was going to stand up her.

I went and had another look at the timetable, wondering where to head for and when, and also wondering where The Virus was thinking of going, because I certainly didn't want to end up in the same place as her.

As I stood by the timetables, I realized that I was getting occasional looks from people who were obviously wondering what somebody of my age was doing out on his own so late on a Saturday night (or early on a Sunday morning, if you preferred to see it that way).

I decided to disappear for a while and so I sneaked through the barrier – there was no ticket collector there at that time of night – and headed for the platforms. It would be best, I thought, to head for the furthest away platform and to spend the night in a nice warm waiting room, if I could find one. Then, in the morning, I would make my mind up where to head for and where to start my new life. I thought I might make for the seaside, as I had fond memories of it, and what with my experience of looking after rabbits, I might even get a job mucking out the donkeys, or failing that, putting deckchairs up.

I walked down into the underpass. The entrances to the various platforms lay ahead of me, up stairwells to the left and right. I went to the far end of the underpass and took the steps up to platform thirteen (I'm not superstitious).

Platform thirteen was long and dark. There was an old-fashioned glass canopy covering it, protecting it from any rain that might fall, but not from the wind or the cold. I shivered again as I walked along. There was a little cafe, but it was locked and in darkness. I peered inside. A sticker on a shiny machine said: 'Why not treat yourself to a nice hot chocolate?' Well, the obvious reason was that the place wasn't open, or I would have done.

I walked on past some benches and trolleys, past a sign reading 'Gents' and one reading 'Ladies'. If the worst came to the worst, I thought, I could pop into the Gents and find myself a nice quiet cubicle, lock the door and sit down and go to sleep in there. It probably wouldn't be all that comfortable, but at least it would be warmer than outside, and I wouldn't have far to go if I needed the toilet.

I sat down on one of the trolleys and drank my milk and ate my biscuits, not much looking forward to the night ahead. But then, at the end of the platform, I saw what I had been hoping for, an old wooden sign, swinging gently in the wind. 'Waiting Room', the sign said. Just what I wanted. So I pulled my collar up to keep out the wind, hoisted my backpack up on my shoulder, and hurried to get out of the cold.

It was a swing door. It creaked as I opened it, and creaked again as I let it close. A single, dim and dusty bulb failed to illuminate the room. But I didn't mind that too much, because the place was as warm as toasted cheese. You could hear the water in the old-fashioned radiator, making its way along bunged-up pipes, like blood in the veins of some poor old soul who was due to have a heart attack soon. But hopefully not tonight.

I yawned, long and loud, for I was pretty tired and whacked by then and ready for my bed. There was a wooden bench around three sides of the waiting room, which looked wide enough to sleep on without fear of falling off when you rolled over. I headed for a dim corner of the room, shrugged off my rucksack and dumped it down on the bench behind me.

To my amazement, the bench spoke.

'Oi! Watch what you're doing, will you? You just dropped that on me.'

To my greater amazement, the bench spoke with a voice I recognized.

It was her. Veronica Melling. She was there on the bench, curled up in a dark corner, with her head on her backpack for a pillow. She had bagged the best place too, right next to the nice warm radiator.

She glared at me from a recently opened eyeball.

'Oh no,' she said. 'It's you.'

'Oh no,' I answered. 'It's you.' (I know it wasn't very original, but it was late and I was tired.)

'What are you doing here?' she demanded.

'Staying the night,' I said. 'Till the early trains start.'

'Well go and find your own waiting room,' she said. 'Because this one's mine.'

'Oh no it isn't,' I said. 'It happens to say that this is a public waiting room outside, and that is me. I am a member of the public. And if you don't like my being here, then either you can lump it and put up with it, or you can clear off.'

'You're not driving me out,' she said.

'And you're not driving me out.'

'Well go and sleep as far away from me as possible.'

'I would,' I said. 'Believe me. Nothing would give me greater pleasure. Only I don't see why you should get to hog the radiator while I have to shiver by the door, so I am going to sleep here, on this bit of bench on the other side of the radiator, and if you don't like that, then move yourself.'

'Huh!' she said. Then, 'Huh!' again. Then she muttered something like, 'What a pain,' then she closed her eyes and turned to face the wall.

I got comfortable on the bench on the other side of the radiator, just like I said I would. I used my backpack as a pillow, just as she had, squirmed around till I was comfy, then closed my eyes.

'Well?'

I heard a voice.

'Well what?' I said.

'Aren't you going to put the light off?' she asked.

'Put it off yourself,' I said.

'You were last to bed,' she said.

'You'd left the light on yourself,' I pointed out.

'You were fast asleep with the light on when I came in.'

'And then you woke me up.'

I could see I wasn't going to get any peace until the light went off, so rather than go on having petty arguments all night, I got up, went to the door, found a switch and turned off the light.

Unfortunately, there was a big wooden table and a long, hard bench in the middle of the room. I banged into both of them on my way back.

'Ahhh! Ahhh! My shins!'

'What is it now?' The Virus demanded.

'I've walked into the table.'

'Then you're stupid, aren't you? What did you do that for?'

'Because it's dark.'

'Then why did you turn the light off?'

'Because you wanted me to.'

'Don't blame me for your stupid mistakes. You should look where you're going.'

'I couldn't see where I was going.'

'Then if you can't see where you're going, you shouldn't go anywhere, should you? You should stay where you are.'

'I could hardly spend the whole night standing by the door! Could I!'

'Then you should have brought a torch, shouldn't you?'

It was becoming increasingly clear to me that

Veronica Melling was the sort of girl who was fond of having the last word. (Mind you, according to my dad, all girls are the sort of girls who like to have the last word. I could distinctly remember him telling me that, because when I pressed him to tell me more, he said, 'Sorry, Bosworth, but that's my last word on the subject.')

I groped my way back to the bench by the wall, and felt my way around it to the radiator. Unfortunately, while I was groping in the darkness, I inadvertently groped a finger up Veronica Melling's nose.

'What are you doing!' she snapped. 'What are you doing!'

'Sorry,' I said. 'I couldn't see you. I think I might have accidentally stuck my finger up your nose.'

'Oh, that is gross,' she said. 'That is disgusting!' And I think she must have got a tissue out, for I could hear her blowing her hooter.

'Well, it's even worse for me,' I pointed out. 'It was only your nose but it was my finger.'

I wiped it on my coat and then felt my way to the radiator. I felt my way along by the radiator and then to the bench and my rucksack at the other side. I lay down, stretched out, and got comfy again, and rested my head on my rucksack.

I thought of saying goodnight to my companion in the waiting room, but felt that it would seem a bit soft and that she would only take it as a sign of weakness and trying to be friendly, so I didn't say anything. I just closed my eyes and tried to get to sleep.

'Oi!'

It was her again.

'What is it now?'

'Did you open a window?'

'What?'

'When you turned the light out, did you think to open the window?'

'No. Why should I?'

'Let some air in.'

'But it's nice and warm. Opening the window'll make it cold.'

'Need some fresh air or we'll suffocate.'

'Then why didn't you open a window before you started going to sleep before I ever came in?'

'Because I didn't need to. There's enough air in here for the night for one, but not for two.'

'Well, you go and open the window then.'

'You were last here.'

I could see there would be no peace until I opened the window, so I got up and headed for the door.

'Ahhh!' I yelled.

'What have you done now?'

'Walked into the table again.'

'I said open the window, not walk into the table.'

I groped around until I found the window.

'It doesn't open,' I said. 'It's stuck.'

'Then open the door.'

'We'll be freezing.'

'Not all the way. Just jam it open a little bit, enough to let some air in.'

'What with?'

'I don't know. Use your head.'

'I'm not standing here all night with my head jammed in the door.'

'Use your common sense. Use a bit of paper.'

I found a piece in my pocket, folded it and used it to jam the door open a touch.

'There,' I said. 'Satisfied?

'I suppose so.'

'I'm coming back.'

'Then stay out of my nose.'

'You don't think I stuck my finger up there deliberately, do you? I mean, what do you think your nose is? Cheddar Caves or something? Some kind of popular tourist attraction that everybody wants to visit?'

'Just be quiet and go to sleep, will you?'

'Chance would be a fine thing,' I said. Then, 'Ahhhh!' I yelled.

'What now?'

'Table again.'

'For crying out loud. You're the clumsiest idiot I've ever come across!' she snarled.

'And you'd be an expert on clumsy idiots then, would you?' I said. 'Being one yourself. Being a kind of leading exponent. Being a sort of clumsy idiot's clumsy idiot. I mean, I expect you've got Oscars and Bafta Awards and all sorts for being an idiot.'

'I am trying to get to sleep!'

'Me too,' I said. And I got comfortable again on my bit of bench on the other side of the radiator. I closed my eyes and let out a long sigh – or something like a sigh anyway.

I was just drifting away again into much-deserved sleep – for it was almost two in the morning by now – when I heard that voice.

'Oi, Mogsworth or whatever your name is . . .'

I groaned, both inwardly and outwardly, mentally and physically.

'Now what? What is it now?'

'I'm cold.'

'Too bad.'

'I'm cold and it's your fault.'

'Why's it my fault?'

'I'm in a draught.'

'So?'

'Well, you jammed the door open.'

I sat up on the bench.

'Now look here,' I said. 'The only reason I jammed the door open was because you wanted me to. Because you said we'd suffocate if I didn't.'

'I've changed my mind,' she said. 'I think we'll be all right now with the air that's come in. I don't think we need any more. And anyway, I'll never get to sleep with that draught. Never.'

There was a silence. A long one.

'I'll never get to sleep with that draught,' she said again. 'Never.'

'Doesn't bother me,' I said. 'I can't feel it. I must be out of it here.'

'Do you want to swap places then?'

'No,' I said. 'Of course not. Why should I be in the draught instead of you?'

'You'd do it if you were a gentleman,' she said.

'If you were a lady, you wouldn't ask,' I told her.

There was another long silence. Then a long sigh.

'I'll be awake all night now.'

'Then go and close the door,' I said. 'I'd have thought it was obvious.'

There was another silence then. An even longer one. I got my head comfy on my rucksack once more and started drifting off into sleep.

But then I heard this strange sound. I didn't recognize it straightaway. I couldn't understand what it was. But then it came to me, the realization. It was a snuffling noise. Not the sort of snuffling that rabbits make – the snuffling noise that humans make.

It was the sound of somebody crying softly to themselves. And yet not that softly either. Sort of softly, but also loud enough for other people in the vicinity to hear.

I put my fingers in my ears. But I could still hear

it. I buried my head in my rucksack, but the crying was still there. In fact it had turned into a gentle sobbing now. I just couldn't stand it any more.

I sat up.

'All right!' I said. 'What's the matter? What is it? What are you crying for?'

There was a bit more snuffling and a bit more silence, then a voice answered tearfully.

'You,' it said.

'Me?' I said, aghast. 'What have I done?'

'You won't close the door,' she said.

'So what?' I said. 'Neither will you! But I'm not crying about the fact that you won't close it. So why are you crying because I won't close it?'

There was a short silence this time, broken by a wail and yet more sobbing.

'You don't understand,' she said. 'You're not a nice person.'

'Understand?' I snapped, coming to the end of my tether. 'No. I don't. I don't understand. What is there to understand? You're a grown girl, aren't you, who's run away from home. If you've got enough gumption to run away from home, what's stopping you getting off your bench and going and taking the bit of paper out of the door and closing it yourself, instead of lying there snivelling!'

There was yet another silence and more muffled sobs, followed by a spot of nose blowing.

'You don't like me,' she said.

I couldn't believe it.

'Like you?' I all but screeched. 'Of course I don't like you. I ran away from home to get away from you. Same way you ran away from home to get away from me. If it hadn't been for the fact that we didn't like each other, we'd both be safely tucked up nice and snug and warm in our beds right now, instead of lying on these hard benches in this waiting room arguing about who's going to get the bit of paper out of the door.'

More silence. More snuffles, but not so many now.

'I never said I didn't like you,' she said.

'Yes, you did,' I said. 'At the zoo.'

'Well, I'll give you a chance to make it up to me.'

'Make what up to you?'

'For saying those things.'

'What things? I didn't say any things that were worse than what you said to me.'

'I'll give you a chance to make it up to me anyway.'

'If I make it up to you will you stop crying?'

She mumbled something. It might have been 'Yes'.

'What?'

'Yes, I'll try. But I can't promise anything.'

'OK, how do I make it up to you?'

'Could you close the door, please? That would be ever so kind.'

I couldn't stand it. I really couldn't. Enough was enough, and I'd had it.

'OK, OK, if it'll stop the flipping racket, I'll close the door.'

Once again I got up. Once again I walked into the table. I located the piece of paper and pulled it out of the door. I groped my way back in the darkness. I whacked my shins on the bench this time. Finally I made it back to my bit of bench and my rucksack.

'There, then,' I said. 'Satisfied now? Will you stop crying now? Will you stop that horrible blubbering? Are you finally happy at last?'

And then her voice rang clear and strong around the waiting room, without a sob or a tremor in it.

'That's much better. Thanks, Mugsworth,' she said. 'You saved me a journey there. I was so nice and comfy on my rucksack that I didn't want to move. Cheers.'

I'd been conned. I could see that my first instincts had been right all along. She was nothing but a deceitful little schemer and a manipulator, who could turn on the waterworks, as and whenever she wanted to, and who'd stop at nothing to get her own way. I'd heard about girls like her. And the sooner I put several miles of distance between Veronica Melling and myself, the better it would be for both of us.

But especially for me.

10

Just the Ticket

Morning came tentatively to the waiting room on platform thirteen, confronted as it was by the several years of grime upon the windows. The new day seemed to hesitate, as if apologizing for intruding, when it so evidently wasn't wanted by the muck on the panes trying to keep it out.

It wasn't much wanted by me either. Dawn had come too quickly and too soon. I felt as if I had only been asleep for a few minutes, instead of the several uncomfortable hours it had been in reality.

The light didn't bother Veronica Angelica Belinda Melling though. She lay on her back on her bit of bench, with her head parked on her rucksack, with her mouth wide open, snoring away like an old tractor.

It was a most unladylike spectacle. Up until that moment, I had only ever seen girls at their best, when they'd given themselves a bit of a rubdown with the old facecloth and the bar of soap and had run a comb through their hair. It had never occurred to me before that they actually snored when they were asleep – at least not that loudly.

I got off my bench, stretched, yawned, and then tiptoed over for a closer look. It was quite a sight and I wished I'd brought a camera with me, if only to record the spectacle for posterity.

And to think, I thought to myself, that if I hadn't run away from home, I'd be getting married to her one day and waking up to that horrible snoring noise every morning for the rest of my life. I'd had a close shave there and the narrowest of escapes.

I tiptoed back to my piece of bench, not wanting to wake her, as it would only start another argument, and I tried to plan my next move.

Pangs of early-morning hunger tweaked at my innards. I thought of home, I thought of my bed. I thought of the cereal packets in the cupboard and the strawberry yoghurts in the fridge. I thought of my mum and dad and how they would feel when they woke and went downstairs to find the note upon the table, explaining that I had run away from home to start a new life as a single man without commitments.

I bet they'd feel upset and I bet they'd feel sorry. I bet they'd regret ever getting me involved in this arranged marriage business. Part of me just wanted to go back. A big part of me wanted to go back. In fact, almost all of me wanted to go back. But one little part didn't. It was my stubborn streak. It's always been my downfall. Even when I was staring sense in the face, my stubborn streak would always argue against it, and, being persuasive, it would usually win.

And besides, I thought, as I glanced across to where The Virus was lying dormant, I couldn't go back home if she didn't. I couldn't be outdone for endurance and adventure and stubborn streakiness by a girl.

No, I had to stick to my plans. If I went home now, I'd never be taken seriously ever again. When the next thing came up that I felt I had to protest against, my reputation would be in tatters. 'Don't worry about Bosworth,' they'd say. 'He is as soft as putty in the hands. He's crumbled before and he'll crumble again. He may have the impulse, but he doesn't have the staying power.' No, I had to see this one through, all the way to the bitter end.

Only where to go? And what to do when I got there? What to live on? Where to hide up? How to avoid the hue and cry and all the people who would surely be looking for me once word got out that I had run away from home?

It was a problem all right – but not one that couldn't be solved.

Quietly, so as not to wake The Virus, I picked up

my rucksack and headed for the waiting-room door. I was halfway there when I got an idea. I put my rucksack down and silently as possible rummaged around in it, searching for the green ink felt-tip pen that I had brought with me, in case I needed to do some doodling to pass the time. I took the cap off and went over to where The Virus was asleep. I took the pen and carefully wrote, in large capital letters on her forehead, the word BIG. I waited to see if she would wake. She didn't. She didn't seem to have felt anything. On her right cheek I then wrote PE and on her left cheek I wrote ST. I stood back to admire the work.

BIG PEST

That seemed to have done it. It would act as a warning, I thought, for the general public, who could now see at a glance the truth of what was heading their way.

My work done and my mission accomplished, I put the cap back on my pen and my pen in my pocket, took up my rucksack once more and headed out of the waiting room. I looked back inside as the door closed behind me. The Big Pest was still fast asleep on her bench, no longer snoring, but still out for the count. The door swung to, and that, I assumed, was the last I would ever see of her. But then, as my mum is always saying, you shouldn't make assumptions.

* * *

Dawn was creeping along the platform like a slow-moving train. I wondered if the cafe was open yet, but it wasn't. I felt hungry. Starving, in fact, and I couldn't help but think of home again and the five different packets of cereal.

Where to go, I wondered. How did other runaways manage? I'd heard of plenty of people who had disappeared from home, but the reports never went into details of how they managed, or what they did for money, or ate for breakfast.

By the sound of it, I was having rumbling for breakfast, and might also be having it for lunch. I took my money out and counted it again, just in case it had doubled in quantity while I'd been asleep. It hadn't. It was enough to keep me going for a few days, I guessed, but then what?

Well, maybe I'd be back home by then. Maybe my mum and dad would have seen the error of their ways and have put out an appeal for me to come home, accompanied by a grovelling apology for ever getting me mixed up in the arranged marriage business in the first place.

Just as I was thinking this, I heard a train. It was the first one of the morning, coming in over on platform number one. I checked on the timetable, to find its destination. It was heading for one of the big cities, but on the way it stopped at several other, smaller places, one of the names of which I recognized – Stompton Sands.

Stompton Sands. My mouth formed the words and my brain formed the memories. We'd gone there loads of times when I had been smaller: sometimes just for the day, sometimes for a long weekend. Stompton Sands. Happy days and happy memories. It was a place I knew and somewhere I felt I could start again. I needed to buy a ticket to Stompton Sands.

The train wasn't due to depart for another twelve minutes, so I went down into the tunnel that connected the platforms, and ran back towards the ticket office. A bleary-eyed clerk peered out at me from behind the glass, looking a bit like one of the animals I'd seen in the nocturnal house at the zoo.

'Stompton Sands, please,' I said.

The clerk gave me a suspicious look, as if I had no business travelling anywhere at that time of morning, and especially not on my own, and at my age.

'Stompton Sands?'

'Please.'

I got my money ready.

'Single? Or return?'

There was a question. Did I need a return? Would I ever be coming back? Maybe not. Not if my new life in Stompton Sands took off. A new life, with a new identity. I might get a job there as a deckchair boy, or I could start up on my own with a small rowing-boat and a couple of lobster pots. But before I could answer, the clerk advised that: 'You may as well have a return, mate. They're the same price.'

Which seemed a bit mad to me. You'd think that half the journey would mean half the cost. But if there wasn't any difference, well . . .

'I may as well have a return, in that case,' I said, dreaming to myself of how I would go home one day, with my return ticket in one hand and my fortune in my rucksack, coming back to show everyone what a great success I had made of things and how sorry they ought to be for not having treated me better while I was still there to cherish.

'Return it is.'

He pressed a button and his machine spat out the tickets.

'How long is the return part valid for?' I asked.

'Indefinitely,' the clerk said. 'It's open-ended. Why, how long are you going to be away?'

I didn't know if I was ever coming back, but I didn't want to tell him that. The less attention I drew to myself the better. I didn't want him remembering anything about selling tickets to boys travelling solo to Stompton Sands.

'Not sure,' I said. 'Better go, though.' I paid and I took my ticket and hurried to get on board the train.

It was all but empty. The morning looked as if it was going to be a fine one now, but it was still too early for day-trippers to be on their way, and anyway, who'd go on a day trip to the seaside in February?

I found myself a seat and sat looking out of the carriage window for a while. Eventually I heard the slam of a door and the blow of a whistle. The train jolted and the couplings jangled as it pulled out from the platform and resumed its journey. At the far end of the carriage I was in, a man sat muttering to himself. He hadn't seen me, and seemed totally absorbed in his conversation.

'She was wrong about that,' he said. 'She was wrong. I was right, and she was wrong.'

But as she wasn't there, and she probably wouldn't have agreed with him anyway, I couldn't much see the point in going on about it. I did wonder though if I might end up one day, sitting in public places talking to myself. My dad used to say that talking to yourself was the only way to get an intelligent conversation.

After five or ten minutes, I decided that I needed to use the toilet, so I walked back down through the carriage to the corridor. There was a toilet there all right and the little sign read 'Vacant' but when I tried to push the door open, it wouldn't budge.

Strange, I thought. Maybe I should be pulling instead. But no, the instructions definitely read 'Push'. So I pushed once more, but again the door didn't open. So I tried again. I gave it a good, firm shove this time, and although the door still didn't open, it seemed to give a bit and I thought I heard a sort of 'Ooof!' noise, as if something inside was being squashed.

It's a body, I thought. A dead one. Lying there on the floor, and I've squashed the final breath out of it. It's probably been murdered, like in one of those crime books, only instead of Murder on the Orient Express, this was Murder on the 7:51 to Stompton Sands.

I was getting quite excited now, and I could see that running away from home was about to turn into a great adventure. I thought I'd better run and fetch the guard – or at least try to find him, because I didn't know where he was. One last effort first though, I thought. If I could get the door open, I might find not only the body, but the murderer as well. Then not only would I get a pat on the back for discovering dead bodies, I'd get another one – and possibly a big reward – for apprehending murderers too.

So I took a few steps back, bunched my shoulder up, and charged at the door.

Woomph!

This time it gave, and before I knew it, I was inside the toilet – and I wasn't on my own. But I wasn't standing facing a murderer with a bloodstained weapon in his hand and a body at his feet either. No, it was far worse than that. I was standing there face to face with . . .

Veronica Angelica Belinda Melling.

'You!'

'You!'

'What are you doing here?'

'Never mind that. What are you doing?'

She looked at me with all innocence. I noticed that she had washed the words Big Pest off her face. Not that this was any kind of an improvement to her appearance. Nor did it make her any less of a pest.

'I,' she said, in answer to my question, 'am here to have a wee. And if you were any kind of a gentleman – which I sincerely doubt – and not the cloth-eared moron you seem to be, you would have the good manners to clear off and let a lady do her business in peace.'

My eyes narrowed. I wasn't falling for that one.

'I know what you're up to in here,' I said. 'You're hiding from the ticket inspector.'

'Oh?' she said. 'And what makes you think that?'

'Because you didn't lock the door,' I said, 'and slide the little bolt across. Because if you had, then the ticket inspector would see the Engaged sign and he'd know that there was a shifty fare-dodger in there on the fiddle.'

'How dare you,' The Virus said. 'I've never been so insulted.'

I didn't believe that for a minute.

'But if you just left the sign as it was and held the door closed when anyone tried to get in, then they'd just assume the door was jammed and walk down the carriage to the next one. And you'd be able to travel without a ticket.'

'What a low and despicable idea,' she said. 'What sort of a mind does a person need to think of things like that?'

'Pretty much the sort of mind you've got, at a guess,' I told her. But she didn't even have the decency to be embarrassed, never mind ashamed.

'Very kind of you to tell me I'm pretty,' she said.

'I never said—'

'And who am I to spurn the compliments of my admirers?'

'Your whaters?' I said.

'But such an idea as travelling on a train without a ticket and hiding in the loo to conceal the crime would never occur to me. It's the pettiness of it I find so distasteful more than anything. The very notion that a girl of my flair and style would stoop to skulking about in the bogs on trains just brings me out in pimples – or it would do, if I didn't have such good skin.'

She didn't fool me though, not one bit. I could tell she was blustering and that hiding in the loo was exactly what she had been doing. And when I heard a distant voice call, 'Tickets, please! Have your tickets ready now!' and when I saw the look of sudden panic in her eyes, I knew that I had her bang to rights.

'Well,' I said. 'The ticket inspector seems to be on

137

his way.' I took my ticket out from my pocket and waved it under her nose. 'And seeing as I do have a ticket to show him, I shall have the pleasure of watching you being thrown off the train at the next stop. Or, with a bit of luck, he might not even bother about the next stop, and chuck you straight out of the window into the nearest cowpat.'

With that I turned on my heel and went back to my seat, deciding that I didn't need the loo now after all, or at least I could hold on a while until I'd had my ticket inspected.

'Tickets, please.'

The man who had been talking to himself looked up at the inspector, somewhat startled.

'Ticket, sir?'

'Oh, right, yes.'

He fumbled in his pocket and produced a ticket. The inspector inspected it, punched a hole in it and strolled on down through the carriage, whistling to himself.

Then, to my great astonishment, Veronica Melling appeared. She waltzed into the carriage, flounced past, and plonked herself down on a seat a few rows along from me. Then she draped herself all over the place, just like she was some kind of Hollywood film star, looked around as if to say, 'It's all so frightfully boring, darlings, I don't know how I'm going to endure it,' before taking out an emery board from her pocket and giving her fingernails a seeing-to.

What a nerve, I thought. About to be unmasked by the ticket inspector as a fare-dodging delinquent, and is she bothered – not in the slightest. Look at her sitting there, cool as brass and bold as cucumbers. Talk about brazen. She didn't have a gram of shame in her. No wonder her parents had wanted to marry her off.

And I then started to wonder if she wasn't one of those 'brazen hussies' I had sometimes heard my mother talk about. I wasn't exactly sure what a brazen hussy was, but they usually seemed to be the characters in the soaps who had gone off to live with someone else's husband.

'That woman,' my mum would exclaim, 'is nothing but a brazen hussy.' But it never stopped her watching.

And while Veronica Melling was no doubt too young to actually be a brazen hussy yet, I did suspect that maybe she had been having lessons, or was possibly doing a correspondence course.

'Tickets, please. Ticket, please, miss.'

The inspector stopped and looked down at her.

I waited for it. I knew what she would do. She'd be all innocence again and all 'deary, deary me', and 'whatever could I have done with it?' as she went through the pretence of searching for her non-existent ticket. But the inspector would have seen all that sort of 'deary me, what a poor little forgetful girl am I' stuff before, and he wouldn't be taken in. He'd get straight on to his little radio and arrange to have the police waiting to arrest her at the next station.

It was all I could do not to laugh.

'Ticket, please, miss.'

She put a hand into a pocket, and to my amazement, she pulled a ticket out from it.

'There you are, inspector,' she said. 'There's my ticket. I think you'll find it's all in order.'

She'd found a used one, that was what it was. Or so I thought.

The inspector took a look at it. But he didn't scowl. The ticket seemed to be fine.

'Stompton Sands?' he said.

'That's right,' she said.

Stompton Sands? I felt cold and trembly. Was that my hands that were shaking? She couldn't be going to Stompton Sands too. Surely they wouldn't let her get off the train at Stompton Sands. There had to be a local by-law against it.

'Next station down the line,' the inspector said. 'Be there in about twenty-five minutes.'

'Thank you,' she said, and she gave him such a big, beaming smile that if you hadn't known any better (which he plainly didn't) you'd have thought that Veronica Melling was quite a nice person really, and not the scheming maniac with psychopathic tendencies that I knew her to be.

The inspector moved on to where I was sitting.

'Ticket, please, young man,' he said. And while he

140

was cordial enough, he was no way as friendly towards me as he had been towards The Virus.

'Here it is,' I said, reaching into my pocket.

Only it wasn't. It had gone. I felt myself go red.

'That is, it must be in here . . .'

I felt in another pocket.

'Or here.'

I felt in all my pockets.

'That is . . .'

I took all the stuff out of my pockets and began to rummage through it. I opened up my canvas wallet and looked in there.

'I mean I'm sure . . . I know . . . I definitely had it a minute ago . . .'

The inspector was staring down at me now, his face like cold concrete, set into a hard, impenetrable expression. He no longer seemed the same man who had been beaming and smiling and exchanging timetable pleasantries with Veronica Melling a moment ago. Now he seemed like a man with a heart of granite and features chiselled from stone.

'Tut, tut, tut . . .'

That wasn't him though. That was her. Veronica Melling, a couple of seats away, sitting there tut-tut-tutting. The inspector looked at her. She gave him a sympathetic smile. He gave her a conspiratorial look, as if to say, 'Here we are, miss, you and I, honest members of society who always pay our way and buy our tickets – and what are we up against –

toerags and good-for-nothings like shifty-shoes here, who's trying to pull the old "deary me, I've lost my ticket, I'm sure I had it earlier" scam. Well, if he thinks he's getting away with that one he's got other thinks coming. I wasn't born yesterday and I know a fare-dodger when I see one, and I know just how to deal with them too. I like to pick them up by the scruff of their ears and shake them till I get the money.'

(Which, I admit, was quite a lot to convey in a single look, but somehow, he managed to do it.)

Then, of course, it came to me. I knew exactly what had happened and where it had gone.

She'd nicked my ticket. The Virus had picked it right out of my pocket.

And I hadn't felt a thing. She'd done it while we'd been standing in the loo cubicle. I should never have taken my ticket out and waved it under her nose, just to flaunt it. I'd put it back into my pocket and as I turned to go, she must have taken it out again.

She was even worse than a fare-dodger. She was a ticket-nicker. We hadn't even begun to plumb the depths of her depravity yet,

'Well, sir,' the inspector said, in a tone of cynicism and contempt. 'So have we found our ticket yet, sir? Or has it gone walkies – surprise, surprise.'

'Eh, well, I definitely . . . I certainly had it earlier . . .'

' 'Course you did, sir. Isn't that what they all say?'

'I must have just lost it, maybe when I went to the loo.'

'Oh, the loo, sir, yes, the loo. Perhaps you accidentally flushed it away, never to be seen again.'

'Yes, perhaps.'

'I don't think.'

'No, maybe no. No, neither do I, but I—'

I stopped. The inspector couldn't see, but directly behind him, Veronica Melling was making faces at me and mouthing, 'I've got your ticket, fat face, so na, na, na!' and she was sort of waving my ticket around in the air, like an enemy flag, captured in warfare.

I was just about to stand up and yell and say, 'That girl's got my ticket!' but I stopped myself. There was no point. That inspector was never going to believe me, not even with twenty-seven witnesses and photographic evidence.

'Well, sir,' the inspector said. 'I expect we know the penalty for travelling without a ticket, do we?'

We didn't, but we guessed it wasn't going to be pleasure. I just hoped they didn't tie you to the rear couplings and make you run behind the train – which wouldn't be easy once it got up to seventy miles an hour.

'It's an automatic fine, is what it is, sir. It's a criminal prosecution. It's a criminal record.' And then he bent down and got his face very close to mine. 'It's your poor mother I feel sorry for,' he said.

I heard a little voice echo him.

'His poor mother.'

It was her, Veronica. She'd taken a tissue out and was dabbing at her eyes. 'Poor mother. His poor, poor mother. They're always the ones to suffer.'

'Yes, really let the side down today, haven't you, son?' the inspector snarled. He straightened up and took out a notebook.

'All right then. Name and address? And no Bugs Bunny, Mickey Mouse or Homer Simpson stuff.'

But then I found it. Well, not all of it, but half of it. The return half. She hadn't pinched that, it was still there, in my pocket, mixed up with some chewing gum papers.

'Look,' I said. 'There's the return half. That proves I bought a ticket. You can see from the time and the date, see? I only bought it twenty minutes ago. You could even ring the ticket office back at the station and ask. Just ask them if a distinguished, good-looking youngster of intelligent appearance was there shortly ago buying a ticket for Stompton Sands. If I hadn't bought the ticket, I couldn't have the return, could I?'

The inspector seemed doubtful, but more than that, disappointed. Yet he could see from the time and date on the return ticket that what I was saying was true.

'All right,' he reluctantly conceded. 'It does look

like you bought a ticket and you genuinely lost it. So I'll let you off this time. But you should take more care of your tickets in future, young man, or you'll find yourself in trouble. In fact—' and he beamed over at The Virus again, as if she was his long-lost granddaughter who'd made him a card for Grandad's Day saying *You are the best grandad in the world*, 'in fact you could take a few tips from this young lady. Careful, considerate, polite and cheerful. That's the way to be.'

He turned away. Behind him, The Virus stuck her tongue out at me, put her thumb to her nose and flapped her fingers.

The inspector was off into the next carriage.

'Tickets, please! Tickets, please!'

The automatic door slid shut behind him.

'You!'

I was across the carriage and at her table. It was time for a big reckoning.

'Go away,' she said. 'Go and sit back in your own seat or I shall call the inspector and tell him there's a strange boy bothering me.'

'Bothering you? I'll bother you all right,' I told her. 'I'll bother you out of the window and into that cowpat I mentioned earlier. You stole my ticket.'

'What if I did? It only serves you right.'

'For what?'

'For writing "Big Pest" on me when I was sleeping.'

'Oh, I see. So people are to be punished now for telling the truth, are they?'

'If it's the truth you're interested in, you ought to write "Stupid Twerp" on your own face and carry a big sign saying "Stinker: I Smell of Armpits and I Think It Might Be a Camel's".'

'Yeah, and you ought to carry a sign saying "Beware of the Loony – Please Return to the Nearest Asylum".'

'If you don't go away I'm going to start to scream.'

'I told her I was right. I told her I was right.' The man at the end of the carriage had started talking to himself again.

'Well, I'm going,' I said. 'Don't think I want to sit next to you. I'd rather sit on a cactus. You'd just better not get off at Stompton Sands, that's all'

'Oh and why shouldn't I? It's a free country, isn't it? Or are you suddenly Mr I Own All The World, Stompton Sands Included, And I'll Tell Everyone What To Do And Where To Get Off The Train – are you?'

'Look,' I said, 'I've run away from home to get away from you. I've not run away from home to be followed about.'

'Followed about?' she said. 'As far as I can tell, it's you following me.'

'Nothing of the sort,' I said. 'I happen to be heading for Stompton Sands as I was happy there once.'

'Well, me too,' she said.

'Well, stay out of my way then,' I told her.

'As if anyone would want to do otherwise.'

'Well, I'm going to sit in another carriage,' I said.

'Good idea.'

'Even though I was here first,' I pointed out.

'Oh la dee dah!'

'And I hope I never see you again.'

'Mutual,' she said.

And I picked up my rucksack and walked towards the door to the next carriage.

'I told her I was right,' the man who was talking to himself repeated as I passed him. I stopped and looked at him. There was a question I wanted to ask.

'I told her I was right,' he said yet again.

'Did she believe you?' I asked.

'No,' he said. 'She didn't.'

'Doesn't surprise me,' I said, and I went on my way.

'I told her I was right. I did,' he said. 'I told her. But would she listen?'

That was the last thing I heard as the door closed behind me.

11

Stompton Sands

As the train drew near to Stompton Sands, I began to feel just a little bit homesick. Not that I was all that far away from home, but I wasn't actually *there*. I'm a touch prone to homesickness, on occasion, to tell the truth. Sometimes I've even got homesick at school. But then, to be fair, I quite often got school-sick too. I'd sit there in the classroom during one of the more boring lessons, thinking, I'm sick of this, I want to go home. Probably the best thing is to be a snail, and then you can carry your home round with you. But even then you might get sick of carrying it.

I looked out of the carriage window and thought of my mum and dad. I imagined them still in bed, having their usual Sunday morning lie-in. They'd wake and then they would remember that today was the big day, that today was the day of the engagement celebration party at the church hall, when they would announce to the world that their only son, Master Bosworth Hartie (bachelor of this parish), would, at some point in the future, when he was a bit older, plight his troth (whatever it was) to one Miss Veronica Angelica Belinda Melling (a.k.a. The Virus and spinster of the adjoining parish), only daughter of Mr and Mrs Melling, of 29, The Willows.

Mum would be thinking of the food. She was doing the cakes and Mrs Melling was doing the sandwiches. Dad would be worrying about the drink. He was doing the beer and Mr Melling was doing the orange juice. Dad had been brewing up a special Engagement Celebration Brown Ale in the shed over the past few weeks. Three of the bottles had already exploded, which, according to him, was a good omen.

So I thought of them there in bed together, then I thought of Dad yawning and stretching and saying things like: 'Cup of tea would be nice,' and 'Bacon sandwich would come in handy,' and 'Bowl of cornflakes and some black pudding would go down a treat,' and Mum agreeing with him until he gave in and went down to start the breakfast.

And that was when they would find my note. I could hear Dad's cry of dismay. (I presumed it would be dismay. I'd have been disappointed if he started cheering and opening up his Clove Champagne.) I could see him rushing up the stairs with my note in his hand, shouting, 'Mother, Mother, our baby's gone! Rather than get engaged to that girl, our boy has done a runner.'

I could picture the two of them filled with remorse then, each blaming the other, saying, 'Look what you've done now. You and your arranged marriages and your high-handed schemes. You've driven our Bosworth away. The poor boy was barely out of short trousers and knickerbockers, but did you give him a chance to grow up, no. You signed him up for the adult world and the responsibilities of married life before he'd even had a chance to play with his super-soaker and his collection of unused airline sick bags. He was robbed of his childhood. What have you done?'

Then, from blaming each other, they would turn to blaming themselves, with Mum saying, 'It's all my fault, I've been a bad mother,' and Dad denying it, and trying to comfort her, saying, 'It's not you, love, it's me. I've been a rotten father, that's what it is. I should have been firmer with him, and then we'd never have had any of these problems. He didn't have enough discipline, that was where we went wrong. We should have bought some leg-irons. It was tough love he needed. That and handcuffs.'

And then what? I stared out of the train window, wondering what would come next in the sequence of events.

The phone call, I guessed. Would Mum and Dad phone the Mellings, or would the Mellings phone them? It depended who got up first, I supposed. I presumed that The Virus had also left a note for her mum and dad. I thought I'd better check with her, so I ambled up through the carriages and back to where I had left her, and then asked.

'Oi,' I said. 'Just out of interest – not that I actually think you're interesting or anything – but did you leave a note in the kitchen for your mum and dad to find when they woke up, explaining why you've run away and such?'

Veronica looked up from a magazine she was reading. She hadn't had a magazine before, so I presumed she had found it on a seat. It was some women's magazine and I saw she was reading the problem page. I got a glimpse of the letter which had been sent in

Dear Doctor Mincey, it read, *I am engaged to be married, but am now having second thoughts about it as my fiancé does not seem to have once brushed his teeth since I met him five years ago . . .*

The Virus put the magazine down before I could read the rest.

'Leave a note?' she said. 'For my mum and dad? Now why would I do a thing like that? Of course I left a note! What are you, stupid or something?'

'Only asking,' I said. 'No need to be snappy. So what did you say in your note then?'

'I said,' she went on, 'that I was running away from home rather than get engaged to you. And then I wrote that if they ever forced me to actually marry you, first I would commit suicide, then I would get a gun and come looking for those who had driven me to it, and then I wouldn't be responsible for the consequences.'

'Oh. Right,' I said.

'Why?'

'Just wondering,' I said. Then I asked her, 'Are you going to ring your mum and dad, and tell them you're all right, so they won't be worrying?'

'No,' she said. 'Because if I do, they'll try to emotionally blackmail me and talk me into coming back.'

'Aren't you going to get in touch with them at all?' I said. 'Because I'm worried about my mum and dad worrying. They always say that I'm a worry to them but I'd hate to think of them being worried at me having run away from home.'

'I wouldn't worry about it,' Veronica said. 'I'm going to send mine an e-mail from somewhere. That'll do it.'

'I might do that too,' I said.

'Good for you.'

I hesitated a moment, wondering if she might invite me to sit down. She didn't.

'Well? What's your problem?' she said.

'Nothing,' I said. I turned and walked back to my own carriage.

I sat back down where I'd been before. I knew it

was my spot as the seat was still warm. I looked out of the window again and returned to picturing the scene in my house as it would be unravelling at that very moment, even as the train rolled into Stompton Sands, giving its passengers their first view of the sea – which at that moment looked grey and cold and most uninviting.

I'd forgotten that I'd only ever been to Stompton Sands in the summer. In the summer it was warm and glorious, with golden beaches which went on forever. In the winter, it was plainly a different kettle of fish. In fact, judging from the smell coming in from the outside, it was nothing but fish, and mostly old ones at that.

What would be happening at home? Where had I got to? What next? Oh yes. The Mellings ringing Mum and Dad, or Mum and Dad ringing the Mellings, and then they'd all be reproaching themselves for the error of their ways. Then they'd be thinking of what to tell the neighbours and all the friends and relations whom they had invited to the engagement party. Then they'd be wondering what to do with all the food and what to tell the vicar, and also, in amongst all that wondering, somebody, at some point, would insist on ringing the police and informing them that both The Virus and I had run off separately to get away from each other. And then, I guessed, sooner or later, it would get into the newspapers and on to TV. Old and recent family photos would be dug out and handed over. Appeals would be made. Things like: 'Have you seen this odd, peculiar-looking girl?' and 'Have you seen this handsome, athletically-built boy with no more than one or two spots to mar the regularity of his noble features?'

Hmm.

It was going to be harder than I thought to stay out of the clutches of the authorities. I hadn't really thought beforehand how difficult that part of it was going to be. Running away is easy enough, you just make yourself scarce. You ride off on your bike or you grab a taxi. It's like that song I heard on the radio – 'There must be fifty ways to leave your lover' it went. Well, there have to be at least fifty plus another fifty ways to leave your parents too. There's slipping out the back, hopping on the bus, making a new plan, getting on your skateboard, waiting until it snows and putting your skis on – the list was endless.

Yes, it was easy enough to run away, but not to be found, that was the tricky bit. Maybe not tricky if you're grown up. But if you're a child and you're out on your own at times of day and in places where children are not usually expected to be on their own, well, people get suspicious. They soon grow concerned and start asking you if you're all right and where your mum is, and if you don't give satisfactory answers, then they start looking around for policemen. And when there's a missing boy report out, they're twice as vigilant and three times as nosy.

How long, I wondered, before everyone in the country was keeping an eye out for a runaway boy answering my description, and a runaway girl answering The Virus's description (though she was pretty indescribable really). Not long at all, I reckoned. A few hours, a day or two at the most.

And then a thought came into my mind – one of those simple, glaringly obvious things which you so often overlook, even though they are staring you straight in the eyeball, waving their arms and making faces at you, mutely waiting for your attention.

The thought was this.

I had run away from home to get away from The Virus.

The Virus had run away from home to get away from me.

Therefore, people would be looking for a boy on his own and a girl on her own.

It was like one of those logic problems we had done in maths.

If A has run away to escape from B, and if B has run away to escape from A, then the last thing anyone will expect to see is A and B in each other's company.

People would be looking for a boy on his own and a girl on her own.

But nobody would be looking for a boy and a girl together.

It seemed strangely ironical, I thought, that my best method of getting away from The Virus was, in fact, to stick with her. I wondered if the same thought had penetrated her brain, but it probably hadn't. There'd be too many dense layers of bone and gristle to get through before anything like a thought made it into her consciousness.

I leaned over, my head in the aisle. I peered the length of the carriage, through the glass partition door, and into the adjoining carriage where she was sitting, reading her magazine. Only she wasn't reading it at that moment. She was leaning out into the aisle, the same as I was, and peering back at me. I pretended to have dropped something, like a pen or suchlike, and mimed picking it up, so that she wouldn't get the idea that I had been looking at her. She did the same thing, pretending to pick up some invisible earring which she then proceeded to put back in her ear.

'I wonder—' I wondered.

And then I stopped wondering. For one thing, we were pulling up at the platform of Stompton Sands Halt, and for another thing my stomach was rumbling, with pangs of early-morning and overnight hunger.

'Stompton Sands Halt. Stompton Sands. Will passengers for Stompton Sands please take all items of hand luggage with them and prepare to disembark. Thank you for travelling with Network South. Stompton Sands next stop.'

The train creaked and rumbled to a halt. Even new trains always sound old to me. They're a bit like babies, who are only a few days old sometimes but have the expressions of old women and old men. It's not so bad looking old when you're a baby though; at least you grow out of it eventually.

I dropped the window, reached out and opened the door from the outside. Further along the train another door opened. The Virus got down on to the platform, deliberately not looking in my direction. The man who had been talking to himself got out after her and walked briskly along the platform towards the exit, still chatting away, nineteen to the dozen, and still maintaining that 'she was wrong'.

What now?

A cold wind gusted along the platform as the train pulled away, carrying an empty crisp bag with it for a short distance, whirling and flying in the slipstream. Once the train had gone, it floated down and settled on the rail, waiting until the next train came to stir it into action again.

Food, I thought. First things first. Food, and then shelter. That was the right order of priorities, wasn't it? Food, shelter, and then what? What came next in the list of things you couldn't live without? Warmth?

Clothes? (Well, I had them.) Money? TV? Xbox? Mobile phone?

I felt in my pocket, just to check it wasn't there. I'd deliberately left my mobile phone at home, knowing that as soon as the note was found, Mum or Dad would call me up, and I didn't want to answer. I knew I had to sever the ties. If I'd kept the phone, my resolve might have weakened, but if I couldn't hear their voices, then the homesickness wouldn't be so bad.

It was odd to be without your mobile phone though. It was like not having one of your shoes. I felt half dressed. But then I told myself that this was all part of the great adventure of running away from home, and I reminded myself of all the great explorers and travellers of the past, and how Christopher Columbus had discovered Australia – or somewhere like that – and he never had as much as an iPod to his name, never mind a camera-phone with ninety-six different ringtones. And then there was Albert Einstein, the great scientist, who had discovered that time went round and round (though I would have thought that was obvious from looking at your watch) and he never had a mobile phone either, as they hadn't been invented. Nor, as far as I could make out, having seen a picture of him once, did he have a comb or a hairbrush.

The train had gone and in its place was a clear view of Stompton Sands themselves. They went on for miles in both directions, left and right, flat and smooth. Even though the sea was rough and the air was cold, and the water probably freezing, there were already some windsurfers out on their boards. They were all wearing wetsuits and rubber shoes and gloves to keep their feet and hands warm.

It was nothing like the summer though, not like the bucket and spade days I remembered. We'd always stayed at Mrs Purley's Boarding House ('En suite rooms. Breakfast a speciality. Hot milk with your cornflakes'). We'd never gone there for that long, never for more than a few days at a time, as Mum claimed that the British weather wasn't reliable, and you were better off going abroad for your main holiday, as at least you knew the sun would shine.

But I had happy memories of Stompton Sands. The sun had always shone for me. Well, it did in memory, even if it had, in reality, rained every now and again.

'So what are you doing? Standing there all day, are you?'

I looked around to see The Virus behind me, her bag in her hand.

'Look,' I said. 'It seems to me a bit of a poor do that here I am, desperately trying to run away from home, due to you and the thought of getting married to you, and all you do is follow me. Talk about rubbing salt into wounds and making things worse than they have to be.'

'Follow you?' she said. 'Don't flatter yourself. You'd be lucky to get a bloodhound to follow you, even if you rubbed yourself down with a cooked chicken. I've not come here to follow you, no way. As a matter of fact, I've come to Stompton Sands to hide up until the heat dies down.'

'What heat?' I said. 'It's flipping freezing. Even a polar bear would need a fur coat.'

'I don't believe in fur coats,' she said. 'It's cruel to animals.'

'But what if you are an animal and it's your coat?' I said.

'Still cruel,' she said.

'So what are you supposed to wear if you're an animal then?' I said, as it seems to me that sometimes all this political correctness stuff can be taken too far. 'If you're a polar bear and you can't wear your coat, how do you stay warm then?'

'You could get an anorak,' she said.

'How?' I said. 'How can a polar bear buy an anorak? He wouldn't have any money.'

'He could get one in a charity shop,' she said.

I was going to say something back to that, but I stopped myself, as I realized it was pointless. We'd both lost all interest in the truth; the discussion was all about winning the argument, and I was too cold to bother.

'So, polar bears aside,' I said. 'Where exactly do you reckon you're going to hole up then tonight?'

I thought, if I got lucky, I might find an unlocked, empty beach hut, and be able to stay there. It was that or sleep under the pier.

Veronica Melling gave me a smug look and tapped her nose with her finger.

'Where am I going to stay?' she said. 'That's for me to know and for you not to find out, thank you very much. So there.'

'So there what?'

'So there nothing,' she said. 'Just there.'

'So why'd you say it then?' I said.

'Mind your own business,' she said.

'I was,' I pointed out, 'until you interrupted me.'

'Sour grapes,' she said.

'Hard cheese,' I said.

'With knobs on,' she said.

'Double knobs,' I said.

'Triple knobs,' she said. 'With spikes.'

I opened my mouth to say something really sarcastic and cutting to her then, but unfortunately all that came out was, 'So do you mean you've come here to Stompton Sands because you knew you'd have somewhere to stay? Is that what you mean?'

She gave me one of her what-a-birdbrain looks.

'Well, of course,' she said. 'You surely don't think I'd just come here on the off-chance, do you? You surely don't think I'd just run away from home with no idea what to do or where I was going, with no notion of where I was going to spend the night or anything like that?'

'Eh, well—'

'I mean, you'd need to be some kind of a substandard, clueless halfwit to do a thing like that, wouldn't you?'

'Errr—' I demurred.

'Surely you're not telling me that you've just come here on the off-chance and that you don't have anywhere to stay?'

'Eh, no, no, I'm not telling you that or anyone that, of course not, no.'

'So what are you telling me then?' she said.

'I'm not telling you anything,' I told her. 'So mind your own business.'

'Just what I am doing,' she said. Then she stuck her nose in the air, in this annoying sort of stick-your-nose-in-the-air way she had, and she swanked off along the platform in that kind of swanking-about manner she had, which seemed to say, without her needing to put it into words, that everybody in the vicinity – but especially boys – was little better than a dog poo.

I wouldn't have followed her if I could have avoided it, but as there was only one way off the platform – unless you wanted to throw yourself in the path of an oncoming train (which, while she was talking to me, had crossed my mind) – I was obliged to go in the same direction.

We got to the end of the platform and walked up to cross over the lines by the footbridge. I got the whiff of things cooking as we approached platform one and the exit. As, by now, I was almost hungry enough to eat my own leg, I decided to head for the station cafe for breakfast, before going any further. It was not a good idea, I felt, to make any major decisions about what to do next on an empty stomach. I'd learned during history that the great French soldier Napoleon once said an army marches on its stomach. Personally, I thought it was its boots, but I could understand the point he was making. First things first. Cars need petrol and stomachs need food, and when they don't get what they need, they can't go far or do much.

So I put on a little spurt of speed, overtook The Virus on the downhill section of the footbridge stairs, and hastened along the platform to the appetizing smells and the steamed-up windows of the Stompton Sands Halt station cafe.

I pushed open the door and went inside, into the warmth and the aromas, to the sounds and smells of hot coffee and scrambled eggs, of cooking bacon and toasty bread, of chocolate croissants and hot porridge with honey. I took a tray and went to the counter and began to pile things on to plates.

As I did so, I was vaguely aware of the cafe door opening and then closing, and of the presence of another customer behind me, standing there with tray in hand, as anxious to get some breakfast as I was.

I turned and glared at her. 'Not you again!' I said.

She looked at my plate, piled high with bacon, sausages, chips and eggs.

'You're not actually going to eat that, are you?' she said.

'Why not?'

'You don't really eat meat, do you? You're never going to eat that sausage?'

'What else would I do? Have a game of tennis with it? Stick it up my nose?'

She looked at me with complete disgust and, standing an arm's length away, pointed at my sausage and said accusingly, 'That used to be a living creature once. That used to be a human being!'

But I wasn't altogether sure about that. I didn't think that was quite right.

12

One Can Live as Cheaply as Two

It occurred to me, once I'd paid for my breakfast, that at this rate of spending, I wouldn't have many breakfasts left. As for dinners, lunches and mid-morning snacks, they would make even bigger dents in my small savings. In fact they'd do more than put dents in them, they'd probably have the bumpers off too. My savings would be completely wrecked.

I sat at a table and pointedly ignored The Virus as she walked away from the counter with a tray full of 'healthy' and 'ethical' breakfast. She sat at a different table – luckily for her, because if she'd sat at mine, I'd have moved. The cafe was quite small, however, so I couldn't help but be aware of her, and I guess that she, similarly, couldn't help but be aware of me.

'Do you have to eat with your mouth open?' she snarled from her table.

'If I don't open my mouth, how am I going to put the food in?' I pointed out.

She went quiet for a bit then as she munched on her muesli and sipped at her orange juice in what she plainly thought was a sophisticated and ladylike fashion – though personally I had seen farmyard animals with better table manners, or better trough manners anyway.

'Oi!'

I looked up from my sausage.

'Are you addressing me?' I said.

'It's you or the chair,' she said. 'Which is the more intelligent?'

I ignored that.

'So where are you off to now?' she said. 'Not that I'm particularly interested.'

I tried to seem carefree and casual.

'Oh, around,' I said. 'And about. Here,' I said. 'And there. Back,' I said. 'And maybe forth. Though I haven't quite decided on that.'

'Hmm,' she said.

I got the distinct impression that she had something on her mind, something she wanted to talk about but she didn't quite know how to bring it up as a topic of conversation.

To be honest, I was getting worried. I didn't know what I was going to do at all. Here I was, I'd run away from home to escape from the nightmare of an arranged marriage and a doom-laden engagement party, I didn't have much money, I didn't have any plans, I didn't have anywhere to sleep that night, I didn't have a friend in the world, and basically, I wanted my mum. Only I couldn't go home because that would have meant defeat and the admission that I couldn't make it on my own.

I looked across at The Virus and said – in as casual a tone as hers – 'So where are you off to now? Not that I'm particularly interested either.'

She was starting on her low-fat yoghurt now, and lifting the spoon to her lips.

'Places,' she said.

'What sort of places?' I said.

'Places,' she said again, then she spooned some more yoghurt in.

As I ate my breakfast, a phrase kept coming into my mind. I think I'd heard my dad say it, or maybe my mum, or, well, somebody.

Two can live as cheaply as one. That was the expression. I thought that maybe there might be some truth in that, and that if I had somebody to pool my money with, it might well go a whole lot further. Only I didn't have anybody to pool my resources with. I was all alone.

'Oi!'

I was getting a bit fed up with *Oi!*. She seemed to think it was my name, and that *Oi!* was what was written on my birth certificate, and when I had been christened, the vicar had said, 'I baptize this child in the name of *Oi!* Hartie.'

Bosworth was bad enough. But it was better than *Oi!*.

'*Oi!*'

'What?'

'A lady's talking.'

'What lady is that then?'

She ignored that one.

'I suppose you do realize,' she said, 'that everyone'll be looking for us now.'

'Yes,' I said. 'Dare say I do.'

'I suppose,' she went on, as she spread honey from a little pot on to her piece of wholemeal toast, 'you do realize that they'll be looking for a boy on his own and a girl on her own, and there's a pretty good chance that a girl on her own or a boy on his own will get spotted by somebody and picked up by the police in no time.'

''Course I realize that,' I said. 'I'm not stupid, you know.'

'Oh, really? So the rumours aren't true then?'

I just ignored that as it was beneath me.

'So what about it?' I said.

'What about what?'

'What you were on about?'

'Well, I was just thinking that a boy and a girl together would be less suspicious and less conspicuous than a girl and a boy on their own.'

'I'd already thought of that.'

'No you hadn't.'

'Yes, I had.'

'You're only saying that so as not to seem slow.'

'Think what you like,' I said. 'You'll still be wrong.'

She chewed her toast for a bit. Then, 'How much money have you got?' she said.

'Enough,' I said. I wasn't going to be any more precise about my money in case she wanted to borrow some.

'Enough for what?' she said.

'Enough for a while,' I said, still not giving much away. 'What about you?'

'Enough to live on,' she said. 'For a time.'

We both chewed and said nothing for a while. Then she looked across at me again.

'Oi!'

I lost patience.

'Look,' I said, 'my name isn't *Oi!*, it's Bosworth.'

'I know,' she said. 'And it's a stupid name. It's half the reason I ran away. Fancy being engaged to somebody called Bosworth. I'd rather put my head in the oven.'

'Yeah,' I said. 'I'd rather you put your head in an oven too.'

'Bosworth!' she sneered. 'What a name.'

'No worse than Veronica Angelica Belinda Melling,' I said.

We went quiet again.

'You haven't got anywhere to go, have you?' she said, after a while.

'I'll find somewhere,' I said. 'I'll be all right. What . . . what about you?'

'I,' she said, with a note of malicious triumph in her voice, 'have got a caravan.'

My eyes all but goggled out of my head.

'A caravan? What do you mean?'

'Well, you don't think I've come here for no reason, do you?'

'Well—'

'Just hoping that something would turn up?'

'Well—'

'Oh no, I've had this planned for ages. I'm going to hole up in the caravan and hide there – for weeks, months, years if I have to. And I'm not going home until I get it in writing that this engagement is completely off and that I will never have to marry you or ever see you again. And I want it signed, by witnesses.'

I have to confess that I was both surprised and taken aback by this piece of news. I thought that I had been pretty bold and resourceful in running away from home with nothing but a carton of milk and a change of pants wrapped up in a spotted handkerchief in my rucksack (along with my iPod and three chunky KitKats). To have made the sort of detailed plans and preparations that The Virus had

170

made smacked of cold-bloodedness to me, but I was impressed all the same by the news that she had a caravan to go to.

'Eh, this caravan—' I said.

'What about it?'

'Is it yours?'

'Not exactly.'

'Only—'

'Only what?'

'Well, if it's your mum and dad's, won't it be the first place they'll think of looking?'

'No. Because it isn't theirs.'

'Whose is it then?'

'Great-auntie Boo's.'

'Boo's?'

'Her real name's Betty, but we call her Boo.'

'And what's she going to say when you turn up? She'll ring up your mum and dad immediately.'

'She's not going to be there.'

'How do you know?'

'She went off to Spain last month.'

'Oh.'

'And anyway, she doesn't live there. She just uses it in the summer, or lets us go there. The rest of the year it mostly stands empty.'

'But how are you going to get in? Have you got a key?'

'No.'

'So how are you going to get in?'

'I know where she leaves the spare one.'

'Where?'

'I'm not telling you.'

'But what about the neighbours?'

'There won't hardly be anyone there. Not at a seaside caravan site, not in the winter.'

'But if anyone notices you on your own . . .'

She looked a touch despondent.

'Yes, I know . . .'

'And they've heard on the telly about a runaway girl . . .'

'I know . . .'

'And it's the same with me too, I guess,' I sighed. 'People hear about a runaway boy and then see me on my own . . .'

'Yes . . .'

'Whereas, if I wasn't on my own . . .'

'Umm . . .'

'Or if you weren't on your own . . .'

'Hmm . . .'

'Nobody would be looking for a boy and girl together, not when they had run away from home for the express purpose of never seeing each other again.'

'Hmm,' she said. 'There may be some truth in that.'

'And I don't know if you've ever heard the expression,' I continued, 'but they do say that two people can often live as cheaply as one.'

'Do they now?' she said. 'Is that a fact?'

'Yes,' I said. 'Or at least it is a theory.'

'Yes. I may have heard something like that myself.'

'And, of course, if it were true,' I said, 'and if say, for instance, I had enough money for three days, and say you had enough money for three days, if we pooled our money, we'd have enough for six days for two, rather than just three days each.'

'Oh well done,' she said sarcastically. 'You passed the elementary arithmetic then. You know how to do two and two then. It'll be big hands and little hands next.'

'No need to be sarky,' I said. She glanced up at me, as if being sarky was a habit she – or maybe both of us – had got into, and that it wasn't really necessary after all.

Or maybe it was.

She finished her toast.

'Well then,' she said. 'I must be off.'

She opened up her backpack and sorted out some stuff in it – not for any discernible purpose, as far as I could see, maybe just more to pass the time, to delay the moment, if anything. Then she stood up.

I felt a sort of dread. I don't know why. Or maybe I do. It was because she was going, and she was the only person I knew, in the whole great winter waste of Stompton Sands. And even though I was there to

173

get away from her and had only ended up in the same place by bad luck and coincidence, I felt suddenly – well – lonely, and all on my own.

'I'm off then,' she said – though she'd already said it once, and she didn't really need to say it again. All she had to do was to go.

'Right then,' I said.

'I'm going.'

'OK.'

I tried to sound as indifferent as I could, but to be honest, a part of me, a tiny, little, unpredictable part of me – didn't want her to go. I tried to ignore it. It's just a small fear, I told myself. I'll get over it. It's just a little needlepoint of anxiety. But I'm not afraid to be on my own. I'll manage. I always have. I've been on my own before and I'll be on my own again. Everyone's alone at some time in their life. We all have to deal with it.

'I'll see you then—'

I wondered if she felt it too, that small, needlepoint of loneliness, of fear of the unknown, of the big, empty beaches and the windswept sand, and the mist clouding in upon the water. She's only human after all, I told myself, hard as that may be to believe.

'See you then,' I answered.

'Or maybe not, with a bit of luck,' she said, as if she was under an obligation not to be pleasant, even if it killed her.

'Yeah, well you won't be seeing me if I see you first,' I promised her.

'Well, it's up to you then,' she said.

I finished my last mouthful of breakfast. It was time for me to go too – to wherever I was going. Out on to the beach, I supposed. I looked at my watch. It wasn't even ten o'clock yet. Ten o'clock. There was a whole, long, infinite day to fill, and I had nothing to fill it with, no money, no desktop PC with internet connection and on-line gaming, no snacks, no room of my own, no warm radiator, no cosy slippers, no hot drinks, no Mum, no Dad, no rabbits, no collection of international airline sick bags (unused). There was just me, and the cold winter beach and the empty, frozen town, and the time going by, one long, eternal minute at a time.

'What's up to me?'

'If you want to go round on your own and get discovered as a runaway in no time at all, then that's up to you.'

'Oh, is it?'

'Yes, it is.'

'Well, same for you too,' I said. 'If you want to wander round all on your own, when a girl on the loose on her own is just what the authorities are looking for, well, that's your business. Especially when you could be wandering round with somebody else, if only you weren't so pigheaded and obnoxious all the time and always having to be in the right.'

'Oh, is that so?' she said. 'Well, if you're so vain and conceited that you can't even come out with a simple apology that would enable you to not be on your own but to walk around with another person, and possibly even get an invitation to share a person's caravan with a person – well, if that's the sort of person you are, you're not much of a person at all.'

'Well, it's up to you then,' I said.

'No, I don't think so,' she said. 'From where I'm standing the shoe's on the other foot and it's very much up to you.'

'Well, from where I'm sitting, the glove's on the other hand, and it's very much not up to me, but up to somebody else.'

'Is that so? Well, from where I see it, the button's in the other hole.'

'Well, from where I see it, the cheese is in the other sandwich.'

'From where I see it, the burger's in the other bun—'

'All right,' I said. 'I don't really see what I'm supposed to be apologizing for – and I'm not really apologizing at all – and certainly not to you. But if I did do anything – and as far as I can see, I didn't – then I would apologize. But as I haven't, I'm not going to, but if I had, I would. So I'm sorry, but I'm not going any further than that, and you can take it any way you like.'

'Very well,' she said. 'I am prepared, this once, to accept your measly, squirming apology and your admission that you have been totally in the wrong from the word go—'

'Eh?'

'But you'd better see that it doesn't happen again. And now, as you have finally come out with this long-overdue grovelling apology—'

'What?'

'I might be prepared, for the purposes of evading the authorities, and to make the money last longer on the basis that two can live as cheaply as one, even when one of them is a glutton – if the size of your breakfast was anything to go by – I might be willing to let you tag along behind me at a discreet distance and possibly even stay an hour or two at my Great-aunt Boo's caravan.'

'I might be willing to consider that,' I said. 'But only as a special favour.'

'And I'm only inviting you along,' she said, 'so as to help make my protest to my parents that I hate the sight of you, that I don't want to get engaged to you, that I'm never going to marry you – not while there's a good-looking toad left in a pond somewhere – and that I never want to see you again, ever, for as long as I live and possibly even longer.'

'Mutual,' I said.

'Agreed?'

'Agreed.'

'Understand?'

'No problem.'

'I want nothing more to do with you – got it?'

'Absolutely,' I said. 'And I want nothing more to do with you. You've got a deal.'

'Right,' she said. 'You may come and stay in my caravan then. But only until my mum and dad back down and agree that I don't have to marry you.'

'Fine. Just what I want.'

'Are you coming then?'

'Might as well.'

We were heading for the cafe door when the assistant behind the counter called to us.

'Excuse me,' she said. 'But I think I've overcharged you. I charged you both for large orange juices when you only had regular ones. Hold on, I'll give you a refund.'

We returned to the counter to get our money. The assistant opened up the till and reached for some coins.

'Do you want your change separately?' she said. 'Or are you together?'

I looked at The Virus in absolute horror; she looked back at me with an expression of disgust.

'Together?' she said. 'With him? Most certainly not!'

'No way,' I said. 'I'm not with her. I've never seen this girl before in my life – except by accident once, when she was on a day out from an institution.'

'Oh, beg your pardon,' the assistant said, handing us our refunds separately. 'I just thought you were a couple.'

We took the money, thanked her, and then left the cafe. I stopped outside to shoulder my backpack.

'She's probably got bad eyes,' I said.

'Very bad,' The Virus agreed. 'Probably mentally impaired as well.'

'She'd have to be if she thought I was with you.'

'Quite what she thought a girl of my standing would be doing with a complete divot and a total nerd in tow I really can't imagine. Unless she thought I was doing charity work.'

'She probably thought I was in charge of you,' I said, 'and taking you out for walkies.'

'I'm going now,' she said. 'To my caravan.'

'Good riddance,' I said. 'To bad rubbish.'

'Are you coming or not then?' she said.

'All right,' I said. 'I've got nothing better to do.'

So we walked on down the road.

Sort of together, and sort of not.

It was kind of hard to tell.

13

Messages Home

'Is it any good?'

'Is what any good?'

'Your Auntie Boo's caravan.'

'Basic,' she said. 'Adequate, but basic. Why?'

'I'm used to my comforts,' I told her. 'Home cooking and regular meals and feather beds and deep pile carpets and stuff.'

'Well, try a park bench, if you'd rather,' she said. 'You don't have to come to my caravan. You're not doing it any favours.'

I spotted a park bench across the street. It looked sort of hard and uncomfortable, and as if it might be very cold and lonely, round about half past midnight.

'It's all right,' I said. 'I can probably put up with your caravan for a while.'

'It isn't a question,' she said, 'of you putting up

180

with my caravan. It's more a matter of me and my caravan putting up with you.'

We walked on in silence. I wondered why everything we said to each other and every topic we addressed or subject we discussed always seemed to end up in an argument.

Why was that? I asked myself. Was it because she was a girl and I was a boy? But it couldn't be that, could it? Not all girls argued with all boys. Some of them seemed to get on quite well. So why didn't we?

It was her, I guessed. It was her fault. There was something about her. She always had to be in the right, that was the trouble. Personally I don't care who's in the right and such things never bother me, as I am one of those easy-going types who don't mind if people don't do any washing-up or eat spaghetti with their teaspoons or wear the same clothes for a couple of weeks.

The silence continued. In some ways, it was worse than the arguing. It wasn't a relaxed, pleasant silence, not the sort you get when you're at peace with your rabbits at the end of the day. It was more of a strained, tense, nervous silence, with resentment in it on both sides, full of what my mum calls 'unresolved issues'.

We passed a row of shops and offices. I saw a sign outside one of them for a thing called the Relationship Advisory Service. 'Marriage on the rocks?' the notice said. 'Relationship not what it used to be? Has the sparkle and magic gone out of your togetherness?' I looked at The Virus from the corner of my eye. She had spotted the sign too. 'If so, call now for an appointment—'

I looked away. I didn't say anything, but in my opinion, a bit of therapy and some relationship guidance was exactly what she needed. She might have been able to get on a bit better with people – especially boys called Bosworth. A step-by-step programme and a bit of the old couch work would have done her no end of good.

'Is it far?' I asked. 'To the caravan?'

'Complaining about a little walk now, are we?' she sneered.

Now, this is just what I meant. I'd only asked how far it was. Why couldn't she have said, 'Not far' or 'Quite a way' or 'We'll be there in a couple of minutes.' But no. Even a simple question had to be turned into an excuse for being sarky. It was a bit depressing, I don't mind telling you, not being able to ask a simple question without someone jumping down your throat and biting your head off.

'Only asking,' I said. 'No need to be snappy.'

'I'll be as snappy as I like,' she said. 'I'll be as snappy as a crocodile sandwich if I choose and it still won't be any of your business.'

Then I had an idea. Instead of my thinking of her as The Virus all the time, it might break the ice, or at least crack it a little, if I tried to be a bit friendlier. So . . .

'Veronica . . .' I said.

She turned and looked at me.

'*What* did you call me?'

'I said – Veronica.'

She stared at me suspiciously, like I was one of those untrustworthy con artists you read about and she was trying to work out what the scam was.

'Well? What is it – Bosworth?' she finally asked.

'Is it far to your Auntie Boo's caravan?' I said. 'If you don't mind my asking.'

'Em, no, not really, not all that far. About fifteen, twenty minutes maybe.'

'Right. Thanks.'

She gave me another of her funny looks.

'You're welcome,' she said.

We walked on.

We were going along the seafront by now, on the wide promenade. Old men and elderly ladies were whizzing by on electrical scooters, almost as if they were having races, to see whose wheelchair was the fastest.

There were even more windsurfers out braving the cold sea, along with half a dozen maniacs in swimming costumes, who didn't even have wetsuits on. They had all run down the beach together, and had plunged hooting and yelling into the freezing water.

'Probably a mass suicide attempt,' I said to The Virus, pointing them out to her.

'It's supposed to be good for your heart,' she said, 'a swim in the sea in winter.'

'I should think it's more likely to turn you into an iced lolly,' I told her.

She did something unusual then. She gave a smile. I mean, it wasn't a big smile, or even a little smile, but it was definitely the glimmer of one. It soon disappeared though.

The sea was to our right. There was a long pier stretching a few hundred metres out into the water, sitting on spindly metal legs, sunk into the sand. At the far end of the pier – as I knew from my summer visits – were dodgems and slot machines and candy floss stalls. But the pier was closed now and the little train which ran the length of it stood empty and covered in plastic sheeting to protect it from the elements.

To our left, the cliffs rose and fell, like waves. In the distance I could make out the white shapes of mobile homes and caravans against a background of green.

'Is that it?' I asked, pointing.

'What?'

'Where the caravan is?'

'That's it.'

On we walked. We passed a few cafes and beachside stalls, almost all of them closed and

184

boarded up for the winter. 'Ice cream's' a sign read: 'Tea's'.

'That apostrophe's in the wrong place,' The Virus said.

I took her word for it.

It was grim sight, sure enough, was Stompton Sands, at that time of year. All its summer glory had gone, and the beach smelled of seaweed.

Down by the waterline, men in big waders and thick anoraks were standing with fishing rods, casting spinners into the sea. They were all men. There weren't any ladies. I wondered if they were single men, with nothing better to do, or maybe they were married, to Viruses of their own, and were giving each other a break by getting out of the house for a while.

Either way, it was a bit rough on the fish.

There were quite a few dog walkers too, with their dogs scampering along the sands behind them, hoping for a stick to be thrown. The summer wasn't so good for dog walkers. Dogs weren't allowed on the beach between March and September. They probably liked the winter, I supposed, and couldn't wait for all the visitors to go.

We passed a sign reading 'Donkey Rides'. It was nailed to a hitching post, but there were no donkeys anywhere.

'I wonder where the donkeys go for the winter?' I said.

'They go to the West Indies,' The Virus said.

But I had my doubts about that.

As we went along, I spotted a cafe ahead which seemed to be open. There also appeared to be a few people inside, sitting in the window with cups of coffee, staring at screens and tapping on keyboards.

'Hey, look,' The Virus said. 'Internet cafe.'

'What about it?'

'Let's go in,' she said.

'What for?' I asked.

'Send an e-mail, of course,' she said. 'To my mum and dad.'

'Oh yeah,' I said. 'Good idea.'

She stopped and looked at me.

'What did you say?'

'I said . . . I said . . . not a bad . . . idea.'

'No you didn't. You said *good* idea.'

'Did I? Well, it was just a slip of the tongue.'

'We going in then?'

'All right.'

'We'll just have half an hour's worth, shall we? So we can both e-mail home and tell them we're all right and outline terms and conditions for a possible return.'

'OK,' I said. 'Wouldn't want them to worry too much.'

'No. Don't want them panicking.'

So in we went.

* * *

'No looking.'

She'd paid for the use of the computer, so I decided it was only gentlemanly to let her go first. This is the sort of stuff which can make you a big hit with the ladies, or so I'd heard my dad say.

'These days, Bosworth,' he had said to me one night when we were having a 'man to man', 'these days, a woman is looking for a certain kind of chap. A woman has expectations these days. And as soon as I've got the top off this beer bottle, I shall tell you what they are.'

(Dad and I frequently had a 'man to man', usually when Dad had been drinking his home-made lager or home-made cider. He would invite me to join him in the shed for some 'straight talking' and some 'lads and dads bonding'.

Personally, I dreaded these sessions, as having a 'man to man' usually consisted of Dad doing all the speaking and me doing all the listening and never getting a word in as I was too young to have any opinions and all the ones I did have were wrong anyway. They also meant that I missed my TV programme – the American one about the vampire who is also a detective and who works nights in the ambulance service.)

'There are a few things you ought to know about women and girls, son,' Dad had said during our last 'man to man' session, before I had run away from home. 'Especially now that you're getting engaged.

You need to know, Bosworth, about the facts of life.'

I wondered if I should make a run for it then. The last thing I wanted was Dad explaining the facts of life. We had already done them at school and I didn't want Dad going through them all over again, as it would have been too embarrassing and he'd probably have got them all wrong anyway.

'Women have certain expectations these days, Bosworth,' he said. 'They're liberated and out in the world there, earning a living for themselves. They're not expecting to be just mothers and housewives like back when I was a lad. Oh no. They're looking for equal treatment and husbands who'll do their share of the housework—'

'Like you, do you mean, Dad?' I said, as I had always been under the impression that Dad would have had great difficulty in identifying a vacuum cleaner, even if there had been twelve of them lined up in a police station.

'Well, obviously I make my contribution in other ways, like taking the bins out and such,' Dad said. 'And fixing the car. Or at least fixing for the garage to fix the car.'

'Right.'

'The thing is, Bosworth, as you're getting engaged now, you need to know the formula for a happily married life – like what your mother and I have, most of the time.'

'So basically, Dad,' I said, 'following your

example, the recipe for a happy life, once I'm married, is to do as I'm told and to take the bins out.'

'No, no, not at all, Bosworth. You're getting hold of the wrong end of the stick entirely here. No. You have to be true both to each other and to yourselves.'

'All right, Dad, if you say so.'

'Of course taking the bins out does help, there's no denying that. But what man wouldn't take the bins out for the woman he loves?'

'True, Dad. I'm sure you're right.'

'Look at Romeo and Juliet. Didn't Romeo take Juliet's bins out?'

'I'm not sure, Dad. We've only just started reading it at school.'

'Antony and Cleopatra then. Solomon and the Queen of Sheba. Elvis and Mrs Presley. Didn't King Solomon take the Queen of Sheba's bins out for her? Of course he did. And why? He did it for love.'

'But, Dad, if he was a king, wouldn't he have had a bloke to do it, like a bin man or something?'

'Yes, maybe, but the thought would have been there.'

'Right.'

'So you remember what I've told you tonight, son, and one day, you'll be grateful for it. Meantime, have you seen my bottle-opener?'

Thanks to Dad, therefore, I had considerable

insight into the ways of girls, and could all but read them like books, and know their innermost secrets.

So that was how I knew that if a girl has paid for half an hour on the computer, you'd better let her go on it first, or she'll probably kick you.

'No looking.'

'I'm not looking,' I said. (Even though I had been.) 'Look, I'll even sit over here so you can see I'm not looking.'

'All right. But no looking.'

I sat on another chair and angled my head so I seemed to be staring out of the window, but so as to get a good look at the e-mail she was typing and sending to her mum and dad without my being detected.

Dear Mum and Dad, **she wrote.** I guess by now you will have discovered the note I left on the kitchen table and that you will know I have run away from home rather than get engaged to that repulsive boy Bosworth Hartie, who has taken on the dimensions of the Human Pimple to my mind.

I felt my jaw twitching, but as I wasn't supposed to be reading her e-mail, I just had to stay quiet.

I know that you both love me and only
want the best for me and you sincerely
believed that finding someone for me to
marry would help with my homework and
my marks at school. I appreciate that
you meant well and felt that getting
engaged would bring some order and
stability into my life. I can see this
and understand it, but what I cannot
understand or begin to forgive is how
you could have thought I would ever be
happy with a great big bogy like
Bosworth Hartie.

I had a sudden coughing fit then and had to slap
myself on the back.

She turned to me from the computer.

'What's your problem?'

'Nothing,' I said. 'Choked. Cola went down the
wrong way.'

'You're not reading my e-mail, are you?'

'No, no, of course not, no. I'm looking out the
window.'

'Well, see you don't then.'

'I'm not interested in your rotten e-mail.'

'Good.'

I went back to my Coke and to pretending to stare
out of the window. She sat, deep in thought for a
time, then resumed her typing.

I know, dear Mum and Dad, that you will be very worried about me, and the last thing I would want to do is to cause you any pain or distress or anxiety like that. All the same, I must stand up for myself on this occasion. I want you to know that I am safe and well and I am sorry I had to do this. But there seemed to be no other way. I tried to tell you, time and again, that I didn't want to get engaged to the great pimple, but you would not listen. I also want you to know that I am not coming home while the threat of Bosworth Hartie is still hanging over me. I shall not come back until I hear that the engagement is off and that such a thing will never happen again. And even then, I shall not be coming home immediately, as I feel that lessons have to be learned and points have to be made, and that if I give in too soon or come home too readily, you will not take my protest seriously and just think it was a silly whim. Therefore, I shall not be coming home for at least a week, maybe two.

If you want to get in touch with me, you can do so at this new e-mail

address I have. But you won't be able
to trace it, and even if you do, it
won't help you as I'm never going to
use the same connection twice.

Please don't worry about me. I am
safe and sound and can look after
myself. I'll be in touch again soon, in
a day or so. I hope that we can work
our way through all this and that one
day we will be reconciled and be a
happy family again. Meantime I have to
show that I am not a person to be
trampled on or fobbed off with the
Bosworths of this world, who nobody
else wants.

I had another coughing fit.

'Are you sure you're all right?' She eyed me
suspiciously.

'Fine. It was just that cola that went down the
wrong way coming back up again.'

'OK, well, I've nearly done now. Just got to send
it.'

She did, and off the e-mail went.

'OK. Your turn.'

'Thanks.'

She moved away from the screen and I took over.

'No looking,' I said.

'Like I'd be interested!' she said.

She went and sat where I had been sitting, and pretended, just as I had, to be looking out of the window.

I went into Internet Explorer and found a place where I could set up a new e-mail address for myself. Once I'd done that, I started my letter to my parents. I thought it best to get to the point immediately and not to beat about the bush.

Dear Mum and Dad, **I began.** Rather than get engaged to Veronica Melling, the human wart and international bad smell, I have run away from home—

I heard a spluttering noise, and looked over to where The Virus was sitting.

'You all right?' I said. 'What's your problem?'

'Drink,' she said, indicating her glass. 'Went down the wrong way.'

14

A Site for Sore Caravans

Once we'd sent the e-mails off, and once The Virus had spent ten minutes surfing the net, clicking on to the websites of her favourite bands (none of whom were any good as they were all stupid), we left the internet cafe and headed on along the promenade towards the distant caravan site.

The wind had picked up and seemed colder than ever, driving the air back down into your lungs before you had properly got it out. We passed more signs of summer activities, long since gone into winter hibernation.

'Trips round the bay' a notice by the small harbour read. 'Magic Mystery Tour' said a torn poster by a bus stop. 'Coaches leave from here, every afternoon at 2.' Well, not that afternoon they weren't.

Everything was grey: the sea, the sky, even the

sand had a greyish tinge to it. We passed the lido. The gates were locked and the place deserted, but you could see the open-air swimming pool inside, empty of water, with old iced lolly wrappers lying in the diving end, and sand piled up in the shallow.

It was bleak all right. Summer dreams turned to winter nightmares. You never know a place till you've seen it in all its moods and seasons. And maybe that was true of people too. I glanced at The Virus, wondering about her moods and seasons, and if I'd seen them all yet. I doubted it. I hadn't seen any of her sunny days or her clear blue skies yet, if she had any. And I didn't think I wanted to be there when her storms started.

We continued on our way in silence, plodding along the promenade at a short distance from each other, still sort of together and sort of not.

I'd noticed that about people sometimes – how some of them are so clearly together, and how others are obviously strangers. But there's a third category too, of people you can never quite be sure of, who are sort of together and sort of not. Some of them might have been married for half a lifetime too, but they still can't seem to decide if they're with each other or if they aren't.

'Better cross the road,' The Virus said.

We left the promenade, crossed the road, and took a steep footpath leading up to the top of the cliffs.

Up we went. There was no one around. Just us and the seagulls, and even they looked cold. Who'd be a seagull, I thought, with nothing to eat but cold fish, even in the middle of winter, when you really needed something to warm you up from the inside, like a nice cup of cocoa.

'It's at the very top,' she said. So we went on climbing. I felt a bit unfit and out of breath, but I wasn't going to show her that, so I kept on going regardless.

At the top of the cliff, the footpath diverged; one part continued on around the coast, the other turned inland to the left, and that was the way we went.

'This is just the footpath,' she said, 'for going down to the sea. There's a road around at the front of the site so you can drive in with your car.'

We walked under a little wooden archway with a board on one of its posts announcing that we were now entering the 'Cliff Top Holiday Park: Private, Residents Only'. It didn't seem like a very imaginative name, but it was certainly accurate.

'Come on,' she said. 'Don't dawdle.'

Only I wasn't dawdling.

She was starting to sound like my mum.

There must have been hundreds of caravans in the Cliff Top Holiday Park, some big enough to live in permanently, others too small to be comfortable for much more than a long weekend.

There were some mobile homes there too, set on concrete bases, which made them look anything but mobile to me. In fact, I've never seen a mobile home go anywhere; as far as I can make out, they all stay put.

'This way.'

We threaded our way along concrete walkways, which criss-crossed between the caravans and the mobile homes; they nearly all seemed empty and shuttered up, waiting for the summer to come, like the rest of Stompton Sands. One or two, however, looked occupied. There were bright curtains in the windows, pulled back or tied up, and the glass was steamed up from the inside, as if warmth and life and simmering kettles were in there.

'Oi!' I said.

If Oi! was good enough for me, it was good enough for her too.

The Virus turned and looked back at me.

'I do have a name you know.'

Yeah, I thought, I could think of several.

'Do some people live here all year round then?' I said. 'Because some of these caravans look like they're being used.'

'Yes,' she said. 'There are a few people who live here all the time. Not many though and most of them are old.'

'So what do they want to stay here in the winter for?' It looked that bleak and depressing to me that you'd have been better off finding the nearest squirrel hole and squeezing in to hibernate with him.

'Because it's cheap,' she said.

'Oh.'

She seemed a bit nervous.

'What's up?' I said.

'Keep your head down.'

'Eh?'

'I don't want the people who own the site seeing us.'

'Where are they?'

'Don't know. They might not even be here. I think they usually go abroad in the winter. But they might have left somebody to keep an eye on the place. Over there – that's the office.'

Some distance away was a collection of small concrete buildings, consisting of an office, a small shop (closed) and what could have been a block of showers and laundry facilities.

'Doesn't look like there's anyone there to me.'

'Well, let's hope not,' she said. 'But keep your head down.'

We wormed our way along between the empty caravans and the deserted mobile homes. Finally we stopped next to a medium-sized, if somewhat rickety caravan with peeling paint and spots of rust on it, perched precariously on some piles of bricks.

'Here we are.'

'Is this it?'

'Yes.'

'Bit of a dump, isn't it?'

'And why are you getting so choosy all of a sudden? You haven't even been inside yet.'

'If it's anything like the outside, I'm not sure that I want to.'

'Then in that case go and find your own caravan then.'

'No, no, it's all right,' I said. 'I'll give it a go.'

'Well, no looking.'

'No looking for what?'

'No looking while I find the spare key. It's in a special hiding place that nobody's supposed to know about.'

'Yeah, like under a brick or somewhere original like that, where nobody would ever think of looking.'

'Look, do you want to stay in this caravan or don't you? Because if you don't, then clear off, and if you do, then keep quiet and look the other way.'

'All right,' I said. 'No need to be so touchy. It's easy to see you got out of the wrong side of bed this morning.'

'I slept on a waiting-room bench, actually – remember?'

'Then you got off the wrong side of your bench then.'

I looked the other way. A few seconds later she reappeared, brandishing a key.

'Got it.'

'Good.'

'We can go in then.'

She fitted the key into the lock, turned it and opened the door.

'Well, this is it.'

We went inside. I looked around the dim interior of the caravan, at the faded fabrics and the spots of mildew around the windows.

'Smells a bit.'

'Just musty, that's all. Hasn't been used for a few months. Be all right once we get some air in. Just need to open the window.'

It was rusted and she couldn't open it.

'Here,' I said. 'Let a man have a go.'

'Sure. Where is he?' she said. 'Bring him on.'

It was so rusted, I couldn't open it either, and not only that, I cut my finger.

'Oh great,' she said. 'Now you're going to get blood-poisoning and need your hand amputated.'

'I'll be all right,' I said. 'I'll rub it with a bit of spit.'

'Well, use your own,' she said – as if I'd have used anyone else's.

'I'll leave the door open a while,' she said. 'Let the air circulate.'

'It's cold.'

'Well, make your mind up – do you want it musty or do you want it cold?'

'Neither, actually.'

She turned and glared at me.

'You know something?' she said. 'Do you want to know something about yourself? Two things actually. One, you're absolutely impossible to please, and two, no matter what anyone else does, you always find fault with it.'

She'd just described herself.

'Well, I like that!' I said.

'Good,' she said. 'Then you finally like something.'

'I mean,' I said, seeing that sarcasm was wasted on her, 'that I don't like it.'

'There's a surprise – you, not liking something.'

'The only nit-picking, fault-finding, impossible-to-please person round here,' I said, 'isn't me – it's you!'

'Huh,' she said.

'Huh, yourself.' I looked around the caravan. 'And by the way,' I said. 'Where's my bedroom?'

'Your what?'

'My bedroom?'

'There isn't another bedroom. What you see is what there is.'

I looked around. There were two beds, at right angles to each other, underneath the windows, and a sofa under another window, which could probably be turned into a bed if needed.

'So this is it?'

'Yes. What you see is what there is and what there is is what you get.'

She crossed to the small sink by the tiny kitchen, and she turned on a tap to see if the water was connected.

'So you mean,' I said, 'that we're stuck in one room, both of us, all the time, and there's no escape?'

'Well, if you think it's any pleasure for me . . .'

'I'll go stir-crazy.'

'So go home then.'

But I couldn't do that. Not yet. I had points to make and my reputation to consider. I couldn't go home before she did. If I had, well, she'd have sort of . . . won.

'Anyway,' she said. 'We won't be in here all the time.'

'Won't we?'

'I wouldn't have thought so.'

'So you'll be out a lot then, will you?' I said, noticing with some relief that there was a small telly on a stand in a corner, so at least I'd have something to do to pass the time.

'Well, I will be going out, yes. But then so will you, won't you?'

'Will I?'

'I would have thought so.'

'Why's that?'

'Well, you're not expecting to lounge around my caravan all day, are you?'

'What else is there for me to do?'

'Well, obviously,' she said, 'you'll have to get a job.'

My legs gave way under me and I sat down heavily on one of the beds. A fine spray of either dust or moisture rose from it.

'A job?' I said. 'How do you mean, a job?'

'Well, we can't live on fresh air,' she said.

'But we've got enough money between us for a few days.'

'Maybe, but we might be here for weeks.'

'So?'

'So you'll have to get a job.'

'I can't get a job,' I told her.

'Why not?'

'I've got a bad back,' I said.

'No you haven't.'

'I have.'

'You never mentioned it before.'

'It's just come on.'

'No, it hasn't.'

'And besides . . .' I said.

'What?'

'I'm too young to get a job.'

'Lie about your age then.'

'No one'll believe me.'

'You're not too young to get a paper round.'

'I might be. I'm not altogether sure where we stand on the legal position.'

'Well, you look old enough for a paper round, so just say you are.'

'It's not worth it anyway,' I said. 'A paper round won't pay enough to keep us in the style to which I'm accustomed.'

'Then you'll be able to get two paper rounds, won't you? One first thing in the morning, the other in the late afternoon, for the evening paper.'

'First thing in the morning!' I said. 'I can't go doing paper rounds first thing in the morning, not at the crack of dawn, when the snow's still on the ground and the ice is still in the bird bath and—'

She lost her temper.

'Oh for heaven's sake, Bosworth,' she said. 'Do stop going on. Do stop whingeing, will you? You sound like a great big fairy.'

'Fairy?' I said. 'Me? A fairy? Me, who's well known for being rough and tough and fearless in the tackles on the football field? Me, Bosworth the brave, a fairy? Do you know what you're saying, woman? Pull yourself together. You must be delirious. You're suffering from the vapours.'

'Well, stop going on,' she said. 'You just go on and on all the time. I hate to think what you must be like when you're ill, or when you get a cold, or a touch of flu or something. I bet you drive your mother mad.'

I had to put her straight on this.

'Look,' I said, 'when it comes to me and being ill, the words "brave little soldier" are never far from people's lips. I bear my sufferings without a murmur, I do, and expect no more than the occasional hot lemon drink and a paracetamol. And another thing—'

'What?'

'Why can't *you* go out to work?'

'*Me?*'

'Yes, you. Why can't *you* go and do a couple of paper rounds? Why can't *you* get up first thing in the morning and go out when it's freezing and crack the ice on your socks?'

'Well, obviously because I shall be busy in here doing the housework and looking after the caravan.'

'Will you? Well, I've got a better suggestion – you go out to work, and *I'll* stay in and look after the caravan.'

'You? Do housework?'

'Why not? Why do I have to go out to work, just because I'm a boy? Why do you have to do the housework because you're a girl?'

'I don't,' she said.

'Exactly,' I said. 'Those days have long gone, haven't they?'

'Of course they have,' she said. 'I quite agree.'

'You're entitled to a career,' I said, 'every bit as much as I am. Right?'

'Absolutely right,' she said.

'Well, there you are then,' I said. 'You can have your career as a newspaper delivery person, and I – being the new man, forward-thinking, liberated type

206

– can stay at home and look after the caravan and the babies.'

'No,' she said. 'You don't understand. I am not staying in to look after the caravan because I have to. I am staying in to look after the caravan because I choose to. Because I don't want to get up and go out in the cold.'

'But what about me? What about my choice?'

'You don't have one.'

'That's sexist.'

'No it isn't,' she said.

'So what is it then?'

'It's my caravan,' she said. 'And that's what I've decided for now. If I get bored, I shall go and find a job, and if I don't, I won't. And that's it. And if you don't like the arrangements, well . . . you know what to do.'

I sat on the bed brooding, wondering how my running away from home had turned out so wrong.

First off, I had run away from home to get away from Veronica Angelica Belinda Melling. But instead of getting away from her, I was now stuck in a caravan with her. And second off, I was at a decided disadvantage, as it was *her* Auntie Boo's caravan and if I didn't toe whatever line she chose to draw, she would throw me out.

It seemed to me as if I had no rights. Or maybe I'd had some once, but somehow they'd been sneakily taken away from me.

'All right,' I said. 'I'll maybe think about it. Only, when you say housework – will that include you doing the cooking as well?'

'Might do,' she said. 'I'll have to see.'

I looked at her.

'Do you like cooking?' I said.

'Don't mind it,' she answered.

'Have you done much?'

'A bit. At home, and a bit at school.'

'We did a bit at school too,' I told her. 'I've cooked things as well.'

'What did you make?'

'Burned stuff the first time,' I said. 'And then undercooked stuff the second time. There was something wrong with the oven.'

'What was wrong with it?'

'I forgot to turn it on. So what sort of stuff can you cook then?'

'All sorts.'

'Pies?'

'Yes.'

'Meat pies?'

'I am not cooking meat. We are not having dead animals in this caravan.'

'Might be an idea to check the beds then,' I said. 'Judging from the smell, the dead animals might be here already.'

She almost smiled again. Almost, but not quite.

'Do you have any favourite things to eat then?'

she said. 'That don't have dead animals in them?'

'Crumble,' I said. 'Can you make crumble?'

'I think so – that is, I have done – my mum helped, but I think I can remember . . .'

'I love crumble,' I said. 'Apple ones. Or apple and blackcurrant.'

'I'll get the ingredients then,' she said. 'And make one.'

'Will you?' I said, forgetting for the moment how much I couldn't stand her and how she was the blight of my existence and the bane of my life. 'Would you make me an apple crumble? All toasting hot? With thick double cream to go with it? There waiting for me, when I come home after a long, hard day at the paper rounds.'

'Could do,' she said. 'For a treat,' she said. 'Maybe. I could try. Why, would you like that?'

'Yeah,' I said, visions of crumbles filling my brain. 'Yeah, that would be great. It's nice to come home to a crumble at the end of the day.'

And my eyes grew misty, and a picture came into my mind, of this little cottage in the country, with a beautiful garden, and roses round the door, and the sun shining, and the lambs bleating, and someone coming home on a bicycle along a country lane, while from the open window of the cottage, the smell of freshly baked apple crumble wafted out into the evening air.

But then I was brought back to cold reality by a

loud and staccato knocking at the caravan door.

'Hello!' a voice cried. 'Hello! I know you're in there! Open up!'

I looked at The Virus, and she looked at me. We couldn't have been discovered already, could we? It surely couldn't be the police?

15

Old Prudence

'Hello? Can you hear me?'

It wasn't the police. Not unless they had started recruiting people who could impersonate the voices of old ladies. I peered out of the window, just to double-check.

'She's not wearing body armour or carrying weapons,' I said. 'I think we're safe.'

'Must be one of the neighbours,' The Virus said. 'Better let her in.'

The Virus opened the caravan door, and there on the concrete path stood a small, old lady, somewhere between the age of seventy-five and two hundred, with wet hair and a towel around her shoulders. She also had on a pair of glasses which she was having trouble seeing through – not so much due to their thickness as to what seemed to be dried salt on them. It was plain that the window cleaner had not visited for some time.

In one hand, the old lady held a carton of milk, and in the other a slightly squashed, very home-made-looking sponge cake with jam dribbling down its sides.

'All right, my dears?' she said. 'I live in the mobile home over the way. Only been here a few weeks myself. I saw you moving in and I thought, now there's a young couple starting off life together in their tiny little caravan, I ought to go over and make them feel welcome. So I've brought you round a little house-warming present – well, I suppose it's a caravan-warming, really. Not that you want your caravan too warm, or it'll be up in flames.'

She peered at us both through the murky glasses.

'Oh my, you do look young,' she said. 'But youngsters today, they grow up that quickly. Oh, my. You only look about twelve or thirteen at the most to me. Just a couple of babies. But I know, I know. You're going to tell me that you're eighteen at the very least, or even twenty-one. Kids today, my oh my, you all grow up so fast. Can I come in and put the cake down?'

Given a free choice, my answer to that question would have been no. But in the circumstances, we couldn't afford to offend anyone, so we had to invite her in, thank her for the cake and milk, and offer her a cup of tea. There were some old tea bags in a can above the sink.

'Very kind, thank you,' she said. 'I'm Prudence – Mrs Bagsholt, as was, before I was widowed. And what are your names?'

'Eh . . . Bartholomew and, eh . . .'

'Patricia . . .' The Virus told her. 'I'll put the kettle on, shall I?' she said, filling the rusty kettle with some brownish-looking water from the tap. The stove was connected to a gas bottle under the sink, which she seemed to know how to open and light. I guessed she had seen her Auntie Boo do it, at some time.

'Oh, Bartholomew and Patricia – Barty and Patty. How nice. So how long have you been . . . em . . .' our new (if somewhat old) neighbour Prudence asked conversationally. (Though I felt that basically she was starved for a chat and that was why she had come over.)

'Been what?' I asked.

'Married?' she said.

I nearly dropped the cake.

'Married!' I said. 'Married!'

'Are you on your honeymoon?' Prudence went on. 'Pity you couldn't have come in the summer. It's much nicer here when the sun's shining. But I'm sure you'll still enjoy yourselves. And I dare say it won't be long now before we're hearing the patter of tiny feet.'

'Why's that?' I asked. 'You get a lot of rats here then, do you? Will we need to put some traps down?'

'No,' Prudence said. 'I mean it won't be long before you're starting a family.'

'Family!' I said, clutching at the table for support. 'Family!'

'Or maybe you'll be wanting to wait a few years,' she said. 'No hurry is there? Enjoy yourselves while you're young, that's what I say, because when you get to my age, there's not so much left to enjoy – except your morning dip in the sea, of course.'

Which explained the wet hair and the towel. She was one of the loonies who jumped into the sea. It also accounted for the dried salt and tidemarks on her glasses.

'You've rented the caravan, have you?' she asked.

'Eh, that's right,' Veronica said, lying again. 'We have.'

'Right.' Prudence peered at her. 'Have I seen you round here before?'

'I don't think so.'

'Ah. Well, I have to say that your husband here seems like a very personable, very pleasant, well-built and handsome chap.'

The Virus nearly set fire to herself on the gas ring when she heard that. Personally, I was starting to warm to our neighbour Prudence and could see that for all her foibles, she had many sound qualities, and even with her mucky glasses on, she had quite a lot of insight.

'Yes, you're a lucky young woman having a chap

like him to keep you warm at nights,' Prudence said.

The Virus dropped the kettle.

'Warm at nights!' she said. 'Him! Warm at nights! I'd rather stick my feet on a sack of well-rotted manure and set fire to the mattress!'

Fortunately, Prudence missed that, as she was fiddling with her hearing-aid.

'Beg pardon, dear,' she said. 'Didn't quite catch that. It's my hearing-aid. I think I've got water in it again.' She took it out of her ear and banged it hard on the table before putting it back in. 'Ah, that's better,' she said. 'I can hear again now. You were saying?'

The Virus had recovered her composure. We couldn't really afford to lose our tempers, either of us. Sooner or later there would be bulletins on the TV, about the two runaways who had left home to avoid getting engaged to each other. Prudence looked like a bit of an avid TV watcher to me, dirty glasses notwithstanding. It was something to do with the shape of her eyes, which seemed rather rectangular. And while nobody would ever expect two runaways – who had disappeared in order to get away from each other – to actually end up together, I didn't want to take any chances with old Prudence's powers of observation and deduction.

'Yes, he's a lovely chap, isn't he?' Prudence continued, smiling and nodding in my direction and giving me favourable looks, as if I was her long-lost grandson back from the wars, formerly given up for dead. 'A bit chubby and knock-kneed, maybe, but none the worse for that. And all his own hair too, by the look of things. Yes, you're a lucky young woman, right enough,' she told The Virus again. 'I expect you count your blessings every day.'

'Oh, every minute,' The Virus said. 'Never stop.' And she went to get a knife to cut the cake with.

I noticed, once the knife was in her hand, that she seemed to have some kind of battle of will with it, as though the knife had a mind of its own, and if she hadn't controlled it and got the better of it, it might have stabbed someone.

'Oh good lord!' Prudence exclaimed. In fact it was more of a scream than an exclamation. She raised a finger and pointed at the knife.

'No, it's all right,' The Virus said, rather shamefaced, 'I wasn't really going to stab you—'

But Prudence wasn't listening.

'Your ring!' she said, pointing at The Virus's hand. 'You've lost your wedding ring! Or maybe it's been pinched. Yes, off on your honeymoon and your wedding ring's been stolen! Quick, quick! Let's call for the police!'

And she was up on her feet, spryer than you could ever have imagined (it must have been all that sea-dipping that had kept her fit), and to my astonishment she whipped a mobile phone out of

216

her pocket and started dialling 999. I looked at The Virus, who looked back at me.

'Bosworth,' her look said. 'We have to stop her.'

I sized the situation up. I guessed that if I dived, I'd probably just about be able to rugby tackle her before she dialled the last number.

But The Virus stepped in with the brains before the brawn could spring into action.

'It's all right, Prudence,' she said. 'I haven't lost it. I had to take it back to the jeweller's, for alterations.'

'Oh. Thank heavens. I thought it had gone.' She cancelled the call.

'No, no. Nothing like that,' The Virus said. 'It was a bit loose, that was all. So I dropped it off at the jeweller's to be fixed before we set off on . . . on . . . our honeymoon.'

'Well, that's a relief,' Prudence said. 'You wouldn't want to lose your ring, would you?' Her voice dropped a little and she took a step closer. 'It is, after all,' she said, 'the symbol of your undying love, for your husband here.'

I suddenly saw that Veronica The Virus had picked up the knife again. I felt it was time for me to intervene and lighten things up a little.

'So, eh, Prudence,' I said. 'Have you lived in the caravan park a long time?'

'Not that long,' she said. 'I moved here after my husband died. It's very economical and I like my

217

mobile home. I know it's small, but it doesn't take much looking after, which suits me, at my age. Gets a bit lonely in the winter, mind, but I'm sure the summers are fine, there'll always be company then. And by the way,' she said, sidling up next to me, 'congratulations.'

'Thanks,' I said. 'On what?'

'Oh, having such a lovely young lady take you on.'

'Who's that then?' I said, not quite twigging on immediately.

'Your dear lady wife,' she said.

'You mean The Virus?' I said.

'Beg pardon, dear? Hearing-aid's gone again.'

She started banging it on the table. For some reason, my own hand was now grasping out for that same kitchen knife. The Virus noticed, and moved the knife out of my reach.

'Yes,' old Prudence said, her hearing-aid back in place, 'it must be lovely to be young and in love.'

'Wouldn't know,' I said. 'I couldn't help you there.'

'Don't know what's wrong with this hearing-aid this morning,' she said. 'It's making all sorts of funny noises. Perhaps I should take it out when I go in swimming. But then if I did, and if a shark crept up on me, I wouldn't hear it.'

The Virus handed her a cup of tea and a slice of the sponge cake she had brought.

'So tell me,' old Prudence said. 'Was it a church

you got married in, or a registry office? Or somewhere unusual, like a lighthouse, or a stately home, or somewhere fancy like that? I don't suppose you'd have any pictures of the wedding with you, would you? I do so love a wedding. And how many bridesmaids did you have? And who gave you away?' she asked.

'Nobody,' I said. 'I gave myself away.'

'I meant your wife,' old Prudence said.

'Oh.'

Finally, about an hour later, we got rid of her. To our great credit, she was still breathing and had no injuries.

'Well, I'm sure you two young lovebirds will want to be left on your own for a while,' she said. 'To bill and coo, and to pour sweet nothings into each other's ears, and to spoon,' she said.

'Spoon?' I said. 'Spoon what?'

'You know,' she said. 'Spoon. As in spooning. Spoon. It rhymes with moon.'

I didn't have a clue what she was on about. I wasn't all that keen on her sponge cake, either. Too much jam in it for me. At last she left, wishing us a happy honeymoon and hoping that the weather might change so we could get a few days on the beach.

'How long are you here for, by the way?'

'Oh, a couple of weeks or so,' I told her, keeping it vague.

'Well, I'll see you again, no doubt,' she said. 'I'd better go and find my cat.'

So off she went to find it – a task which, judging by the state of her glasses, could easily be a five-hour job. And even then she'd probably come back with a mop-head instead of a moggy and spend the rest of the day encouraging it to eat a tin of pilchards.

There was a long, uncomfortable silence after old Prudence had gone. I think it was due to what she had said, and her (for us, fortunate) misinterpretation of events.

True, it was good that she thought we were far older than we were; true it was lucky that she didn't think of us as runaways or anything like that, but for her to actually think that we were—

Married.

Me? Married? To her? To The Virus?

It was horrifying. It was all your worst dreams, all your nightmares come true. I felt quite queasy. In fact I said as much.

'I need the toilet,' I said.

The Virus, who was clearing the tea things away, and wrapping what remained of the sponge cake in some clingfilm, which she had found in the cupboard, looked moodily across at me.

'So if you need the toilet, go to the toilet,' she said.

'Eh, right,' I said, looking around the caravan. 'So where is it then?'

She pointed out of the window.

'Over there.'

She was indicating the concrete building which I had seen when we arrived.

'Over there?'

'Over there.'

'I've got to go all the way over there?'

'If you want the toilet you have to.'

'What – even if I wake up in the middle of the night and want the loo, you mean I've got to go out in the freezing cold and walk miles to the toilet block?'

'It's the same for everybody else.'

I looked around the caravan again.

'What about the sink?' I said.

'Don't you dare,' she said. 'Don't you even think about it.'

So the toilet block it was. I had to trudge all the way there and then all the way back.

'This isn't going to be a lot of fun,' I told myself. 'Having to make a trip like this any time you want to use the loo or to have a shower. Especially when it's dark.'

By the time I returned to the caravan, The Virus had tidied up a little, and had even managed to get one of the windows open to let some fresh air in. She had also got the TV to work.

'Shh!' she snapped as I came in. 'News is on.'

I sat on what seemed to be my bed – as she was

sitting on the other one – and we watched the news. There was plenty about the Prime Minister and international events, but not much about anything else.

'There's nothing on about us,' I said. 'It's too soon.'

'Shh!'

I stood to turn the set off.

'Wait.'

'It'll be hours before they put an appeal out.'

But I was wrong.

The face of The Virus appeared on the screen. I could imagine people in houses all over the country, crossing themselves and reaching for lucky rabbits' feet with which to ward off the evil eye.

'The police put out an appeal this morning for help in locating the whereabouts of two missing children. The youngsters, a girl, Veronica Melling, and a boy' – my face appeared on the screen. It was me in my school uniform, the photo Mum kept on top of the bookcase – 'named Bosworth Hartie, both ran away from home during the night, due to personal and domestic reasons. The police believe that they have run away separately and it is extremely unlikely that they will be together. Anyone who spots either of the runaways, or who has any information which might help in finding them, is asked to—'

Then they gave a phone number, and that was the end of it. The Virus turned the set off.

'Well, they can't be that worried,' she said. 'They must know we're all right. They'll have our e-mails by now.'

'Exactly,' I said. 'They know we're safe and OK.'

'All the same . . .'

I knew what she meant, and how she felt – guilty. Guilty for causing all this worry and distress which my mum and dad and her mum and dad would no doubt be going through. But then, on the other hand, they'd more or less asked for it: they wouldn't listen, they wouldn't pay attention, they thought they knew best . . .

'Send them another e-mail tomorrow,' The Virus said.

'Yes,' I agreed. 'Regular bulletins, then they won't have to worry.'

'And meantime,' she said, 'I'm going to change my hair.'

'Eh?'

'So I don't look like that photograph of myself.'

'Oh, right. I'll just wear my beanie hat when I go out,' I said. 'Then no one'll recognize me anyway.'

She spent the next twenty-five minutes titivating herself and experimenting with new looks. The only trouble was, she wanted my opinion on them, while all I wanted was to have a nap, as it had been a bit of a rough night in the station waiting room, and I hadn't slept very well.

'How does my hair look like that?' she wanted to know.

'Fine,' I told her.

'Or does it look better like this?'

'Yeah, that's fine too,' I said.

'Or do you like it better when I do this with it?'

'Whatever,' I said, wishing I'd packed a book with me.

'Or do you think I look better when I have it like this?'

'No,' I said. 'You look like a ferret.'

'No need to be rude.'

'Well, you did ask.'

'So you prefer it when I have it like this?'

'That or the other way.'

'Or how about this?'

'Yeah, that's fine too. Whatever.'

'Well, which one then?'

'Any of them.'

'This? Or this?'

'Either.'

'But if you had to choose. This way? Or this way?'

'All right. The first way then.'

'The first way?'

'Yes.'

'So you don't actually like the second way then?'

'No, I didn't say that.'

'You think it makes me look frumpy and my bum look big?'

'What? No. I never said that.'

'Because if that's how you feel, why don't you say so?'

'Eh?'

'I'm not talking to you any more.'

'Eh? What did I do?'

'As if you didn't know.'

She was as good as her word. She sat there and didn't talk to me for ages. I started to nod off.

'You're snoring!'

I opened my eyes to see she'd changed her hair again.

'I've tried a new style,' she said. 'Do you like this one?'

'Fine,' I said.

'Do you prefer this one now?'

'I don't mind it,' I said.

'Or do you like me better when I put it up like this?'

'Whatever you think.'

'But if you had to choose,' she said, 'which would it be? This way? Or like that?'

'Like that,' I said. 'Second way.'

'I see. So you don't actually like the first way at all?'

'I didn't say that.'

'You think it makes me look cross-eyed and my ears stick out?'

'I never said that!'

'You're so shallow,' she said.

'What did I do?' I wanted to know.

'You disgust me,' she said.

'Why?'

'Huh! As if you needed me to tell you. I don't think!'

She went back to not speaking to me.

I looked around to see where the knife was, but she must have put it back in the drawer.

I was glad of that, in many ways.

I didn't want to do something I might regret.

You can get quite a long prison sentence for attempted murder.

And the fact that you were provoked beyond all human endurance is no defence at all.

16

A Good Job Too

We had the rest of the sponge cake for lunch, and then the day took a bit of a dip.

'I'm bored now,' The Virus said.

So was I. And not only that, I was accustomed to having my own space. I wasn't used to sharing, and I guess that neither was she.

Basically, I was used to having things more or less my own way. It was hard having to share a small caravan with somebody you had gone on the run to escape from. Maybe I ought to go home, I thought. Because, after all, as long as she had disappeared, I was safe. But then I realized that doing so might make me look like a mummy's boy and a wimp, so I decided to sit it out. I wouldn't go home until she did first. There was no way I was going to blink first.

'I think I might go out for a while,' I said. 'And have a look around.'

'Good idea,' The Virus said. 'You might be able to find a job.'

'I'm never going to find a job on a Sunday,' I said.

'Why not? Loads of shops are open on a Sunday, especially newsagents – which is what you want, for a paper round.'

'We'd better get something in for dinner, too, I suppose,' I said, as there didn't seem to be much in the caravan, apart from a packet of lentils. 'How about I get a nice tin of meatballs and a tin of potatoes and tin of ice cream for pudding?'

'We're not having meat in this caravan,' Veronica said. 'We'll have baked potatoes and cheese. I'll do them.'

I looked at her, impressed.

'Do you know how to bake potatoes then?' I said. 'And how to grate cheese?'

'Of course,' she said. 'Piece of cake.'

'But isn't that technical work?' I said. 'Like chemistry and engineering and stuff?'

'Not that difficult,' she said. 'We'll have them with salad.'

'Salad?' I said. 'Why do we have to eat salad when there aren't any adults here?'

'It's good for you.'

'Not for me, it isn't.'

'I like salad,' she said.

'I don't,' I told her.

'Well, we're having some anyway,' she said. 'We'll

get some at the supermarket. There's a small one down the road, about ten minutes' walk from here.'

I didn't want another argument just then, so I didn't say anything. You can make as much salad as you want, I thought, but I'm not eating it. The only salad I was having was chocolate.

She put her coat on.

'Well?' she said. 'Are you coming?'

'You go ahead,' I said. 'I'll maybe go out later.'

I thought I could have a quiet hour without her before looking for a job.

'Well, who's going to push the trolley round the supermarket and carry the bags back here?' she said.

'Eh – you?' I suggested.

But she didn't seem very keen on that.

As we locked up and walked away, I saw the curtains move in what had to be Prudence Bagsholt's mobile home.

'She's watching us,' I said.

'I know,' Veronica said. 'Just smile and wave and be friendly.'

So we did. I put my beanie hat on then, so as not to be recognized.

'How do I look?' I asked.

'Stupid,' she said.

'Good,' I said. 'No one will recognize me then. I suppose for nobody to recognize you, you'd have to try and look intelligent.'

It could have been an accident, but she seemed to

stumble then, and she inadvertently caught me up the backside with her knee.

We walked on through the nearly deserted caravan park, which seemed less holiday-like than ever. The site shop was closed up and had a sign in the window which said 'Open in April' – which was too long for my stomach to wait.

After leaving the entrance to the caravan park, we followed the road down to the town and soon came to a parade of shops. There was a newsagent there, right enough, along with a hairdresser, and across the street was a decent-sized, cut-price supermarket, the kind that sells all the usual stuff but in packets you don't recognize.

'How much have you got on you?'

I told her how much money I had, keeping a bit back for myself.

'We'll just get enough for dinner tonight and breakfast tomorrow, OK? Then we'll see how it goes.'

'All right.'

So we went in, and I pushed the trolley while she put the stuff in it. Nobody paid us much attention. Either they were short-sighted like Prudence Bagsholt, or they thought we were brother and sister, shopping for our mum.

Brother and sister – it gave me the chills.

'Here,' I said to Veronica. 'Has it crossed your mind that people might think we're brother and sister?'

'They're hardly going to think that – with your looks – are they?' she said. 'You look more like a plate of leftovers.'

I didn't say anything in reply, but I did accidentally-on-purpose run the trolley over her foot.

We got some potatoes, some stuff for her salad, and some breakfast cereal and orange juice for tomorrow, then we paid and went. I looked at the clock on our way out. It was still only two in the afternoon. There were hours to go before evening. What were we going to do?

It was funny, but of all the things I'd imagined when I'd decided to run away from home, there was one thing I'd never contemplated at all – that I might be bored. But now, how to fill the day seemed like the most difficult thing of all. And then there was tomorrow, too, when normally we'd be going to school. What were we going to do instead?

'Eh, Veronica—'

'What?'

'What are we going to do for the rest of the day?'

'Eh – well, can't you think of something?'

'Is there a cinema here?'

'In the town.'

'Anything else to do?'

'There's the beach.'

'Bit cold for the beach. We have to do something though. We can't just sit in the caravan. We'll go mad.'

'*Go* mad?' she said. 'What do you mean, you'll *go* mad. You're there already, aren't you?'

'Well, how do we pass the time, with no computer and no PlayStation and no—'

'There are plenty of books in the caravan,' she said. 'In case you didn't notice. I'm happy to curl up with a good book myself.'

'Me too,' I said. 'But not for the rest of my life.'

'Well, go and look for a job then,' she said. (She kept going on about this job. I was starting to think that she meant it.)

'All right,' I said. 'I will. You take the shopping back, I'll try and find a job.'

It was only one bag of shopping, so she didn't object to carrying it.

'And don't come back till you've got one,' she said, then she turned and headed back to the caravan park.

I mooched about for a while and had a look around town. Stompton Sands wasn't a big place, and in the winter it seemed to shrink. There were a few shops open though, and even one of the amusement arcades had its lights on. I went inside to play the slot machines, thinking that if I won enough money, I wouldn't need a job. Only I lost two pounds. I thought I'd better stop before things got worse.

On my way along the High Street, I came to a newsagent's. It had a lot of small ads on cards in the window. And there, in among them, was a large handwritten notice saying 'Paper Delivery Person Wanted. Urgent. Apply Within.'

So, only taking a couple of seconds to think about it, I did.

'Paper round? You?'

The man behind the counter wasn't unfriendly exactly, but he did seem a bit suspicious.

'Eh, yes.'

'Do I know you then?' he said.

'Eh, no,' I said.

'You go to school round here?' he said.

'Eh, not far away.' (Well, it was only an hour away on the train.)

'How old are you?'

'How old do I have to be?'

'You've got to be old enough to do a paper round.'

'That's how old I am then.'

'Are you sure?'

'Oh, yeah.'

'I'll need to see a birth certificate.'

'No problem,' I said. I could tell that he was desperate for someone to deliver the papers and he wasn't going to do too much checking up on my credentials if he didn't have to. 'I might have to send off for it first, to get a copy, as we lost the original, so it could take a few weeks. Or even a month or so.'

'All right then. And I'll need a note from your parents.'

'I'll get one. When do you need it for?'

'Oh, some time will do.'

'OK.'

'Do you know the area?' he asked.

'Pretty much,' I said – thinking that what I didn't know I could soon find out.

'Got a bike?'

'Eh – got stolen.'

'Never mind, I've one out the back you can borrow. Have you any experience of delivering papers? Or putting things through letterboxes?'

'I posted a letter once.'

'Fair enough. Can you start tomorrow?'

'Eh – guess so.'

'Can you do mornings and evenings?'

'Eh – probably.'

'All right. You've got a job then. See you first thing tomorrow morning.'

I hadn't bargained on that. I'd been hoping for a late start on my first day.

'When you say first thing – what sort of thing do you mean?'

'About seven,' he said. 'At the latest.'

Seven o'clock. That meant I'd have to be up by half six. Still, I could always go back to bed when I'd finished the paper round, I supposed.

'OK,' I said. 'I'll be here.'

So he told me how much money I'd be getting, and we left it at that, and I went out and headed back up the hill, relieved to be in employment, as at least I'd have some money coming in now and I wouldn't be stuck in the caravan all day, getting cabin fever and going stir-crazy, all cooped up with The Virus.

But when I got back and told her I'd found a job, she wasn't that impressed.

'I've got one too,' she said.

'Eh? But I thought you were going to stay in and do the housework.'

'Changed my mind. You can do that.'

'What? *And* two paper rounds?'

'We'll do a bit each then.'

'How did you get a job?'

'There was a card in that shop window, by the supermarket. They were looking for a dog walker at the local kennels.'

'Dog walker?'

'Two or three hours a day.'

'How much do they pay?'

She wouldn't tell me at first, but she did eventually.

She was getting paid more than I was!

The rest of the day passed uneventfully. We had cheesy baked potatoes and salad for dinner (though I left my salad – I thought about my rabbits and how they would have appreciated it), followed by a yoghurt each. As she'd cooked, I washed up. Then we had a game of Scrabble. There was a board in a cupboard in the caravan, along with Monopoly and draughts. It wasn't a very good game of Scrabble though, as she cheated, and kept making up all these words I had never heard of and which I was sure did not exist, but as there wasn't a dictionary around, I couldn't prove anything.

After that we watched the telly for a while, then it seemed to be time for bed.

'I'm going to brush my teeth,' she announced. She took her toilet things and headed for the shower block. A few minutes later, I did the same. But although I went out after, I was back before her. I don't know if she had more teeth to brush and more face to wash than I did, or perhaps she just took more time over it.

I realized then that I hadn't brought any pyjamas. I hadn't packed any in my rucksack. It hadn't really seemed like a running away sort of thing to do. Running away was bold and dangerous, a perilous adventure, like being in the commandos. I couldn't see blokes in the commandos packing their pyjamas somehow, not when they were off on an assignment behind enemy lines, or anything like that. It didn't seem very fearless, really, packing your pyjamas.

I wondered if The Virus had packed hers. Or

maybe she wore a big nightie, made out of old bin bags.

Before I could decide what to do about not having any pyjamas, she was back smelling of soap and toothpaste.

'Oh—' she said, surprised to see me still up. 'I thought . . . you might have gone to bed . . . and put the light off.'

'Eh – just about to. Which is my bed again?'

'Whichever. That one, if you like.'

We each had a sleeping bag. I spread mine out on my mattress.

'OK, well . . . I'll get into my sleeping bag then,' I said. 'But I might . . . have to take my trousers off,' I warned her.

'Oh,' she said, as if she hadn't been prepared for that. 'Oh, all right then. I'll look the other way.'

So while she did, I took my trousers off and hung them on the back of the chair, and got into my sleeping bag, taking my top off but leaving on my T-shirt. I was wearing my *Lord of the Rings* one, with Frodo the hobbit on the front.

'I'm in,' I said.

'Well, I'm getting ready now,' she said.

'I'm closing my eyes and going to sleep,' I said. And I closed them. I heard all this rustle, rustle, rustle, as she got ready for bed and squirmed into her sleeping bag. She must have reached out and put the small light out, as I could see that it had gone dark, even through my closed eyelids.

All was silence in the Cliff Top Holiday Park. It was quiet and lonely, empty and cold. I thought of my lovely warm bed at home, of my mum and dad, still no doubt worried about me, despite my reassuring e-mail of earlier in the day. How did I come to be here, I wondered. Had I done the right thing? What did the future have in store? How on earth was I going to get out of bed at half past six in the morning?

Then I heard a voice.

'Bosworth?'

'Yeah?'

'You awake?'

'Yeah.'

Then there was a pause before she spoke again.

'Night, Bosworth.'

'Night . . . Veronica.'

'See you in the morning.'

'Yeah, see you in the morning then.'

Then little by little, I drifted into sleep, and as I did, I began to dream that I was at home, in my own bed, in my own room, and I was small again, and Dad and Mum had come in to say goodnight, and when they'd read me a story and tucked me in, they turned to go. As they did, I seemed to hear a voice, distinct and clear, not one in my head, but one right there in the caravan. It seemed distant, detached, a sleepy, drifting voice, like the voice of another dreamer, sinking into a sleep of their own.

'Love you,' the voice said. 'Night, night.'

'Night, night,' another voice answered. 'Night, night. Love you too.'

And the next thing I knew, Auntie Boo's alarm clock was screeching right next to my ear, and it was six twenty-five in the morning. I gave it a thump to shut it up.

To my disgust, I looked over to see that Veronica Angelica Belinda Melling was still lying there, fast asleep.

17

A Hard Day's Work

I didn't see The Virus for the rest of the day, in fact not until the evening. It took me hours to get the paper round done, as I didn't know where anywhere was.

I shouldn't think many people on my round got their papers in time that morning, and most of them left for work without anything to read. I knew there would be complaints, but I wasn't worried. It was only to be expected, really; it had to happen every time there was somebody new starting the round. The newsagent must have known this and that I'd soon get the hang of it and be faster once I knew my way about.

It was almost ten o'clock when I returned to the caravan. It was empty and The Virus had left a note. I got in by using the key, which she had left under the stone.

'Gone dog walking,' her note said. 'Dinner at seven, if I don't see you before. Something special. Don't be late. V.'

I put the note in my pocket, and then – oddly enough – decided to tidy up a bit. I don't know why. Normally I wouldn't have bothered. But strangely, I began to hear this little voice in my head, asking questions like, 'What would Veronica think? What would Veronica say, if she came back to find the caravan in a mess, and you hadn't even tidied up a little?'

Part of me answered, 'I don't care what she says. She can get knotted.' But another part felt slightly uneasy, as if all it wanted was a quiet life. So I did tidy up – a bit, anyway, but not too much.

I decided to go back out then and wander around until it was time for the afternoon paper round and I could earn some more money.

I locked up, put the key back under the stone, then walked down the cliff path to the beach and along the prom to where we had found the internet cafe. I paid for an hour's browsing and bought a drink and sat down to surf the net and to check my e-mails. There was, as I had expected, one from Mum and Dad.

Bosworth! it said. (They hadn't even bothered with a 'Dear'.) Bosworth! You must come home *at once*! Whatever put it into your head to run away? What a mad and totally irresponsible idea. You must call us now, right this minute, the moment you get our e-mail. Or ring the police – immediately! Everyone is looking for you and even though we have your assurance that you are all right, we are still worried sick. Your mother is losing pounds rapidly. Where are you? What are you doing? Where are you staying? Have you fallen in with a bad crowd? Bosworth, whatever made you do this! **(But I thought I had explained all that. Typical, I thought, they simply don't pay any attention.)** Just come home, and we can talk things through. Ring us now, that is all that matters. You cannot possibly stay out there on your own. There are many good people in the world, but there are also a lot of weirdos. **You're telling me, I thought. I'm living in a caravan with one of them.** You have no idea of the peril and danger to which you have exposed yourself. You could be abducted or kidnapped and exploited. You could all so easily end up in a carpet factory in Taunton. Or making trainers for a pittance in the Third World. Or be forced to work in a call centre in Luton. Don't think we are exaggerating, Bosworth – these things happen!

Telephone us the instant you read this, please, Bosworth. We are both terribly worried and your rabbits miss you and are pining away. **But I felt that was just emotional blackmail.** We would also like to point out that you will fall behind with your essays and coursework if you don't come home, which is the last thing you need. Call us *now*, Bosworth, if only to say that you are all right. Or just hurry home. We promise that there won't be any trouble or any lectures or remonstrations. Simply come home, Bosworth. Come home now. Come back to the bosom of your family and to those who love you.

PS – Your mother says that if you come home, you will not have to learn the tuba after all, and she will stop putting spray-starch on your pants when she irons them.

Up until the point where I read 'We promise that there won't be any trouble,' I have to admit I had been weakening. As soon as I saw those words, however, they gave strength to my resolve.

It is my experience that whenever people say to you 'We promise there won't be any trouble,' then you are headed for the biggest trouble you have ever seen. Because if there really wasn't going to be any trouble, why would they even think of it?

Why would they go all to the trouble of denying there was going to be trouble unless there was going to be trouble? At least that's how I see things and in my opinion I have yet to be proved wrong.

It is like when your parents say (after some unfortunate incident that shall be nameless), 'Well, that's all in the past now, Bosworth. That's all over and done with and behind us now. We shall move on and never mention it again.'

Well, when they say that, you know that you will never hear the end of it ever, and they will still be going on about it for the next forty-seven years.

I decided I was better off remaining out on the run for the time being. And as for the matter of Veronica Melling, my parents hadn't even addressed the issue or taken my feelings seriously enough to even think it was worth discussing.

I sent them a quick e-mail back, just to put their minds at rest but also to let them know that I wasn't a man to be trifled with.

Dear Mum and Dad, I wrote. (Even though they hadn't put a 'Dear' in their e-mail, I wasn't one to hold a grudge or to be petty.) 'Thank you for your e-mail. I understand where you're coming from, but feel that we still have a lot of unresolved issues here that aren't being addressed – namely this engagement you have got me into against my will and better judgement. I feel I am not being taken seriously on this and that I have to make a stand. I am not coming home therefore until the matter is sorted out and I get an assurance that I don't ever have to get married to anyone. Meantime, just to let you know I am OK and surviving and have somewhere to stay. Please tell the police not to bother looking for me, as I'm sure they have more important things to do like give out speeding tickets. I hope to be back home one day, but not yet. Love to you both, your son, Bosworth.

PS – Please keep an eye on my collection of unused airline sick bags from around the world and don't use them for rubbish.

I hit the send button and off the e-mail went. The rest of the hour passed playing on-line games, then, when my time was up, I went for a wander along the beach. I watched the fishermen for a while, then I found a burger bar where I got some lunch, then I went for another wander on the beach. Under the pier I met a bloke with a metal detector who told me he was looking for money, so I had a look as well, but I didn't find any. Then I went for another wander and got a bar of chocolate. As I was standing eating it, I saw a figure in the far distance, with two dog leads in either hand, walking briskly along the sand. I couldn't be sure, but it looked a bit like The Virus, doing her dog walking. So I went into town then and had another go on the fruit machines in the amusement arcade, where I won yesterday's two pounds back, and then I headed for the newsagent's and my afternoon paper round.

And that was what caused the trouble.

I made some friends. It was some of the other paper boys, doing the other rounds. They got back to the shop about the same time as me, and they all seemed to know each other, and were standing around chatting and eating crisps.

'What's your name?' one of them asked me.

'Blenkinsop,' I told him.

'Do you play football?'

'A bit,' I said.

'We're one short for a five-a-side.'

'All right then.'

So I followed them down to the beach and we had a few games of football; after that we went to a cafe and drank a few Cokes, and then we had a wander round the town and ended up in the amusement arcade. And although time was getting on by then and it was growing late, all thoughts of The Virus and the note she had left in the caravan had gone from my mind.

By the time I got back to the Cliff Top Holiday Park, it was dark and quiet. I threaded my way past the empty mobile homes and found Auntie Boo's caravan. I opened the door and went in.

'Hello!' I said, cheerfully. 'I'm home.'

The Virus was sitting on her bed, reading a magazine. There was a delicious smell of cooking in the air, and yet no plates were laid on the table, no pans were to be seen. Something seemed to be up, something was bothering her, I could tell.

'Hello,' I repeated. 'I'm home.'

She turned a page of her magazine, but still didn't speak.

'Hi,' I said. 'Good day with the doggies?'

She looked up. She didn't seem very happy for some reason.

'Oh,' she said coldly. 'So you're back, are you? Finally condescended to come home, have you?'

'Beg pardon?'

'And what time do you call this!' she said, holding up the alarm clock.

'Eh, well, it's quarter past—'

247

'I can see what time it is. You don't have to tell me.'

'But you just asked and . . .' And then, before I could stop myself, I let out this enormous burp. 'Oh dear,' I said. ''Scuse me.'

She stood up. Her eyes narrowed. She took a step forward.

'You – you've been drinking!' she said.

'No, I haven't!' I protested.

'Yes, you have,' she said. 'I can smell it on your breath.'

'It was just a few Cokes,' I said. 'And a couple of Red Bulls, maybe – and perhaps a lemonade.'

'A few Cokes,' she said. 'Look at you. You're practically hyper.'

'No I'm not. I only had two cans. Three at the most. With the lads.'

'Oh – the lads. And who are the lads?'

'Just some mates I made – other paper boys. We sort of went for a bit of a kick-about and a drink after.'

'Oh, really? Did you just? So here I am, left on my own all night in the caravan, cooking and slaving over a hot stove, while you're out drinking and boozing with your mates.'

'No, no, we just – you know – went to the amusement arcade for a while.'

'Oh, marvellous, wasting even more money. And how much did you lose on the slot machines?'

'Well, not that much. Only a little bit. And I did work for it. I have been working all day. I'm entitled to a bit of relaxation with my mates.'

'And who do you think's going to pay for everything else? While you're squandering your money on fruit machines.'

'I did earn it.'

'And what about me? I'm working too, you know. Out walking dogs half the day in the bitter cold, then coming home to start the cooking and to put a meal on the table. I even left you a note, asking you not to be late. All you had to do was to get back here at a reasonable hour. But did you? Well?'

I sniffed the air. The smell was familiar, delicious even; it was a smell I knew, a smell I loved.

'What . . . what is that smell?' I said. 'What were you cooking?'

'I was making,' she said, 'an apple crumble, if you must know.'

'Apple crumble?' I said. 'Apple crumble? Real, home-made apple crumble, with real apples, and real crumbles?'

'Yes,' she said. 'And I even bought some ice cream to have with it.'

'Oh, lead me to it,' I said. 'Put a plateful down in front of me. Hand me a spoon and I can do all the rest myself.'

She just glowered at me.

'So where is it then?' I said. 'Where's the crumble?'

'The crumble? Simple,' she said. 'My share is in my stomach, thank you very much.'

'Oh, you started without me?'

'Yes, seeing you're more than two hours late for dinner, yes I did!'

'Oh . . . so where's my bit of crumble then?'

'Your crumble,' she said, 'is with the rest of your dinner.'

I looked around for the rest of my dinner but it was nowhere to be seen.

'So where's that then?' I said. 'Where is my crumble and the rest of my dinner?'

'You'll find it,' she said, 'in the bin.'

I took a look. With luck I'd still be able to salvage something. The bin was empty.

'Not that bin. The big wheelie bin. Outside.'

All hope was gone then. And my dinner had gone with it. I stood there staring at her. I couldn't believe she'd done it.

'You put my dinner in the bin?'

'Yes, I did. So let that be a lesson to you. And tomorrow night, it's your turn to cook. And don't forget, Bosworth, that what's sauce for the gander is sauce for the goose.'

'Isn't that supposed to be the other way round?'

'Don't worry about it. It will be.'

And she flounced off across the caravan (which is quite difficult to do in a confined space), sat down with her magazine again, and didn't say a word to me for the rest of the night.

I had bread and cheese for dinner followed by bread and jam for afters.

She still hadn't spoken to me, even when we'd gone to bed.

'Veronica,' I said, when the light was off.

I finally got a response.

'What?' she said. 'And what do *you* want?'

'Sorry,' I said. 'About being late home. I hate it when there's an atmosphere. Let's not go to sleep in a bad mood.'

'Who's in a bad mood? Not me,' she said. 'I'm in a perfectly wonderful mood, thank you very much.'

'OK, well – sorry, anyway.'

'Huh!' she said.

She seemed a bit unforgiving, I thought. I was glad I'd left home to get away from her. I'd have hated to have been stuck with somebody like her for the rest of my life, who wouldn't even forgive you for a little mistake. I mean, if she'd been late for dinner, I wouldn't have gone on about it.

I lay awake for a while, brooding on things, and wondering why it was so hard to get on with other people sometimes, and yet lonely on your own sometimes too. It seemed to me there was no easy answer, and that it was as hard to live with people as it was to live without them.

It had never been like this with my rabbits.

The next day, I made a special effort. I went to the shops after my paper round and I bought a recipe book and some ingredients. I read up the recipe and I made a veggie flan and a treacle tart for pudding. I had it all ready for seven o'clock. But at eight o'clock, I was still waiting. By nine o'clock – even though it was only The Virus and I hated her and good riddance to bad rubbish – I was worried sick. It was dark, it was cold, she was a girl, out on her own. I'd no idea where she'd gone. She hadn't left me a note or anything.

What if something had happened to her?

I decided to go out and look. I was just rummaging around, trying to find a torch, when the caravan door opened and in she came. She was a bit flushed and out of breath.

'Oh – hi.'

'Hello,' I said. (I managed not to say, 'And where have you been?' I was trying to play it cool.)

'Oh,' she said, looking at the food. 'Did you cook something?'

'Yeah,' I said. 'I did. It's a bit cold now but I can warm it up.'

'Oh, none for me, thanks,' she said.

I looked at her suspiciously. 'Why not?' I said. 'What's wrong with it?'

'Nothing, I'm sure,' she said. 'But I'm not hungry. I've already eaten.'

'Oh?'

'Yes.'

'Where?'

'Oh, I just went out with a couple of the girls from the kennels. We had some chips.'

'Oh did you now?'

It was true. I could smell the vinegar.

'And where did you have those?'

She gave me an odd look.

'At the chip shop.'

'Oh? And what's the big attraction about the chip shop, when there's a hot meal waiting here at home?' I said.

She tossed her hair.

'Different people, that's all,' she said.

'What different people?' I wanted to know.

'There were a few boys there, that's all.'

'Boys?' I said. 'What boys? What boys are these?'

'Just some local boys that the girls happened to be friendly with.'

'Did they now?' I said. 'Is that so? So you've been off chatting to boys then, have you? I see.'

'One of them asked me out, as a matter of fact.'

'Did he now?' I said. 'Did he just?'

'I haven't decided whether to go or not.'

'Well, it's all the same to me,' I said. 'Makes no difference to me ... So, are you going then or—?'

'Haven't decided.'

'It's all the same to me. I don't care if you go out with boys. It doesn't matter to me at all.'

'I think I'll go and have a shower,' she said. 'Excuse me.'

Off she went to the shower block. I sat and had a slice of cold quiche, followed by a slice of cold treacle tart. They weren't bad, even if I say so myself, but they lay like lead in my stomach somehow, as if I'd swallowed a couple of shoes.

I had an early night that night. She was still up reading when I turned in.

'Goodnight,' she said.

I just mumbled.

'Aren't you speaking?' she said.

I just mumbled something else.

'There's no need to be like that,' she said.

I pretended I was already asleep and didn't say anything. I mean, I'm not one to have a moody about things, but I'd gone to a lot of trouble to cook that dinner, and she couldn't even be bothered to get back to eat it. She'd just gone hanging round chip shops so she could go out with other boys. Not that I was jealous as there was nothing to be jealous of and I couldn't have cared less anyway as it was nothing to do with me.

But I thought it was a bit bad not getting back for my treacle tart.

Some kinds of behaviour are just unforgivable.

18

A Close Call and Headline News

We had a narrow escape the following day, when we strolled down to the internet cafe in the evening to send some e-mails. As we were coming back, keeping five paces apart as usual, a woman out walking her dog saw The Virus and began staring at her, like she was suspicious, and half recognized her as the runaway from the TV.

'Quick,' The Virus said, sidling up to me. 'I think she might have rumbled me. Throw her off the scent. Look like we're together. Hold my hand.'

'Your hand?' I said. 'You must be joking. I'll hold your neck for you if you like, and squeeze tightly.'

Before I could say anything else, she'd grabbed hold of my hand, and then my arm, and next thing we were walking along like we were going out with each other or something.

'Gerroff me,' I said. 'I'm coming over queasy.'

She rested her head on my shoulder.

'You don't think this is any fun for me, do you, you great der-brain?' she snarled. 'It's for your benefit as much as mine. If she calls the police, they'll get you too and then we're both done for.'

The woman was still watching us. She didn't seem so suspicious now, but nor did she appear entirely convinced.

'Stop here and sit on the bench,' The Virus said.

'What for?'

'So we look like we're watching the sun go down.'

There were quite a few couples, sitting on benches and on the beach wall, viewing the sunset. So we joined them, and sat holding hands, watching the sun go down on Stompton Sands. The woman was still loitering and eyeing The Virus curiously.

'Put your arm around me,' The Virus said.

'Give you a punch on the nose, was that?' I said under my breath. 'Kick up the bum, did you say? Certainly. No trouble.'

'You heard,' she said. 'Get on with it. Quick!'

The woman was still staring. I draped my left arm around The Virus's shoulders so we looked all lovey-dovey, and we sat like that for a while.

Finally the woman called her dog and they went on their way. The Virus shoved my arm off.

'That was horrible,' she said. 'It was like being smothered by a greasy octopus. Has she gone now?'

'Seems to have.'

'Thank heavens,' she said. 'But what a price to pay.'

'You're telling me,' I said. 'How do you think I feel? Putting my arm round your shoulders – I could be traumatized for life.'

We sat awhile in silence, watching the sun drop into the water on the far horizon.

'You're still holding my hand, you know,' The Virus said.

'Ecch!' I said, recoiling and letting go of it. 'I didn't know. I thought it was a burger.'

The sun was like a great huge red ingot now, like a glowing coal. You almost expected it to sizzle as it sank, and to see steam rising from the sea.

I heard The Virus sigh, and turned to look at her. She seemed thoughtful and far away.

'Terrible when you feel that everyone's after you, isn't it?' she said. 'And that the world's against you.'

'Yeah,' I said. 'You and me against the world, eh?'

It was out before I thought about it really, before I knew what I'd said.

She looked at me, quite seriously.

'Do you feel like that sometimes?' she said.

'What?'

'That no one understands you?'

'Maybe.'

'No one understands me either,' she said. 'They think I'm weird. It's just 'cause I'm a bit different, and don't like to do what everyone else does all the time.'

'Me too sometimes,' I said. 'People think I'm weird too.'

'You are weird,' she said. 'You collect sick bags.'

'It's just a hobby,' I said. 'No worse than stamps. Or beer mats.'

'I suppose not.'

'We can be outcasts together,' I said. 'And then there'll be two of us, and we won't be quite so outcast any more. We could form the Outcast Society.'

'What – a society of two?'

'It's a start.'

The sun had gone down now. It was time to go back to the caravan.

Funnily enough, as we walked together along the prom, it was a good few minutes before either of us realized that we were somehow holding hands again.

'I'm only doing this in case that woman's still around,' The Virus said.

'Me too,' I said. 'As a precaution. It's the lesser of two evils.'

Once we were on the cliff path though, we walked on our own. I mean, I'd only held her hand out of self-preservation, to stay at large and guard my liberty. I'd never have done it otherwise, if I hadn't been under duress.

The following morning, when I went to start my paper round, I picked up the bundle of newspapers

I was to deliver, and instantly dropped them.

'You all right, Blenkinsop?' Mr Cramms the newsagent called. 'You haven't done your back in, have you? I've no money for compensation.'

'No, no. I'm fine,' I said. 'Slippery fingers, that's all. No problem.'

But there was a problem, not that I was going to mention it to him. The problem was right there on the front page of the morning paper – going under the name of Veronica Angelica Belinda Melling.

Have You Seen This Girl? the front page headline asked.

Well, I had. And I wished I hadn't. I'd seen more than enough of her, and I didn't much want to see any more. But there she was, notwithstanding, staring out at me from the *Daily Examiner*.

Runaway Girl Still Missing.

Parents Distraught.

Well, she wasn't properly missing, I thought, not really. And they couldn't be that distraught. She'd been sending her mum and dad e-mails, the same as I had.

I put my newspapers into the shoulder bag Mr Cramms had provided and went out the back to borrow his bike. Once I was a safe distance from the shop, I stopped and got the paper out and had a proper read. There wasn't much to see on the front page, the bulk of the report was on the inside.

It struck me as peculiar – before I turned the page

– that there was only concern for her, and none for me. After all, I'd gone missing too. When I turned to page two, however, all was revealed.

Beauty and the Beastie, the inside headline read. And there was a photo of me now, next to another one of her. Her photo was under the word *Beauty,* and the *Beastie* caption seemed to apply to me.

No wonder she ran away! the article began. *A narrow escape.*

Young Veronica Melling ran away from home rather than get engaged to this boy. And who can blame her? Veronica's parents say she has been in touch over the internet. She claims that she is safe and well, and not being held prisoner – but how do we know? Is it really her sending these e-mails, or some abductor? We must find her, before something terrible happens. She could be in grave danger. If you have seen a girl who could be her, don't hesitate. Get in touch with the police immediately, or call our help line.

And then, in much smaller print, the article ended by saying, *Bosworth Hartie, the boy who caused lovely Veronica to run away, is also still missing. Police say they are keeping an eye out for him, but he is not on the top of their list of priorities.*

Well, of all the cheek, I thought. Talk about biased reporting.

I opened up a different newspaper, the *National Newsday,* to see what they had written. To my relief, it was the other way round in there. On page three was a recent picture of me – quite a good one – and a horrible one of The Virus.

Boy flees home rather than be forced into engagement with plain and 'homely' girl.

(I hoped The Virus didn't see this newspaper or my life wouldn't be worth living when I got back to the caravan.)

The police have issued further pictures of Bosworth Hartie, the schoolboy who has run away from home to avoid the possibility of an arranged marriage. Having studied the pictures of the girl in question, some might say, who can blame him? Not the National Newsday. *What the* National *says is, 'Go, Bosworth, Go!'*

It went on, in similar vein, to put the schoolboy side of the case. The report appealed for anyone who spotted me to tell the police (which I wasn't so keen on) but not to tackle me personally, as I might be mad by now (which was true up to a point, as I had been feeling a bit irritable lately, though I had put that down to the early mornings).

I put the *National Newsday* back into the bag and pedalled on along the road. I kept my beanie hat low down over my forehead. I didn't look like anyone with that beanie hat on. No one would recognize me from any front or inside page photos as long as I kept wearing that. What was worrying me was The Virus. She was too vain to wear a beanie hat, and even with her change of hairstyle she still looked too much like herself for comfort. I was concerned that by the time I got back to the caravan, she would already have been rumbled.

When I returned to the site in the mid-morning – a little worried that she might have read the *National Newsday* and its description of her as plain and homely – my worst fears were confirmed. I opened the door, and there she was, trying to drown herself in the sink.

I leaped across the short distance that separated us.

'No!' I yelled. 'Veronica! Don't do it! Think of your mum and dad! It's not so bad to be plain and homely! You can still have a life. Don't do it. Don't drown yourself. Please!'

I went to pull her out of the basin, but got a mouthful of bad language and abuse for my trouble.

'Get off!' she said. 'What are you doing?'

'Never mind me. What are you doing?'

'I'm not trying to drown myself, you idiot. I'm dyeing my hair!'

'Oh.'

'Twerp.'

'Sorry,' I said. 'How was I to know?'

'We were on the telly again earlier,' she said. 'Both of us. Another appeal. So I nipped up to the shop and bought a hair dye kit. No one'll recognize me if I change my hair colour. It was a close thing with that woman the other night.'

'Oh. What colour are you changing it to?'

'What does it look like? Blonde.'

'Who's that going to fool though?' I said. 'It's not going to fool the people down at the kennels, is it?'

'It's not them I'm worried about. They only read dog magazines and watch doggy programmes. It'll fool strangers though,' she said. 'And anyway, I can't un-dye it now.'

And half an hour later, that's what she was – a blonde. It was quite a major improvement. She didn't look too bad at all.

'Right,' she said, when it was all dry, done and finished. 'I'm off to the kennels for the dog walking.'

'Don't they wonder why you're not at school?'

'It's half-term here,' she pointed out. 'Haven't you noticed?'

But I hadn't. I was sort of pleased and disappointed too. Running away during half-term meant I wasn't missing out on any lessons – but on the other hand, it meant I wasn't missing out on any school either.

Off she went to walk the dogs. I went outside, thinking to wander down to the amusement arcade. I didn't get very far before I was accosted by old Prudence Bagsholt as I passed her mobile home. She was standing outside, pegging her swimming costume up on the clothes line.

'So there you are! Shame on you,' she said.

I stared at her, not understanding at first. Then I

realized that she must have recognized us as the runaways and was upbraiding me for all the worry I'd caused my parents.

'D-do you know then, Prudence?' I said. 'Did you work it out? You won't tell on me, will you? Please.'

'I've a good mind to,' she said. 'And you only just married!'

'Eh?' I said, confused. If she knew we were the runaways, then she knew we weren't married.

'Betraying her already! You unfaithful swine.'

'Eh?'

'Your lovely little wife!'

'Eh?'

'Don't play the innocent with me, you two-timer,' she said. 'I saw her. I saw that blonde-haired floozy sneaking out of your caravan a few minutes ago. Your poor wife. That lovely girl.'

'But that was her,' I said. 'That was my . . . well . . . that was her . . . that was . . . eh . . . what did she tell you her name was again?'

'You can't fool me,' Prudence said. 'Your wife's a brunette.'

'She's dyed it,' I said. 'For fun. I liked her as she was, of course. But no, she fancied a change—'

'Oh, I do apologize. Yes. Now you mention it . . . oh, silly me. It was her, wasn't it? Oh yes. Sorry.'

'No problem,' I said. 'Anyone can make a mistake.'

(And I should know, I thought. Look at me. I'd ended up in a caravan with Veronica Melling. Mistakes didn't come much bigger than that. Not in Stompton Sands.)

'Oh dear, oh dear,' Prudence said. 'What an embarrassing mistake. You'll be thinking now that I'm just a silly old woman.'

'Nothing of the sort,' I said, as sometimes it does no harm to tell little white lies. 'I don't think that at all.'

So we parted on good terms and I went off to send Mum and Dad another e-mail and then to win some more money on the slot machines.

There was an e-mail message waiting for me in my in-box. Very short and snappy it was too.

```
Bosworth! Enough's enough! This is
beyond a joke. You're wasting
everyone's time - including the
police's time - and causing untold
worry and distress. You must come home
immediately without further ado. We
mean it now!
    Yours sincerely,
    Your Parents.
'PS According to the bathroom scales,
your mother has lost ten pounds.'
```

I felt that signature was a touch cold and formal. No

Mum and Dad. No *Lots of love*. Just *Yours sincerely* and *Your Parents*.

Well, three can play at that game, I decided.

```
Dear Parents, I replied. I am afraid I
cannot come home yet, as nothing has
been resolved as far as I can see, and
no concessions have been made. Also, I
need some space and some time to
myself, as I am still trying to find
myself and my direction in life and to
get in touch with the inner Bosworth.
Thanking you for your patience and
understanding. I will be in touch again
soon. Please remember to clean the
rabbits out.
   Yours faithfully,
   Your Son
```

That should hold them for a couple of days, I thought, so I fired the e-mail off, and then made my way to the amusement arcade, where I lost that morning's newspaper round money on the Fruity Fruits machine.

I decided that I would give the amusement arcade a miss for a couple of days, as I was getting worried that I was turning into a compulsive gambler and would soon be attending Gamblers Anonymous – in fact I was almost prepared to bet on it.

I had some lunch – just a takeaway sandwich and a drink – then, as the weather had improved, I went down on to the beach. I found an old plastic spade and built a sand sculpture of a fortress, which was quite magnificent and took me hours. I thought of when I was little, and when I had come to Stompton Sands during those wonderful summers, with my mum and dad. I thought of that expression, 'Happy as a sandboy', and I felt that it was right – you could be happy with a spade and some sand.

By the time I had finished the fortress, the tide was sneaking up the beach. I had to go to start the afternoon paper round. As I left, I looked back and saw the water lapping around the foundations of my castle. Soon the tide would be all around it, and my sculpture would be washed away.

It made me think of me, back when I was little again. I was the fortress and the water was time, and the tide had come in and washed me away, and I wasn't there any more, for those days had gone. I felt a bit sad then, and kind of lonely, and I wished someone had been there with me, someone who would have understood, even The Virus, maybe.

I thought maybe I would tell her about it later, when I got home. It was nice to have somebody to tell things to. You can only tell so much to your mum and dad. It's someone more your own age you need, when it comes to confiding. They're better able to understand, at least that's what I think.

But instead of returning to a warm welcome and some human understanding, I got back that evening to a caravan full of cold silence, mute recrimination and sour grapes.

The Virus was sitting there, moodily turning the pages of another magazine she had bought. She seemed to spend a lot of money on magazines – more than I was losing at the amusement arcade.

'Hi,' I said, as I came in. 'Good day? How were the dogs?'

She gave me a hurt and bitter look. She looked at my hands, as if she'd been expecting to see something in them. But what, I couldn't imagine.

'The dogs were fine, thank you very much,' she said. 'Nothing wrong with the dogs. No, the dogs are no trouble. Very nice, friendly, faithful, loyal and loving creatures are dogs. Dogs don't meet you one day and forget you the next. No, dogs remember things. Dogs don't betray you and trifle with your feelings and let you down.'

I was flummoxed. She was plainly peeved about something, but I'd no idea what.

'Eh, is something the matter, Veronica?' I said.

'Nothing at all!' she snapped, and she flipped over a page in her magazine.

'Have I done anything?' I said.

She gave a hollow, bitter laugh.

'Done anything? You? Oh no, Bosworth. You haven't done anything. No. You haven't done anything at all.'

'Do you mean then,' I said, 'that there's something I should have done, but haven't?'

'I really don't know, I'm sure,' she said. And she turned another glossy page, which made a noise like a cracking whip.

'Eh – it's not your birthday, is it?' I said.

'No,' she said. 'It is not.'

I couldn't think what else it could be.

'Well, what's up then?' I said. 'What is it?'

'Like he doesn't know!' she said, talking to the magazine now.

'Like I don't know what?'

'Like he doesn't actually know what day it is!' she said, still talking to the magazine.

'Why? What day is it?'

'It's only Valentine's Day,' she said. 'That's all. It's only Valentine's Day! It's only February the 14th, that's all it is! And you didn't even buy me a card!'

And with that she left the table, threw herself down on to her mattress, pulled her sleeping bag over her head to hide her face, and then—

—then—

—it was horrible—

—awful—

—I didn't know what to do, or how to deal with it—

She started to cry.

And then she began to wail as well.

'Veronica,' I said. 'Veronica—' I kind of reached out, hesitantly, not knowing what I was reaching for.

'You don't love me!' she wailed. 'You don't love me!'

'No, true,' I said. 'I hate you.'

She wailed even louder.

'But then, be fair,' I said. 'You hate me too.'

She appeared briefly from under the sleeping bag.

'I can't stand the sight of you!' she said. 'You're a toad!' And she went back to covering her face and crying.

'Well, there you are then, fair's fair,' I said.

'You could still have brought me some flowers,' she said. 'Or a card.'

'Yeah, but I didn't even know it was Valentine's Day.'

'How could you not know it's Valentine's Day? It says so everywhere. In every shop you go into. I bet that newsagent's is full of Valentine cards!'

Now she mentioned it, I realized there had been a few out for sale.

'But you didn't remind me,' I told her. 'You never said anything this morning.'

'I shouldn't have to. That's not the point. You don't understand. You don't know what it's like when it's Valentine's Day and nobody sends you flowers or buys you a card and nobody loves you.'

'Yeah, but hold on,' I said. 'You didn't buy me a card or send me flowers or get me any chocolates either.'

There was a snuffling noise then and some congested sounds coming from under the sleeping bag.

'Ook oncha air.'

'What?'

'Ook oncha air.'

'What?'

She partially emerged.

'Look on your chair!'

And there, on my chair, was an envelope, a little white envelope, and inside it – was a card.

I felt so awful. I really did. Awful, and ashamed, and mean, and selfish, and a real monster.

Here we are, I thought, stuck together in this terrible situation – her and me, who can't stand each other, and we've run away from home to get away from each other. Here we are, and nobody loves us, and everyone's after us, and they're all against us, and our parents are angry with us, and don't understand us, and will probably never forgive us for what we've done.

Yes, here we are, all alone in the world, and she went and bought me a Valentine card, even though she hates me, just so I wouldn't feel alone and unloved on this special day.

I felt so bad. I didn't know what to say. I just turned and left. I walked out, and closed the door behind me. I walked and walked. I don't know how long I walked for. It was late and it was dark by the time my steps turned homeward.

She still had the light on when I came in. Her eyes were a bit red, but she wasn't crying.

'Hello,' she said.

'Hello,' I said.

'I was starting to worry,' she said.

'Sorry,' I said. 'I didn't realize how late it was getting.'

Then I handed her the flowers.

'What are these?' she said.

'For you,' I said. 'I passed a shop, and got them for you. For Valentine's Day.'

'Oh, Bosworth,' she said. 'They're lovely. You shouldn't have.'

'Just a small thing,' I said. 'Just a little something.'

'I'll put them in water,' she said, and she did.

Later on, when we'd both been to the shower block and had brushed our teeth and were getting ready for bed, she looked over at me and said:

'Bos—'

'Yeah?' I said.

'Night,' she said.

'Night,' I said.

'Bos,' she said.

'Yeah?' I said.

'Would you like a kiss?' she said. 'For Valentine's Day?'

I didn't answer straightaway. Then, 'Wouldn't mind,' I said.

So she kissed me, on the cheek.

'Can I kiss you back?' I said.

'If you want to,' she said.

So I did. I kissed her too.

Not that I liked her or anything. More that I felt sorry for her. Because she was all alone, on Valentine's Day, and didn't have anyone to send her a card.

I mean, it doesn't cost much to be nice to people, does it?

It costs nothing to be a bit friendly sometimes.

19

This Relationship . . .

First thing next morning, normal hostilities resumed.

I had to get up at half past six for my paper round, and when I fell over a chair and caused the table to collapse, and as a result woke up The Virus when she'd plainly been expecting a lie-in, she reverted to her usual ill manners and bad behaviour.

'Keep the noise down!' she snarled at me. 'What are you doing? Elephant impressions?'

'No need to snap!' I told her. 'You and your nagging, they get me down!'

'And make your bed before you go,' she said.

'I'll do it when I come back,' I said. 'Stop going on.'

'My mother was right about you,' she said. 'She never liked the look of you from the word go.'

'And my dad said you looked like a nagger, the

first time he saw you, and he was right.'

I drank some orange juice, had a bowl of cereal and went.

'Do your washing-up!' were among the last words I heard as I left for the paper shop. 'Don't just leave your bowl in the sink.'

'I'll do my washing-up when it suits me, not you,' I said. 'And see if you can remember how to use a vacuum cleaner while I'm out.'

There was no way I was having her telling me what to do. A boy has to assert himself.

When I got back later that morning, it was to find old Prudence loitering outside her mobile home, pottering around her flower tub, obviously wanting a chat, but trying to look casual about it.

'Oh, hello,' she said. 'How's the wife?'

'Fine,' I said. 'Still breathing.'

'Good,' Prudence said. 'I know it's not my business, but did I maybe hear a little tiff earlier?'

'Eh, perhaps,' I said.

'Oh, you lovebirds,' she said. 'You and your little quarrels. Still, falling-out makes making-up even sweeter, doesn't it?'

'I wouldn't know,' I mumbled, wondering if I should ask her if she knew where I could buy some rat poison, but deciding against it, as it might look suspicious at the trial.

'Anyway,' Prudence said, 'I just thought that as young newly-weds, and not having a lot of money to spend on trips and what have you, you might like to borrow my old tandem to get out and about.'

'Your what?'

'My tandem,' old Prudence said. 'My husband and I used to ride it, back when he was alive.'

I wondered why she said that, as he'd plainly have had trouble riding it once he was dead, unless she tied him on and did all the pedalling herself.

'Anyway, you and your good lady are welcome to borrow it. It may need a drop of oil and you might want to pump the tyres up. You'll find it round at the back, covered in a tarpaulin.'

'Oh, right, OK,' I said. 'Thanks very much.'

I tried to sound keen and grateful, but there was no way I was going out on any tandems with The Virus. Absolutely none.

Unfortunately, she was still in the caravan, and she must have overheard every word, as the door suddenly opened and she poked her head out and said, 'Thank you very much, Prudence, that's very kind of you, We'll go out on it this afternoon. Lovely.'

I decided that once Prudence was out of the way, me and The Virus needed a talk.

As soon as the caravan door closed behind me, I got down to it.

'What's the big idea?' I said. 'Telling her we wanted her rotten tandem?'

'I want to go out somewhere,' she said.

'So go out. I'm not stopping you.'

'I'm fed up with being cooped up in here day after day.'

'You get to walk those dogs.'

'That's not the same. That's work. I'm talking about relaxation. You never take me anywhere.'

'Why should I? You never take me anywhere, come to that.'

'I don't know what's wrong with us,' she said. 'We never do anything together any more.'

'We never did anything together in the first place,' I pointed out.

'You just sit there in front of the telly with your tins of cola watching the football, night after night.'

'I do not!'

'Well, I want to go out.'

'All right,' I said. 'All right. Anything for a quiet life. Where do you want to go?'

'Let's go along the coast road,' she said, 'and down to West Quay.'

'That's ten miles or more.'

'So? We've got all afternoon until my paper round.'

'I'm not sure I know the way.'

She rummaged in a drawer and pulled a dog-eared Ordnance Survey map out.

'I've got a map,' she said.

'Well, there's no way I'm sitting on the back of the tandem,' I said, 'and looking at your bum. Not unless you paint a target on it and I get a bow and arrow.'

'Well, don't think it'll be any sort of a pleasure for me to sit on the back of any tandems and have to look at your fat, smelly bum either.'

'Well, I want to drive,' I said, 'or I'm not going.'

'Oh, typical man,' she said. 'Wants to be in charge of everything whether he's any good at it or not.'

'I'll drive and you can navigate or I'm not going.'

'Oh, all right then, if you're going to sulk. But don't forget that I'll be behind you, and if you make any smells it'll be no trouble for me to hit you with the bicycle pump – and you won't even see it coming.'

'Look,' I said. 'If there's anyone making any smells in this caravan, that anyone isn't me.'

'Well, it certainly isn't me. I've never made a smell in my life, as ladies don't do that sort of thing.'

'Oh really?' I said. 'Then I guess it must have been Mister Pooh-Pooh, the Phantom Smell Maker of Stompton Sands, who sneaks into people's caravans late at night and slowly tries to suffocate them.'

'Yes,' she said. 'I guess it must have been – well, either him, or his creepy assistant Bosworth.'

But I just treated that remark with the contempt that it deserved.

About half an hour later, we got underway. I had checked the tandem over and pumped up the tyres and had made sure the brakes were working. The

Virus had made some cheese sandwiches and had filled a bottle with squash. She put it all in a rucksack which – naturally – I got to carry. Then we said cheerio to old Prudence, who had come out to wave us off.

'Careful on the downhill,' she said. 'Don't go too fast.'

And we were away.

The first half an hour wasn't too bad, although the tandem did seem quite heavy and my legs were feeling the strain – I put that down to it being an old bicycle and made of steel instead of aluminium. It was a nice day though, cool, but clear and sunny. The Virus was quiet as well for a change, which added to the pleasure. We followed the coast path, which kept us away from the traffic. But the path turned inland after a while, and we found ourselves in this warren of country lanes, and there seemed to be no signposts anywhere.

I stopped the bike.

'Well?' I said, twisting round in the saddle. 'Which way?'

No answer.

'Which way now?'

Still no answer.

Then I realized why.

She'd fallen asleep. No wonder my legs were tired. She hadn't been doing any pedalling, not for miles.

'Oi!'

She woke up.

'Yes?' she said.

'You were asleep,' I said.

'No I wasn't. I was enjoying the sun.'

'Look,' I said, 'I'm not your flipping chauffeur, you know. I'm not Bosworth the rickshaw boy or something. I'm not here to pedal you around. So do your share or get off and walk.'

'Keep your hat on,' she said.

'Well, we're lost,' I said. 'And you're supposed to be navigating. So which way?'

'Oh, let me see now—'

She got the map out, unfolded it, and had a look.

'That map's upside down,' I pointed out.

'I know that!' she said. 'I was using it for reference.'

She turned it the other way round and spent a while going 'Hmm . . .' and 'Umm . . .' and 'Ahhh . . .'

'Let me see it,' I said, reaching back.

'No, it's all right. I know where we are now. It's straight on, left, and then right at the crossroads.'

We went straight on, turned left – no crossroads, just a T-junction.

'Well?'

'Must be right here.'

'If you say so.'

So right it was. After about a mile, the road narrowed to a track, and then suddenly, as we turned a tight corner, I saw a stream fording the road – straight in front of us.

'Brake!'

I did, but it was too late. We rode straight into the ford. We didn't fall over, but we slowly came to a halt, up to our middles in freezing cold, fresh, running water.

'You idiot!' she yelled. 'You and your reckless driving! Now see what you've done.'

'What I've done?' I said. 'If you learned to read a map properly, we'd never have come down here. It's all your fault.'

We got off the tandem and pushed it out of the water.

'My trousers are wet now!' I said. 'I'm soaking. Thanks to you!'

We rested the tandem against a tree. I took off the rucksack and threw it down on the grass verge.

'That's it!' I said. 'I've had it. I've had it with you! I've had it up to here!'

But instead of her getting angry too, she got all annoyingly calm.

'Yes, that's it,' she said in a teacher-knows-best sort of voice. 'Fly off the handle like you usually do. The first sign of adversity, and off he goes on one of his temper tantrums – spoiled boy Bosworth.'

'Nagging girl Veronica,' I said.

I hit the mark there. She sort of winced. She knew it was true.

We sat on the grass verge in silence, waiting for the weak sun to dry us out a little. If we went back, we'd have to recross the ford and get soaked again: there was no way but forward – only where was that going to take us?

I decided to have my cheese sandwich.

'And I've still got to get back for my evening paper round too, you know,' I pointed out.

'And I've got my dog walking. You and your driving.'

'You and your useless map-reading. You couldn't find your way out of a paper bag – or find your way into one, come to that.'

We ate in silence, then halfway through her sandwich, she looked at me and said, 'Bosworth—'

'What?'

'This relationship isn't working.'

'Huh!' I said. 'You think I need you to tell me that?'

'I think,' she said, 'that we need to go to counselling.'

I gawped at her.

'Your mouth's open,' she said. 'I can see half-chewed cheese. It's not pretty.'

'Counselling?' I said. 'How do you mean counselling?'

'To try and make this relationship work.'

'But I don't want it to work,' I reminded her.

'No, neither do I,' she said. 'But that's not the

point. The point is that we are stuck in that little caravan for the time being until we decide what to do next. And if all we're going to do is to bicker and argue over everything, it's not going to be a very pleasant experience, is it?'

I was about to say something sarky then, but for some reason didn't.

'Look,' I said. 'We can't go and get counselling. You have to be grown up, don't you? It costs money.'

'One of my friends at the dog kennels is thinking of doing counselling one day when she leaves school. I'm sure she'd be willing to do it if I asked.'

'Does she know about me then?'

'I might have mentioned you – I mean, she doesn't know about us running away or anything, or living in a caravan together.'

'So what did you call me?'

'Well—'

'Well? How did you describe me to her?'

'Well, I had to say . . . I said . . . I told her . . . well, I didn't know how else to put it . . . I said you were . . . my . . . boyfriend.'

I nearly dropped my crusts.

'Boyfriend!' I said. 'I'm not your flipping boyfriend.'

'Don't flatter yourself,' she said. 'There's no way you'd ever be. I just had to refer to you as something and I thought boyfriend might be a little better than the truth.'

'Which is what?'

'Take your pick – Dog Face? Poo Head?'

'All right, all right. For someone who wants to improve this relationship, you aren't saying much to make it any better.'

'Sorry.'

We passed the bottle of squash back and forth. I still hadn't agreed to anything, but maybe a little counselling would do no harm, I thought.

'So this friend of yours – this girl you know, at the kennels – what qualifies her to give advice and be a counsellor then? I mean, what does she know about it?'

'Her mum's a hairdresser,' The Virus said.

'Oh,' I said.

I didn't see what that had to do with anything. But I didn't want to start an argument. Well, not another one. Somehow you get argued out in the end. All you want is peace and quiet.

We got to West Quay eventually, and we got back to the caravan too, just in time for The Virus's dog walking and my evening paper round. We found another road for the return journey, which avoided the ford and a second soaking.

I took the tandem back to old Prudence. She wasn't in, so I left it where I had found it, under the old tarpaulin. I scribbled a thank-you note and put it under her door, then went off to deliver newspapers.

When I got home, The Virus was already back from dog walking. She was peeling spuds at the sink.

'Need any help?' I asked.

'You could do a few carrots,' she said.

'OK.' I didn't really like carrots, but if she wanted them, her being a veggie and everything – I mean, I suppose you have to be a bit tolerant, live and let live and all that.

She didn't mention any more about counselling, so I didn't ask her. Maybe her friend hadn't been there.

As the dinner was cooking, there was a tap at the door. It was old Prudence, who was carrying something – something which looked sort of alive.

'Hello! Only me!'

I hoped she wasn't going to stay long. I'd had a long hard day and wanted to put my feet up after dinner and watch the telly.

'Thank you for letting us use the tandem,' The Virus said.

'Not at all. Glad you enjoyed it. Now, I won't keep you as I can see you're going to have your meal. I just called because I wondered . . . well . . . my friend Mrs Copple, she lives not far away – her cat Bubbles, well, it was all very unexpected . . . we just thought she was getting fat . . . but she's had quite a big litter you know, and Mrs Copple has been looking for homes for them, these past few weeks, and well, I'm a bit too old for a kitten myself, and I've got a cat already, but I promised I'd ask – just say no if you'd rather not – but I wondered if you'd like to have a kitten. This is him. His name's Bodger.'

And she set a small piece of fur down on the table.

I can't say I liked the look of him. He looked like trouble to me. But The Virus was over the moon. It was all hey-diddle-diddle for her.

'Oh, Prudence! He's so lovely! Isn't he lovely? He's so cute, isn't he? Oh, isn't he though? He's such a little cutie. Oh, let's keep him. Shall we?'

'Well – a kitten,' I said. 'It's a big responsibility – and he's probably not even house-trained yet and—'

But I may as well have talked to the moon she was over.

'Oh, can we keep him? Just for a while. Just to try him out. On probation? How's that?'

'Well—'

'Thanks, Boz,' she said. Then she remembered that as far as old Prudence was concerned, I was supposed to be called Bartholomew. 'Barty, I mean.' (Which, I've just realized, rhymes with farty.) 'Thanks. I knew you'd agree.'

Not that I had.

'Just try him for tonight,' old Prudence said. 'If it doesn't work out, I can take him back tomorrow.'

'OK,' The Virus said. 'Is that OK with you?'

I didn't want to have another argument, and certainly not in front of old Prudence.

'All right,' I said. 'But only on trial.'

286

'OK. That's great then. Thank you, Prudence. We'll try to give him a good home.'

'I'll leave him with you for now then,' old Prudence said. 'And as I say, just bring him back if it doesn't work out.'

'Oh, I'm sure we'll be fine, just fine.'

So Prudence went, and left us with Bodger. He sat there, his little whiskered face looking up at us, as if we were his mum and dad or something.

'Ah, look at him,' The Virus said, and started making girly noises. 'Love him,' she said. 'Ah, bless! Iddles, diddles, oozum, doozum den.'

I wished I'd brought one of my sick bags with me. I could have spared one from the collection.

She picked the kitten up and cradled him in her arms.

'Who's a lovely boy then?' she said. 'Who's a lovely boy?' Then she looked at me and she said, 'Bosworth—'

'What?' I said.

'We've got responsibilities now,' she said.

'Have we?' I said.

'We have Bodger to look after. So no more nights out now, Bosworth.'

'Eh?'

'We'll have to save our money now, for what he needs.'

'Eh?'

'A basket, and a scratching post, and a flea collar,

287

and his injections at the vet's, and worming tablets and—'

'Hang on,' I said. 'Hang on, I don't know if I'm ready for all this yet—'

'It's no use us just thinking of ourselves any more. We're a family now.'

'We're a what?'

'You and me,' she said, 'and Bodger makes three.'

'I can count,' I told her.

'Ah,' she said. 'Look at his little whiskers. Look at his little pink nose. Look at his little tongue—'

'Look at that stream of water that's trickling on to the floor,' I said. (I felt I ought to mention it.)

'Oh deary, deary me. Has little Bodger done a wee-wee? Never mind. Mummy will put some newspaper down and then go to the shop and get some cat litter. Here you are, Bosworth. Will you hold him?'

'Me?' I said, panicking. 'I don't know how to hold kittens. I've never held kittens before. They make me nervous. Kittens – they give me kittens.'

'Oh, don't be silly. Take him. While I clear up.'

And that was it.

She went all mumsy after that.

If I'd known, for one second, what having a kitten was going to involve, I'd never have agreed to it in a million years.

Kittens today – they're nothing but trouble. They

have it too easy, if you ask me. And are they grateful? Do you get any thanks? No way.

It was murder. I hardly got a wink of sleep all night.

Which was a pity really, because although we didn't know it, it was to be our last one there.

20

The Patter of Tiny Paws (and Some Counselling)

'Bosworth?'

'What?'

It was dark and silent; I was almost asleep.

'Can you hear anything?'

'No.'

'Nor can I.'

'Let's go to sleep then,' I said. 'Ideal sleeping conditions.'

But sleep wasn't on her mind.

'Bosworth—' she said, in a worried voice. 'I can't hear Bodger breathing.'

'What?'

'You don't think he's suffocated, do you? On that old blanket I put down for him.'

'No.'

I heard The Virus get out of her sleeping bag.

'What is it? What are you doing?'

'I'd better check,' she said.

'What?'

'That he's breathing.'

'Look, he's asleep,' I told her. 'And if you put the light on you'll wake him, and then he'll be running round the caravan for the next hour.'

'I've got to see. I'd never forgive myself if he got smothered.'

So she had to get out of bed, and she had to put the light on, and she had to make sure that Bodger the kitten wasn't dead – which he wasn't of course. And of course he woke up then and thought, *Oh, it must be time for us kittens to have a run around and a lark about,* so he scampered round the caravan for the next hour, playing with a piece of string and jumping up on to the surfaces and sharpening his claws on the table leg and chewing up my hat.

'Now see what you've done,' I said. 'We'll be up all night.'

'I hope he's not hyperactive.'

'He is.'

'I did read that if you're hyperactive, you might also turn out to be dyslexic.'

'What?'

'Have trouble reading.'

'All cats have trouble reading.'

'I just wouldn't want to think of him as falling behind.'

'Behind what?' I said.

'All the other kittens.'

'What other kittens?'

'I don't know,' she said. 'There must be some. We want him to socialize, don't we, and make friends? When he's a bit older, I'll sign him up for Kitten Club.'

I stared at her. She was losing her marbles.

'Kitten Club? What's that'

'There must be a local one, surely, where people can take their kittens, so they can get to know each other.'

'Let's go to sleep,' I said. 'I've got work in the morning.'

I put the light off. Finally the sound of a mad kitten running amok in a caravan eased off and slowed down. We could get to sleep at last.

But no.

'Bosworth—'

'What?'

'What's that smell?'

'It's him, isn't it?'

'Did he miss his little tray?'

'Well, it certainly smells like it.'

'Your turn,' she said.

'My turn!'

'I did it last time.'

So I had to get out of my sleeping bag and clean up the mess and go and put it out in the dustbin in the freezing cold. Finally, I got back into bed.

'Right. Now can we get some sleep.'

I closed my eyes. I got ten seconds' peace.

'Bosworth—'

'What now?'

'What do you think he'll be when he grows up?'

'Who?'

'Bodger.'

'What do I think he'll be? He'll be a cat, that's what he'll be. What else can he be? He doesn't have a lot of choice, does he? What do you want him to be? A wheel?'

'I was just thinking that maybe he might work in television.'

'Eh?'

'In the cat food ads. He might be famous one day. Just think – our little Bodger, a film star.'

'Right. Wonderful. I'll look forward to it. Now can we go to sleep?'

Twenty seconds' peace this time. Then there was a faint meowing noise from where Bodger was sleeping.

'Bosworth—' The Virus hissed.

'What?'

'Did you hear?'

'Did I hear what?'

'He said his first meow.'

'What?'

'Bodger. He said his first meow. I must make a note of the time and write it down in my diary.'

'No, don't put your light on, you'll wake him up again and then—'

'He's very young to be meowing, isn't he? Do you think he might be extra intelligent? Perhaps we could get his name down for cat training. He might be a prodigy. Maybe he could play the violin.'

'No, Veronica, don't put the light—'

Too late. She put it on. She got out her diary and wrote down Bodger's first meow. And what did he do? He woke up, of course, and ran round the caravan for another hour, and then he weed on my sleeping bag.

'Great,' I said. 'Just great. Just what you need. With an early start and a paper round ahead of you. Great.'

'Ah, he couldn't help it, bless him,' The Virus said.

'You wouldn't say that if it was your sleeping bag.'

'It was only a tiny wee. You'll be all right. We can go to the launderette tomorrow.'

'Yeah, and take him with us, and stick him in on spin!'

'No need to be like that.'

Finally the kitten went back to sleep and I was able to close my eyes for a few hours before I had to get up again for my paper round.

I staggered off, bleary and exhausted, wondering whatever was I doing and why was I doing it?

If only I'd known. If only I'd have anticipated. But that's always the way, isn't it? You never do know, you never do anticipate. You never know when the day of reckoning is at hand.

But before the reckoning came, there was the counselling to get through.

We met The Virus's friend from the kennels down in a cafe by the beach that afternoon. Exactly why her mum being a hairdresser qualified her as a relationship counsellor, I didn't really understand, but I felt that if I questioned her credentials too closely, it would only lead to further bitterness and disagreement in the caravan, so I kept quiet and went along with things.

This girl's name was Elspeth and she owned a pair of glasses, which she put on when we came in, either so as to see us better or to make herself look intelligent.

We sat down at her table and The Virus introduced us. Elspeth gave me what my dad says is known in the painting and decorating trade as a 'good coat of looking at'. So I gave her an equally good coat of looking at right back.

'Hmm,' she said. 'So this is him, is it?'

'Yes,' Veronica The Virus said. 'I'm afraid it is.'

'Hmm,' Elspeth said again. 'Yes. I see what you mean now.'

I took offence at this, as I thought that we were supposed to be having this counselling on an equal footing. I didn't think it was fair if the counsellor was a sympathetic friend of one of the parties and already had it in for the other party before she had even met him.

'OK,' Elspeth said, and she took out a notebook and put it down on the table, and then sat with her Biro poised, ready to take notes. 'Shall we begin, Veronica? Would you like to say what you feel about Bosworth? What his many faults and flaws are? Where he is going wrong and what he ought to do better?'

'Hang on, just a minute—' I started to say. But I got no further.

'You are not to interrupt, Bosworth,' Elspeth said sternly. 'You are to let Veronica speak for a full five minutes. You are to listen closely to what she has to say. And then, when Veronica has finished speaking, you will get your turn.'

'OK,' I said. 'I suppose.'

'Veronica, then, if you would like to start.'

'Right. Well, it's hard to know where to begin, really, as Bosworth-face here—'

'Hang on,' I said. 'That's not very nice. She just called me Bosworth-face!'

'No interrupting!' Elspeth snapped. 'I've told you once already!'

Well, I just more or less turned off then, and let them get on with it. I could see it was a kangaroo court with a hanging judge, and that they'd already arrived at the verdict, even before they'd had the trial.

'OK,' The Virus resumed. 'Bosworth has many faults. He's selfish, inconsiderate, untidy, smelly, scruffy, he doesn't wash much, he doesn't change his clothes very often, he has gross manners and disgusting eating habits.'

I just had to speak.

'Hang on,' I said. 'What about my good points?'

'Those,' Veronica said, 'are your good points. I haven't started on the bad ones yet.'

'Don't interrupt, please,' Elspeth said. And I couldn't help but feel that if it had been another boy doing the counselling, instead of a girl, I might have got a more sympathetic hearing.

'In addition,' The Virus continued, 'Bosworth is rude, opinionated, argumentative, stubborn, pig-headed, and can never admit he's wrong.'

'Only because I never am wrong!' I said.

'Quiet!' the counsellor snapped. 'Go on, Veronica.'

'Furthermore, he takes other people for granted, he never does his share of the housework, he drinks too many fizzy drinks, eats too many snacks, slobs around the place and never gets enough exercise. He won't do the washing-up unless you nag him, he won't put the cap back on the toothpaste and—'

On she went. I had to sit there for the full five minutes, listening to all about how I was the worst human being ever to have walked the planet and how I should have been strangled at birth, or possibly earlier.

Finally, it was all over.

'OK, Bosworth,' Elspeth said. 'So what have you learned from all that?'

'Well,' I said, 'if I'm to believe what I hear, I'm a complete and utter scumbag who ought to go and throw himself into the nearest sewage works at the earliest opportunity.'

'Excellent,' Elspeth said. 'It's good that you've achieved some sort of insight into yourself. You should thank Veronica.'

'Thanks,' I said. 'For nothing.'

'Now, now, Bosworth,' the counsellor said. 'We're getting petty and spiteful again.'

'So,' I said. 'How about my turn? I get five minutes now then, don't I, to tell you what I think of her?'

'I'm afraid I'm in a bit of a hurry now, actually, as I have to be back at the kennels. But I can give you thirty seconds.'

'That's not fair.'

'Twenty-five.'

'But—'

What was the use, I thought. It was a stitch-up, a conspiracy; they were all against me.

'Well, go ahead,' Elspeth said. 'Make a start.'

I looked at The Virus, thinking of all that was wrong with her, all the trouble she'd brought me, all the woe and misery she'd caused, and yet, when it came to saying what I didn't like about her, it was hard to put my finger on it.

'Well, the truth is . . .' I began. 'The thing is . . . what I'm saying here . . . what I'm getting at is . . .'

'Yes?'

'That Veronica can be really irritating sometimes, and she drives me mad, and she's absolutely infuriating to live with in so many ways . . . and . . . yet . . . I mean . . . despite that . . . I suppose . . .'

'Well?'

'Well, I guess . . . she's sort of . . . all right really, in her way. I mean, we're all only human, aren't we? Nobody's perfect.'

'No, well, you're certainly not, Bosworth, are you?' Elspeth the counsellor said.

I sighed.

'No,' I said. 'I guess I'm not.'

'Well, there we are then,' she said, closing her notebook. 'I think we all know who's in the wrong now and who needs to improve his act and to take a good, long look at himself.'

'Who might that be, I wonder?' I said. 'Like I wouldn't know.'

'Must away then, Veronica,' Elspeth said. 'I hope this has been of some help.'

'Oh yes, I think so, thank you,' The Virus said. 'You've really opened my eyes as to what's wrong with this relationship. I had so little self-confidence before and was even starting to think that I might be to blame in some small way. But now I see that the fault lies entirely with Bosworth-face here – old fat cheeks.'

'Well, I'm glad to have been able to help with those insights,' Elspeth said. 'I shan't be charging you for this session, as I'm grateful for the counselling experience. Well, if you'll excuse me, I've got a big Alsatian to give worming tablets to. So I'll wish you good luck, and say goodbye.'

And off she went, to give the Alsatian some worming therapy.

'Well,' The Virus said. 'What do you think? She's got tremendous insight, hasn't she?'

'She's got a pretty big bum as well,' I said, watching Elspeth manoeuvre herself out of the cafe.

'There you go again,' The Virus said. 'Always being snide and finding the worst in people.'

Then she turned and watched Elspeth as she left the cafe.

'I suppose it is a touch on the big side,' she said. 'I mean, it's huge compared to mine – wouldn't you say?'

But I didn't say anything. I'd had enough psychology for one day.

We made our way back up the hill to the Cliff Top Holiday Park, to our caravan, and our imminent doom. When we got to the top we separated, as I wanted to use the loo.

'See you in a minute,' I said. I headed for the toilet block; The Virus went to the caravan.

It wasn't even particularly dramatic when we got

discovered – which I felt it would be. I felt that if anyone ever found us, it would be the police, in body armour and with truncheons, breaking down the door of the caravan and shining bright lights in our faces, saying, 'OK! Don't move. We've got you covered.'

But no. It happened quite casually and unexpectedly, and so low key. We didn't go out with a bang at all, it was more like a sigh, like a whimper.

I saw the woman as I was walking back to the caravan from the shower block. She was about fifty metres ahead of me, going from the car park to where the caravans were. I thought she was just some resident, on her way home. She was a grey-haired woman, of about sixty or so.

The gap between us was closing, when something made me slow down, and hesitate. She seemed to be going where I was going, heading for the same caravan as me.

Who was she? What did she want? Was she someone from the social services? Had somebody tipped her off that we were living there?

She stopped by our caravan. But she did a strange thing then. She didn't reach her hand up to knock on the door. Oh no. She did something else. She went and looked under the stone, to find the key.

When she saw it wasn't there, she rummaged in her bag and produced a key of her own. She went to fit it into the lock of the door. I stopped and watched her, half hidden behind a tree, as she turned the key and pushed the door open.

As she did, The Virus appeared from inside, with Bodger in her arms. I saw her there in the doorway. She stared at the woman before her, the blood draining from her face.

The woman spoke first.

'Veronica!' she said.

'Auntie!' The Virus said. 'Great-auntie Boo! Whatever are you doing here?'

'I could ask you, Veronica, the very same question,' she said, in a stern and commanding voice. 'And whatever have you done to your hair! And where did you get that cat?'

But before I could react, before I could shout, or gasp, or fall in a faint or run for it, I felt a hand fall on my shoulder.

I knew who it had to belong to. It had to be the hand on the end of the long arm of the law.

But it wasn't. It was a hand belonging to old Prudence, who was standing there behind me.

'You'd better come and hide in my house,' she said. 'If you don't want to get nabbed as well.'

I stared at her, open-mouthed, my jaw as slack as a pancake.

'Prudence?' I said. 'What do you mean?'

'What do you think?' she said, and she smiled and gave me a wink.

'You know?'

' 'Course I do.'

'You know? You knew? All along? Who we are? You didn't think we were newly-weds, or old enough – or anything?'

'Of course I didn't,' she said. 'I didn't believe a word of that for a moment. What do you think I am – daft?'

I didn't answer that, because it was just what I had thought. Which only goes to show, you should never judge by appearances.

'Well?' she said. 'There's no point in your both being caught, is there? And think of the embarrassment – you two, supposed to have run off to get away from each other, and ending up together. No sense in having that made public.'

'I guess not,' I said.

'Then you'd better come with me.'

I hid in Prudence's mobile home, peering out from behind the curtains, watching what was going on.

It transpired – as I found out later – that the weather had turned nasty in Spain, where Auntie Boo had gone for the winter – so she decided to come home early and head for her caravan at Stompton Sands instead. She'd heard about The Virus's disappearance, and of course, when she was found in the caravan, everyone went around saying, 'We should have thought of that and looked there in the first place. What an obvious place to go.' But sometimes the obvious is anything but.

I saw Auntie Boo leave the caravan with The Virus behind her; she was carrying Bodger and her backpack.

'Come along, my girl!' Auntie Boo said. 'I'm taking you straight home.'

The Virus glanced in our direction and saw me at the window. She shook her head, as if to say, 'Stay where you are. Stay there, don't come out, and don't say anything. I haven't told her. And I'm not going to either.'

For a moment I felt I should dash out and say to her Auntie Boo: 'It wasn't all her fault. It was mine too.' But then what would have been the point? As Prudence had said – The Virus had run away from home to get away from me, and I had run away from home so as not to get engaged to her. If people ever found out that we had ended up together, with the very person we had said we so desperately wanted to get away from, well, she'd never live it down.

More to the point, I'd never live it down. I'd be a laughing-stock at school. They'd be splitting their sides right open, every time they saw me. Whereas if I kept quiet, I'd be a hero – Bosworth Hartie, all-star runaway, the man you don't mess with, or he'll be off.

But as it was, nobody knew. Except Prudence. And I didn't think she'd tell, somehow.

We watched Auntie Boo and The Virus go. I heard a car start up.

Then, 'Come on,' old Prudence said. 'Let's go.'

'Where?' I said.

'To get your stuff,' she said. 'She's obviously taking your young lady back home. She plainly doesn't know yet that you've been hiding in there too. So let's get your stuff out and get rid of the evidence.'

'No, she wouldn't have seen anything,' I said. 'I put everything away this morning. Put my sleeping bag under the bench, and my rucksack's in the wardrobe.'

'Let's see if we can get inside.'

We did. Auntie Boo had been in such a hurry to leave and to take her great-niece back home that she had forgotten to lock the caravan. I gathered all my stuff up. Soon there was no sign that I'd ever been there.

'Now what?' old Prudence said. 'Do you need money to get home?'

'Home?' I said. 'Home?'

'Yes,' she said. 'Don't you think you ought to go home now? You've worried your parents long enough. You've had your adventure and you haven't missed much school, if any, if it's half-term for you too. You've made your stand as far as anyone knows and you've made your point. And now you can hold your head up, and go home. Don't you think?'

I thought about it, and I nodded. Yes, maybe that was right.

'And don't worry,' old Prudence said. 'I'm not going to tell.'

'Thanks, Prudence,' I said. 'Thanks for not turning us in— Can I ask you something?'

'What's that, dear?'

'Why didn't you turn us in?'

'Because you're young, my dear,' she said. 'And that only happens once in life. And it's soon over, believe me. And besides—'

'What?'

'Who can stand in the way of true love?'

I didn't get it. I didn't know what she meant by that. I guessed it was some kind of joke.

'Sorry,' I said. 'I don't understand.'

She just smiled and said, 'Don't worry. You will. One day. Now, do you need money to get home?'

'No, I'm all right,' I said. 'I got a return ticket.'

She laughed.

'Some runaway you are,' she said, 'who gets a return ticket before he goes.'

But then, I suppose I always knew, in my heart of hearts, that I was going to go home again one day.

I just hoped they wouldn't be too angry with me when I got there.

21

Home Is Where the Rabbits Are

I said goodbye to Prudence and walked on into town. I left a note for Mr Cramms the newsagent saying I was sorry but I wouldn't be able to do my paper rounds any more, then I made my way to the station.

Two and a half hours later, I was walking along our street, then up the path to our house.

I rang the bell. It was Mum who came to the door. She wasn't that angry, more relieved than anything. She'd lost so much weight while I'd been away, I think she was slightly disappointed to have me back already. She might have preferred it if I'd stayed away a little longer, now that she'd finally found a diet that actually worked – The Worry Diet.

'Oh, Bosworth, Bosworth, my little Bosworth—'

I wasn't that little, but she carried on like I was.

Dad came to see what all the noise and

commotion was, and he was pretty glad to see me too, and I was pretty glad to see them, to be honest.

I got some serious ticking off though. Not just from them, from the police too. They came round and gave me a professional ticking-off and told me how stupid I'd been and what trouble and worry and inconvenience I had caused for everyone and did I have any idea how much police time and manpower I had wasted and how much looking for me had cost?

I was worried that they were going to charge me for looking for me – which wouldn't have been very fair, really, because it wasn't as if they'd found me, was it?

They wanted to know where I'd been, of course. I told them I'd gone to Cornwall and spent my days mooching around and my nights in an old barn. I couldn't prove I had, of course, but they couldn't prove I hadn't.

'And do you know, Bosworth,' Mum said, 'that that appalling girl you were to get engaged to – I see you were right about her now – she actually ran away as well?'

'I might have seen something about it,' I said. 'In a newspaper somewhere.'

'Apparently she went and hid in her aunt's caravan in Stompton Sands,' she said.

'Never,' I said. 'Is that a fact? Stompton Sands – where's that?' I asked.

'You know – where we used to go when you were smaller.'

'Oh, that place, yes. I vaguely remember it.'

'Well, don't worry, Bosworth. We've talked it over, your father and I, and we see that although we meant well, we didn't act well. We should never have pressed you to get engaged. It was a mistake. So don't you worry. You will never have to see that awful girl ever again.'

'Great,' I said. 'Great!'

And yet, for some odd reason, it didn't seem that great. Not as great as it should have done. I should have been delirious really, happy and smiling and over the moon, now that I'd got what I'd wanted and would never have to see Veronica Angelica Belinda Melling ever again.

But I wasn't that happy somehow.

I may as well tell you the truth. I felt a bit – well – sad.

I got over it though. I was soon back at school and back looking after my rabbits and back scanning eBay for any unused international airline sick bags that I didn't have in my collection. It was all back to normal in fact and business as usual. I was quite a celebrity at my school. Everyone thought it was pretty hot stuff, running away from home.

I never told anyone about The Virus, and how we ended up going to the same place, and sharing her Great-auntie Boo's caravan. I've never told anyone and I never will. Just my computer here, and no one else knows the password, so no one will ever read this. Maybe when I'm older, I'll show it to someone.

I used to think about her, wondering how she was, and how Bodger the kitten was, and how he'd be growing up into a cat now. I wondered if he missed me or ever thought of me – if cats ever think of anything apart from themselves.

Once or twice I nearly wrote to her to ask, but I thought better of it. I nearly phoned – but I put the receiver down before the number rang.

I was glad I'd run away. Not for the trouble and distress I'd caused, but for what it had given me. I felt a more tolerant and, well, a better person.

I wondered too if Veronica thought of me, if she had any sort of – fond memories. She obviously never told anyone that we'd ended up in her aunt's caravan. I guessed that at her school she was a runaway hero too. Or heroine, rather.

Months went by. I was on the internet one evening, just after I'd come home from school. I'd gone on to this chat room. Not my usual one. But I like to move around and try new things. I noticed there was someone on-line whose nickname was VAB-M, and I thought, that's a coincidence, those are The Virus's initials. We started talking to each other – just chatting – what school do you go to, how old are you, sort of thing. Then VAB-M asked for a private chat. So, intrigued, I said OK.

Boz, she typed. *is that u?*

who's u? I asked.

u know, she wrote.

yes, I wrote. *itz me. iz it u?*

yes, she wrote. And she sent me a smiley face.

We chatted a while. I asked her how she was and how Bodger was and if she'd got into a lot of trouble when she got home. She said no, not too bad, she'd survived. Her mum and dad had apologized for ever trying to marry her off to 'that appalling boy' (me!) and promised that she would never have to see me again.

We chatted a while longer, and then she said she had to go, as she had a lot of homework.

always remember you, Boz, she wrote.

always remember you too, I answered.

bye.

don't go just yet, I typed.

wot iz it?

Veronica, I wrote. *when u grow up, do u think u'll ever want 2 get married?*

It took half a minute or more before I got a reply.

yes, she wrote back. *i mite do. 2 the rite person. if it was someone I liked and really loved. wot about u?*

yes, I replied. *mite do. me 2. 1 day.*

y do u ask? she wrote back. *any special reason?*

no, I wrote. *just wondering.*

Then there was another pause, and I thought she'd gone, but she hadn't. Another line of text appeared.

bye, Boz. have a good life. mayb we'll meet again 1 day.

mayb, I answered. *that wood b nice.*

must go, Boz.

ok

lotz of luv.

I sat there and stared at the screen. I thought of us, and all our quarrels, and all our arguments and bickering, and how we'd run away from home to get away from each other, and how we couldn't stand each other, and all we'd been through together.

lotz of luv. Now she had the nerve to write *lotz of luv.*

Huh! I thought. *lotz of luv.* Well, there was only one way to respond to that.

My hands reached out for the keyboard.

lotz of luv 2 u 2, Veronica, I wrote. *it was great to know u.*

great 2 know u 2, Boz. never forget u.

never forget u 2, I wrote. *I miz u,* I added. Because it was true. I did. I didn't see it was anything to be ashamed of.

miz u 2, Boz. always will, she wrote back.

Then I saw that she had signed off and gone.

I went outside to the garden and spent some quality time with my rabbits. I wondered what it must be like to be grown up. I guessed that I'd find out one day. Maybe I already had a head start.

I wondered too if, at some time in the future, when I was older and wiser (or at least taller, anyhow), I'd ever meet Veronica Angelica Belinda Melling again, and what she'd be like, when she was grown up.

I bet she'd be quite a head-turner, because she wasn't bad-looking really.

And then I realized, with a momentary pang of regret . . .

. . . that I never did get my dowry.